The train

The train

Roger Wheatley

Roger Wheatley lives with his family in Canberra, Australia. His school years were spent in small-town southern New South Wales. From cattle-station cowboy to international aid worker, he has usually looked for the road less-travelled. And it's a unique setting that his writing is often built around, that and the colourful characters that inhabit such places.

The train is his third novel. *Wolves in white collars*, and *Out of the ruins* are both available on Amazon.

Thanks as ever to my gorgeous wife for her love, support and patience.

1

The older of the two women thought it incongruous. The three of them sitting there, each perched on the end of a concrete railway sleeper, leaning against the bogie wheels of the train. The fragility of flesh, organs and bone, set against the destructive potential of a thousand tons of train and the endless burnished rails. Steel on steel. Flesh on steel. A small movement of the train would end them. Severed limbs, arterial blood pulsing like a smokers cough. Bone splintered. The damage of a second, irreparable.

She thought of such things. Injuries, not trains. They'd been her life. The smell of antiseptic, cold sterile air, the rustle of medical gowns, the muffled speak of masked faces. The arrogance of men. The next patient. The high-pitched scream of surgical tools. Her job, their life, her life.

What she wouldn't give now, for five minutes of that refrigerated air.

They'd swept away the blue metal in the rail-bed from around the sleepers so that each had a flat surface to sit on. She smiled the first time she'd sat, thinking about what her mother said about the effects of concrete on the derriere.

They weren't the only ones there. Along the length of the train their routine was mirrored a hundred-fold. Shot in black and white it might be a Nazi death photo, lifeless forms propped up against the train. A macabre statement of Aryan superiority.

And here and there a gap, a vacant sleeper between groups. Some gaps accidental, some intentional. The three had a gap beside them. But this was no cartel. They were leftovers. They had no agenda.

It had only been three days but already there were factions. It began as class war. First versus economy, platinum and gold, the front of the train against the back—one old man had referred to the rear carriages as steerage, setting off the initial fracas. It was during the first all-train gathering on the second day. The manager framed by the train doorway. A tight shot of him might have looked like a still from a sci-fi movie, the hero standing in the hatchway of his space-craft, the burnished silver of the carriage like the outer skin of his interstellar vehicle.

The bulk of the passengers were fanned out before him in the long late-afternoon shadows cast by the train. The passengers stood on the rough service road running alongside the rail line, the chalky loam scarred here and there by the four-wheel drive tracks of service crews who came this way every couple of months. The edge of the road furthest from the train line pushed up into a jagged mound by the yearly pass of a road grader.

Many glanced nervously for the snakes, scorpions and other creatures that they had convinced themselves lurked behind every rock. It was the farthest some had ventured from the carriages.

In a show of solidarity the two train drivers in their matching dark blue slacks, light blue twill shirts and safety vests stood at the bottom of the stairs. Looking more like security than drivers. The sweat rings under their arms taking some of the gloss from the authority that their uniforms might have conveyed.

The heat was stupefying. There were many sweat rings and the white stains of leached body salts on shirt backs. But the time of day was infinitely more bearable than the early afternoon heat that scorched the air inside the train, threatening to scald the lungs of the elderly who could not or would not clatter down the steps to perch on a sleeper or to lay in the rail-bed under the train.

The drivers had banned anyone from being anywhere near the outside of the train on the first day after the train had come to a stop. These were the rules they said. The rules had only lasted a day. A handful of passengers ignored them on the morning of the second day and to save some face an announcement was passed along that passengers could take shelter near or under the train.

The drivers' concern on day one was not merely authoritarian, they'd wondered about the potential arrival of a goods train during the day. Or worse, during the night. The thought scared the hell out of them. No running lights and who knew what information the other drivers had of their plight. The vision of a thousand fast-moving tons bearing down on them did not bear thinking about, the senior driver had said to the train manager.

In the end the manager agreed to accept the risk of leaving the passengers on the train on that first night. He simply couldn't fathom how he would force people—the average age of whom was around seventy—to climb down and spend the night in the desert.

The night had passed without incident.

It was the afternoon of the second day when the manager addressed them all the first time. The flies were still active, and would be until after sunset. They were driving the passengers mad. Out here with everyone together the constantly waving hands looked like a fight against a bad smell rather than thwarting the tiny black hordes..

Many of the older passengers stayed inside the train, the climb down the steep steps, and the slippery descent from the rail-bed to flatter ground too much for many of them. So they gathered behind the manager in the carriage entryway.

The manager showed both palms, fingers upwards, to call for silence. A gesture that seemed to smack of defeat. He was tall and spare, a face that looked permanently surprised.

—We haven't been able to contact the company as yet. His tone conveyed that he knew they wouldn't want to hear it.

He was right. He seemed to take the questions that hammered him from the front and rear, like physical blows. Jerking a little under each salvo. He raised his hands again.

—Please. Please. Let me speak. When he had mostly silence he continued. Rescue will be on the way. I can guarantee that. He tried to say it with conviction. They will know that we have stopped here. I just can't say when it will be.

—So the train is buggered? It was a simple direct question, the voice younger than many, from somewhere in front of him.

The train manager looked down at the drivers for support and continued.

—Yes, the train is unserviceable.

The hubbub rallied again.

—Look. The train manager raised his voice for the first time. If you don't let me continue we'll be here for hours. Please, he added, thinking he might have been overly abrupt. He waited until the conversation abated.

—The drivers have confirmed that the train's electronic systems have been compromised. He looked down again and received a backwards nod from the older of the two drivers

—We don't know what caused it. And we will not be able to repair the damage without support from company technicians.

—And when will that be? The question came out quickly halting the next salvo from the mass.

The train manager's brow furrowed.

—I can't say. He paused, as if gathering himself for the next statement. And because we are unsure of rescue plans we need to consider our food and water use.

The crowd paused.

—In order to conserve water I will be switching off the train showers.

He had more to say but the crowd had erupted. And when they did quieten sufficiently for a single voice to be heard, it was the old man, standing behind the manager, who made his point that surely this only applied to those in steerage. That was an end to it. The manager gave up and walked away.

The three had stayed mute during this first skirmish, accepting that decisions had to be made.

But many sought the older woman for comment. Her medical skills had already bestowed status upon her, particularly among the older passengers, where she had mostly plied her acumen.

She'd told the man, the third member of their triumvirate, that her treatment didn't amount to much. Hand-patting, water-soaked cloths and a good lie-down was the *treatment de jour*. She'd scoured the train and pooled its medical kits with that of her own, setting up shop in her cabin. But, she told the man privately, the supplies didn't amount to much more than some paracetamol, ibuprofen and a few bandaids.

The man could see why the passengers were drawn to her. It wasn't only the skills she brought, she exuded a quiet, unflappable competence and efficiency. And there was compassion. Underneath the all-business demeanour the man could sense compassion. But where she might have been a leader she instead chose neutrality.

She was invited to sit with various groups. They all wanted the Matron—as she had become known. It was as if having her in their circle would grant them status and influence. Perhaps it would. Many thought this, some said it quietly in their groups. She knew. Avoided it. Sought out only the man and the younger woman for companionship.

So they sat against the bogey wheels, mostly silent, through the worst of the day, staring out across the endless plain, the mirage of heated air dancing like the precursor to a migraine before them. All three wore sunglasses, like observers in a nineteen-fifties nuclear test. But there was no mushroom cloud, only salt-bush, sparse lank grass and the occasional stringy mulga tree casting a mean shadow across the chalky shallow loam.

2

The Matron never seemed to sit for long. A panicked call for her came from the carriage doorway near to where she rested. She climbed to her feet without any acknowledgement of effort or inconvenience. She moved sensibly in the conditions, stepping carefully around and over outstretched legs, along the edge of the rail-bed to the steep steps into the carriage. An old man reached out a hand from the top of the stairs wanting to do something to help, thinking that this was his value-add to the operation.

It was one of the luxury cabins, in the first passenger carriage. The man lay on a single bed—the other packed away, neatly into a wall cavity, to create some space for those in attendance. A woman, presumably his wife, sat on the bedside mopping at his forehead with a damp cloth. The Matron could see that the patient was distressed. His breath came in short gasps in the stifling heat inside the small room, the air thick enough to chew. She knew she could do no more than was being done. Getting him outside and into the shade of the train where it was ten degrees cooler the only real alternative.

As if knowing what the Matron was thinking, and despising the idea of climbing out of the train to sit indecorously in the dirt, the old man drew one final rasping breath. It was eerily quiet for a moment. The gathered group watched expectantly, breath held, waiting for the next breath to come. It didn't. The woman mopping his brow, paused, turned towards the Matron, stricken, speechless.

—All of you out. She said it before the panic came, ushering all but the wife to the doorway, and began resuscitation. She felt the brittle sternum crack within the first few compressions. She gave it her best, knowing that the old man was unlikely to respond, and if he did, was unlikely to survive. Even in a hospital, with his advanced age, she knew his prognosis would not be good. By this stage there would already be long-term ramifications. But here in the baking heat... She ignored what she knew and worked hard and long for the old woman. Some of the sweat rolling from her brow fell onto the old man's face, running down his cheeks. The tears he'd had no time to shed over his demise. When she began to tire she might have called someone in to take over but knew it was hopeless. It seemed somehow disrespectful to continue. So she just stopped and turned to the old woman.

—I'm sorry.

The old woman nodded, taking the blue-mottled hand of her husband and placing it against her tear-stained cheek. By this time the manager was standing in the doorway. The Matron signalled for him to follow, walking to the carriage doorway, as much for fresher air as privacy.

—Likely heart failure induced by the heat, she said before the manager could speak. It won't be the last, particularly if they remain inside the train during the hottest part of the day.

The manager was overwhelmed and could only nod.

—It goes without saying that you will need to bury him as soon as possible, in this heat...

The manager snapped from a reverie. Here was something to be done.

—Yes, yes, of course.

A shovel found, the hole dug that evening, a respectful but not great distance from the train. The man in the Matron's circle volunteered, he and twin brothers from the back of the train, heading home to a wheatbelt farm. The man wasn't much for manual labour. Not out of laziness, it was simply that his business did not afford him the time. But he wanted to help.

The brothers were much more familiar with the effort required and the implement used, making light work of the chalky loam, only the occasional piece of shale thwarting the shovel edge—the scrape of metal on rock a rude interruption to the peace of the desert night. They spoke little these three. The longest exchange respectful agreement on how deep the hole should be.

The man enjoyed the experience, taking turns, digging quietly, torches off, under the light of a waxing moon a day or so from full.

The dingo watched them from a distance, curious but cautious, squatting in the moon-shadow cast by the salt-bush. They were easy to see, such was the power of the almost-full moon in the clear air.

He was a solitary dog, light ginger, lean and hard, built for agility and stamina. He knew trains, saw them most days. Such was his familiarity he was comfortable to remain in one of his favourite sleeping nooks—a rail-line culvert—while a train rumbled overhead. But his territory didn't include a stop so he rarely saw the occupants. It was only the occasional rail-line work-crew or intrepid adventurer following the rough rail service road who he saw. And this might mean months between sightings.

11

He had approached the stalled train on the first night. He'd been at the outer edge of his territory, miles away, when the barest hint of a breeze carried a melange of scents to him. It was only a vague recognition, given his limited experience with humans. But more than enough to see him into a mile-eating trot.

He'd skirted the train throughout that night with no reward. But the smells, and memories of the barely buried shit of service crews and their rubbish, kept him close. And now he watched these three. When they were finished and had moved back to the train he closed, sniffing around the hole, before pissing in it and on the pile of dirt they'd removed. And then he went back to circling the train.

The old man was laid to rest the next morning while the red dawn rolled through the salt-bush like the leading edge of an incoming tide. The manager had explained to the wife as delicately as possible the necessity of burying the old man so soon. And that it would obviously only be a temporary measure until help arrived, and then he could be exhumed and moved. He assured the woman that his company would assist with all arrangements. He hoped he was right in saying this.

Most of the passengers were there. It was the first funeral. The older people at the front of the train had risen early, knowing that it would take time and effort for them to climb down and move out of the rail-bed and into the trackside scrub. The event had the sense of a happy outing. It was the first time many had left the train. They commented on the coolness of the air, and the beauty of the dawn.

The old man had been wrapped in blankets from the train and lay alongside the hole. The logo on the blankets was prominent, along with the tag line, 'travel well'. There was a moment of panic when it became obvious that no-one had thought about how to get him into the hole.

The hole was deep. During the digging the twins had explained to the man that dingoes were prevalent across the plains, and given the ease of digging, a deep hole was preferable. But the hole was barely longer than the old man's height, so no option for someone to climb down and lower the body. And they couldn't very well drop him in.

The train manager whispered hurriedly to a minion who ran back to the train, returning shortly afterwards with a roll of curtain cord. The manager had wanted this service to go well.

A discussion ensued about how best to undertake the tricky task. A lot of older men had opinions.

—Is he stiff enough to lower him from the ends? That would be easiest.

Eventually four strands of the cord were placed under the old man and eight volunteers recruited. The dead man was shifted close to the hole. Four men stood on the far side clasping the thin cord, looking concerned.

—On three. It was the older train driver who took charge. They lifted. Careful, we don't want to roll him over. Right, let's get him over the hole. They all shuffled, little dust devils erupting from sliding feet. Lower on this side, don't tip hiiiiim. Alright, that's good. On three, let's lower, sloooowly. The body was half-way down when an Oxford brogue found it's way out of the blankets.

—Keep going, we can't stop now. The shoe snagged slightly on the side of the hole cascading some of the sandy loam, the shiny black leather dulled on the toe. Ok, that's it, now you blokes let go of the cord and we'll pull it out from this side.

The train manager then stepped in front of the dirt pile to address the crowd. The shovel stood in the mound where the three had left it. It had a casual air about it, a workman gone off for smoko. He'd queried every carriage the previous night, there wasn't a person who held a religious position to be found. He'd spent the next two hours writing and re-writing his words. It wasn't a task he wanted.

He looked across the hole to where the man's wife stood in a circle of women and gave a small nod. For all the time he had spent writing his notes, his comments were brief. But the old woman and some of her friends thanked him for his sincerity and kindness afterwards.

The twins and the man waited for the crowd to move off. The man threw the first shovel-full into the hole, spilling it across the recalcitrant shoe. The sound of the soil hitting leather made the man pause, as if the process had suddenly become more real. But he stopped only briefly, then sent wave after wave of the dry, desert soil down into the deep hole. It was one of the twins who finished it off, patting the pile it into place with the back of the shovel head. The three of them stared briefly at the grave and then in some unspoken agreement, turned together and headed back to the train.

3

The manager had still not been able to speak to anyone outside their new world, a world that was growing smaller and more isolated by the day as the reality of the situation grew. He had been assured several times by the drivers that all the electrical and electronic systems had been fried, as the younger driver put it. They saw no explanation for it, only saying that it was something strange.

It was the first point for discussion when the meeting came to order. The manager felt much more confident in this environment. They were sitting in a dining car, a representative from each carriage, and the train drivers, twenty or so of them. Much more manageable he thought.

Before the manager had a chance to call them to order someone asked what caused the train to stop. They talked for a while about likely causes and then moved onto why no-one had contacted them. Why no-one had come. It didn't make any sense. It had to be something serious, didn't it.

The manager took the opportunity to reinforce that there was no power for any systems, and that meant that the array of high-tech radio communication devices were useless. He finished by saying that he would certainly take this up with the company.

He explained that his staff had scoured the train in search of a satellite phone among the passengers, but none were forthcoming. Everyone had a mobile of course, but there was no reception out here. He asked the lead driver, the older of the two men, to provide an update of where they were exactly.

—Based on the time we stopped and our speed, I can say with some certainty that we are here. He thumped a strong index finger into the middle of a map he had taped to the carriage window. From a distance the map might have been a blank sheet such was the dearth of landmarks and other distinguishing features, like elevation changes, that might have given the map some substance. On closer inspection the context improved little, a few pin-stripe blue lines signifying creeks which would be nothing more than dusty beds, leading to small, non-existent lakes of cracked and baked earth. The only road, the rough service track running beside the rail line. The only real feature on the map some changes in the shading which signified a shift in the density of vegetation, from non-existent to sparse.

—We are between our two stops. Here and here. And a bit closer south to the highway. His look and manner—that of a ship's captain—gave him an air of competent authority, a bit like the Matron, who had declined to be the representative from her carriage. She said she had enough to do.

They talked about when they might expect rescue and what they needed to do to manage key resources until that time. The manager explained that the kitchens had used up as much of the fresh meat as possible with the remainder having gone bad in the heat. His staff had carted this away and buried it.

—Will this attract predators? It was a younger woman from a rear carriage. It's just that I heard a squeal last night, out in the bush.

The old man who'd had made the 'steerage' comment blew air between disapproving lips. It was the train driver who saw the potential for a blow-up.

—Look. The only stupid questions are ones we don't ask. Let's be respectful here. Madam, it may well attract predators, if it's not been buried appropriately. He looked at the manager when he said this. But the only predators are likely to be dingoes or maybe a goanna or fox. None of which are cause for concern.

The woman nodded to the driver, as much in thanks for his respect as for the answer. The manager also nodded towards the driver. The manager went on to explain that there were to be only three meals a day, nothing in between and no self-service. This was met with a groan from several of the front-of-train representatives but accepted without discussion.

—We will all eat the same meals and there will be no charge to those who were previously on a pay-as-you-go fare.

—Well this is hardly acceptable. It was the old man again. I've had about enough of this. I have paid for the most expensive fare on this lumbering rust bucket. You've stranded my wife and I, and our friends, in the middle of the desert, in this intolerable heat, having turned off our shower. And now you expect us not to be provided with a higher level of service than those others.

The group erupted. The manager looked to the driver. The driver stood and slapped a palm on the dining table, the smack resonating around the carriage. Silence was instant.

—Sir. He looked directly into the old man's eyes. Sir. Everyone could sense the restrained anger in the expulsion of this simple word. If you continue in this way, I will ask you to leave. I understand your frustration but your attitude is not helping the situation. He shifted his gaze back to the whole group. We are in this together. And unfortunately sacrifices need to be made. I am sure the company will make good on this situation once we are rescued. But in the mean-time I would ask you to be patient and reasonable.

The old man pursed his lips and mumbled something largely unintelligible except for the word 'lawyer' which came out clearly.

—What about smashing out some of the windows? It was the young woman who said it while the three were sitting in their spot. She was the youngest in the group, the gap in years between her and the man about the same as that between the man and the Matron. She was returning to her job in one of the many pubs in the goldfields where, she said, she made good money serving beers in her undies.

The Matron had finished explaining her concern for the older passengers who refused to climb off the train in the heat of the day when the young woman made her suggestion. The Matron raised it with the manager who was standing with the driver in the shade of the engine. The manager didn't respond but his look told the Matron that it wasn't a suggestion he welcomed. It was the driver who spoke first.

—Let's try knocking out a dining car window from each of the carriages first to trial it. Not too much damage.

—You'll take responsibility? It was more pleading than statement.

The driver tried not to let his irritation show.

—Yes. Leave it with me. The Matron and I can decide which to remove.

They were regal together this pair. He with the square features and trimmed dark whiskers streaked with grey, she with her portly

18

authority, unblemished skin and short reddish hair. Their arrival together into the carriage brought a small amount of excitement.

The residents agreed it was a good idea. A short discussion ensued as to which window would be appropriate. Definitely the south side of the train, said the driver. He inspected the mountings. I think we might be able to do this without smashing the glass. Let me get some tools. He worked with a Stanley knife and pliers on the rubber mounting surrounding the glass and then levered the glass away with the help of the younger driver and the man from the Matron's circle. They stowed the glass and repeated the process in two more carriages. It proved a success, the residents agreeing that the atmosphere was far more bearable during the heat of the day. It was agreed that more windows be removed.

But it didn't stop people from dying.

It was a woman this time. She took a final breath on day four. She'd collapsed in the tiny bathroom cubicle of her suite in the same carriage where the man had died. She'd been washing herself with a cloth from a bucket of tepid water, trying—apart from addressing her hygiene needs—to ameliorate the feeling of faintness and shortness of breath that had been with her for a day or so. She'd not mentioned it to her husband but had suggested that it might be nice to move outside the train for a while. Her husband wouldn't hear of it.

He yelled for help and was attempting to protect his wife's modesty with a monogrammed robe when the Matron arrived. When she realised where the woman had fallen she sent for the driver and her friend to assist. She had to pull the old man out of the doorway.

—Please, we need to treat her. And I don't want you to become my next patient. These men will be respectful.

The old man backed out. His face was pale. The Matron could see

19

that his blood pressure had fallen dangerously and he was likely to pass out. She sat him into the chair while the men extricated his wife, laying her gently on the single bed. The Matron covered her torso with a sheet and checked for vital signs. She began resuscitation but stopped after a much shorter time than she had on the old man.

The woman's husband rocked backwards and forwards slightly on his chair.

—She wanted to go outside.

The old man wanted to speak at the burial. The twins and the man had dug another grave, sighting it neatly in line with the old man's but at a respectful distance. The man suggested to the twins that they find some volunteers among the younger members of the train to dig the next. The boys looked uncomfortable, not so much in finding volunteers but recognising that there would be need for more graves.

Fewer people attended the burial, but not noticeably fewer. That would come.

With a second death, the driver had taken the initiative to construct a simple cross for each of the two graves, as much for identification during exhumation, as for any religious leanings he might have had. He asked the partners of the dead whether they thought a cross appropriate.

He'd scoured the train for something to make them from, taking bed slats from the crew compartment. He trimmed the wood with a hacksaw—the only saw he had—and heated the end of steel knife handle over the gas cook ring in the drivers' cab and burned the names of the dead into the crosses. He'd always had a neat hand.

—Fifty-seven years, the old man began. The crowd was gathered as before, the sun peaking across the plain, the flies beginning to gather.

—Fifty-seven years. He stalled, staring into the hole to the blanket-wrapped body lying inert in the earth. He had no other words. It was awkward. Was it a sadness so deep that the old man was struck dumb by the enormity of the emptiness that confronted him? Or did he suddenly realise that the years together were the sum total of their relationship? No more than a score.

The manager stepped forward, putting a hand on the old man's shoulder, guiding him back towards his friends. The manager had amended his notes but the sentiments were the same. He didn't know what else to say. He'd asked the driver whether he would like to do this one. The driver had smiled. No thanks.

The passengers moved off quickly. The driver and the grave diggers remained behind.

The man—he'd told the twins to call him Ticky, as he was known in the boardroom—watched as one of the brothers took his turn scooping the dry earth back into the hole. When they'd patted down the final shovel-full they used the back of the shovel head to hammer the crosses into the earth. The driver winced a little as the force required slightly flattened and splintered the top of his cross.

The dingo dug furiously, the smell goading him.

Two of the manager's staff had been given the grave shovel and told to bury the rotten meat, deep. But deep was a subjective term. They'd not gone a third of the depth as the grave diggers. And while it was probably enough to ensure that the passengers wouldn't smell the decaying cache, it wasn't near deep enough to avoid sending out a homing beacon to the native dog.

The dog had had no luck with plunder to this point, apart from licking at a few drying piss stains, but something made him stay in the area. The odours that had brought him close were still prevalent, they just hadn't amounted to anything. But he was patient. It went with the territory and his breed. And he wasn't starving. He'd run-down a rabbit the night before, the staple in his diet. It was the squeal the woman had heard.

But here it was. His patience paying dividends. He was head-down in the loosely packed loam, paws scraping furiously, like a duck frantically swimming, the dirt flying between his back legs. He was an expert digger, occasionally sniffing out rabbits and catching them in their burrows, sometimes a litter of babies.

But even in his desperation to reach the source of this unfamiliar efflux, he paused briefly every now and again, glancing around, sniffing the air, listening, ensuring that nothing was going to catch him unawares. The full moon made him more attentive than usual.

He toiled underneath the brightest star in the sky, Sirius—or the dog star as it was known. It was part of Canis Major, the greater dog constellation, which followed Orion the hunter across the night sky.

It wasn't just the presence of people that made him cautious, there was always the possibility of an interloper, another dog, or worse, a pack, coming into his territory, driven by the strong scent of the rotting cache. He was a mature animal at the height of his power. He had carved out his patch, fighting pitched battles, establishing his piss-soaked boundaries that he traversed and re-sprayed with regularity. The only time he strayed was when the smell of a female in oestrous drew him out. It was a dangerous journey, often across multiple territories, arriving to an unwelcome reception and a reward for which he would have to fight. He had returned from his last sojourn sore and sorry, laying up under the culvert for many days, licking at the wound on his front leg. But he would go again.

He'd sniffed around the fresh mounds of dirt on the other side of the rail line the night before. He could smell that something was buried there as well—another foreign odour—but a tentative dig in the soil made him quickly realise that the depth was beyond him.

But this was different. As he pulled away more of the loose soil his excitement grew. And then he was into the rotten flesh. It crawled with a million white maggots and he gorged, the maggots spilling across his snout and into his eyes. Though he didn't know it he was eating some expensive cuts, aged black angus, wagyu, new-season lamb and even some pork. There were no sheep or cattle this far out into the desert so the tastes were alien to his palette but it was of no account. He ate until he could eat no more. He rested for an hour in the salt-bush and then returned and gorged further. But even with this second attempt he left behind still more. But he would return. He walked off, his distended stomach penduluming with each stride. He went to the railway culvert and curled up against the bank, still holding heat from the day just gone, and slept long into the next morning.

4

The Matron sat bolt upright in her bunk. She was drenched in sweat. The train was quiet. She'd been woken by her menopausal night sweats more times than she cared to remember but this one had the added joy of a bad dream. It was the old man, the first person to die. She found it more strange than scary. She'd spent a lifetime working around death. There were dreams in the beginning, back when she was young and learning. Some of them frightening enough to make her wonder whether it was the job for her. But she persisted. Within a few years they had largely stopped. She couldn't remember the last time she'd had one.

She lay in her bunk, sheet bunched beneath her, damp. She had a room to herself, the door propped open and the window removed from the corridor outside. She'd been sleeping well. The nights were cool enough and with the windows removed the day's heat build-up could drain away as the night wore on. She'd visualised the heavy hot air flowing out of the window holes like good custard.

Her cabin window was on the north side of the train so she kept the blind drawn all through the day to keep out as much heat as possible. And with the full moon, she'd been keeping the blind closed at night.

Removing the windows had been a great idea. After removing a half dozen, Ticky had suggested the driver pass his tools to the twin brothers. The driver had enough to do. The brothers moved along the train, firstly asking, and then removing windows. They were task-driven boys, Ticky had said. They needed things to do and were happy to figure out how to do them. The sort of people he liked to recruit for his company. Common sense and a strong work ethic. Traits he said, that were harder to find than one might imagine, especially among the young.

No-one said no to the window removal and within two days almost all the windows on the south side were gone. And while the carriages still shone silver and new under the desert sun, the removal of the windows instilled an air of dilapidation about the train. Even though the job had been done neatly—not one broken pane, the windows stored in the baggage car—there was something about looking at the darkened holes in the afternoon shadows. Like peering into a gap-toothed mouth.

The Matron felt it. She'd said as much to her friend, making the point that she now felt that they were part of the landscape rather than simply passing through it. She told him the story from another holiday. She'd been in the north some years before, on a day trip with a dozen or so people in an old and massive four-wheel-drive vehicle, driving all day, looking at the wild buffalo, crocodiles and birds. She loved the birds. She told the man that she fancied herself as a bit of an amateur birder. No, not a twitcher, she said to him. That was an English word and generally accepted to mean the pursuit of rare species, largely across England and Northern Europe. No, she just enjoyed looking at all and any birds. She did record her sightings and take a lot of photos but was not all that obsessive about it. Not like some.

—Anyway, she'd said, we were out on this all-day outing in this old vehicle with no windows. We had an Aboriginal woman for a guide and a white driver, a man that lived and worked with the Aboriginal communities. It was a grand day. I asked the driver why the vehicle had no windows. And he'd said that he'd removed them. He'd found that with the windows and air-conditioning people were often loathe to leave the vehicle and get involved in activities. But with the windows gone, people never hesitated. It wasn't just the change in temperature, he'd said, it was something about that glass barrier, like being at a zoo. With it gone, they felt part of what they saw, rather than observers passing through it.

—Well, we're certainly part of this landscape, Ticky said. Not much choice there.

The Matron climbed from her bed and walked to the empty window frame and peered into the night. The moon was just on the waining side of full but still casting its strong luminous glow across the plain. So much so that the train offered a giant shadow across the trackside, its square proportions incongruous to the shape of the natural desert elements. The shadow was the reason she was able to watch the dingo move past. She'd seen it almost immediately as it moved around from the front of train. The skin on her neck had prickled when she first saw it. It moved wraith-like under the moon. Trotting, unconcerned, stopping briefly to sniff at something, moving on again, soundless. The night was so quiet that she rubbed the tip of her long finger against the pad of her thumb to make a soft sound to prove she hadn't lost her hearing.

It was a special moment for her. There was no fear. She knew enough to know that the dog presented very little threat to humans.

And so she watched it. She looked down the train's length, hoping that she wouldn't see the outline of someone else peering from a window. She wanted this to be her moment.

And then she almost laughed, smiling in the darkness. The irony she thought. A train full of the planet's apex predators, top of the food chain. Opposable thumbs and big brains. And doing what? Descending into chaos. I can see it coming. And all the while this simple beautiful creature wandering around us, getting on with life. Surviving, prospering, in an environment that will likely end us all. Was it irony, she wondered? She'd never really been able to come up with a satisfactory definition for irony.

The dingo moved closer to the train, slightly past where she stood. It stopped, turning to look up at her, as if hearing her thoughts. She hadn't moved. She found herself holding her breath. The dog's almond-shaped eyes held her gaze, ears pricked, the moon bright enough for the woman to see the lighter colour of the dog's muzzle hair.

And then the dog moved off into the train shadow towards the rear, the darkness quickly swallowing it. She let the breath go, taking a couple of shorter ones to recover her breathing pattern. She smiled again in the darkness, shivering slightly, the night-sweat drying, and turned back to her bed.

The deputation interrupted the meeting. They avoided eye contact with their carriage representative who sat in the group.

—It's been six days. We don't want to wait any longer. We want to go for help. There were five of them. The leader short, broad across the chest, not much neck, shoulders and arms sculpted from hundreds of hours of repeated lifting efforts, a tattoo on the side of his neck—a lion and eagle intertwined.

—No one's coming. One of his cronies added this, as if it was a forgotten part of the leader's speech.

The driver was a good judge of men. People in general. And he'd expected something like this to come up eventually. Had talked to the Matron's friend about it already. Workshopped some ideas about going for help. Nothing much had made any sense. They were just too far from anywhere, the sun too fierce. The shortest walk was to the highway south of them. At least two or three days. West or east along the rails it was probably another day on top of that. They'd agreed the rails made more sense. You couldn't get lost that way and if help was coming then you'd meet it. But whatever direction they went what would be there?

The highway held the promise of traffic, but they agreed that if whatever had stopped them had also stopped the traffic, then whoever made the journey would be in trouble. There was nothing else there. No town, no water. It was death. At least to the west was the next siding. There was plenty of water there but not much else. A family lived there. They'd have food, not enough to feed a train, and how would they get anything back here. If they had a vehicle that functioned surely they'd already have been out to find the train.

The driver had told the man that there might be a goods train somewhere between them and the siding. One had been expected. They should have passed it sometime on that first night at one of the passing sidings. Who knew what was on it, the driver said. It would have a small crew and could be carrying anything. Maybe there were useful things. But still, a long walk.

They'd agreed that if someone was going to go they would need to leave soon, while there was still enough water and food to spare for them. So the interruption had only brought forward the discussion that the driver had wanted to introduce. And it saved the trouble of finding volunteers.

He held up a hand to forestall the response from the disgruntled carriage representative.

—Gentlemen, please find somewhere to sit down.

The driver could see that his welcome to the men had taken the wind out of the leader's sail, his chest dropping slightly with a tense breath being released. It told the driver something about the leader. That he was nervous and edgy in his role. Maybe not a good leader. Emotional, rash even, believing leadership was about physical strength. He thought about the twins. He'd talked to Ticky about them. They'd agreed that they would be useful.

But as it was the driver would need to deal with the five in front of him. He knew who they were. The manager had already mentioned them. Telling him that before the train stopped they'd been drinking a lot and disturbing the other passengers. Trouble in the making. The manager had said that they were all miners, the fly-in, fly-out types so common to the region. Cashed up, and rather than fly off to Bali or somewhere similar, they'd spent their down days on this occasion drinking their way across and back over the desert.

—You boys got a plan? There were no spare seats so the five remained standing, a little awkwardly. The leader looked uncomfortable, having been prepared to argue the right to leave, but not much more than that.

He stumbled for a moment. Look, it's not complicated, we just walk for help.

—Which way had you planned on going?

The leader could see the map, taped to the window. Look, just wanted you to know that we are keen to go. We don't have a plan.

—Thanks boys. It's something we are going to discuss. So we'll come back to you.

The leader knew he'd been dismissed. And he didn't know what else to say.

—Right, he said, and turned on his heel not making eye contact with his cronies but leading them out of the dining car.

The manager, who was sitting quietly in the corner, nodded his approval.

The driver took the opportunity to explain what he had discussed with the Matron's friend. He told them about the distances and what might be there. It was generally agreed that a couple of people should go west. That the goods train might offer succour, and if not, that help might more likely be sought from the railway siding than from the highway.

The meeting concluded in time for dinner. It was meagre fare. The cooks were down to what they could make from tins, bags of pasta and rice, and the few vegetables that held in the heat, potatoes, onions, pumpkin. They were under strict instructions on portion size, the manager stressing, after talking to the the Matron, that the food had to last another two weeks. That was the limit of the water supply, even with strict rationing.

The Matron had gone about the train talking to various groups explaining the water rationing, telling people to stay as inactive as possible. That any effort would increase the body's water usage. To sip at the water rather than slug it down in gulps, letting it rinse around the mouth before swallowing.

Ticky could see that she was happy to be busy and said as much. She explained that she'd had doubts about coming on the trip, that sitting for three or four days without much activity might not agree. But it was something she needed to do. It was something her partner had long wanted to do and the Matron felt she owed it to her memory.

—A bit sentimental. Not very me, she'd laughed when she said it. Though she and the man had been talking for long hours over many days it was the first time she had discussed anything of a personal nature, beyond her career.

Ticky asked what had happened to her.

—Breast cancer.

—Insidious disease, all cancers.

—Yes. I had many opportunities to work in oncological areas in hospitals but could never face it. I preferred the short-term nature of casualty treatment and surgery. It sounds harsh but the way I saw it people either lived or died. You either saved a life or you didn't and then you moved on. No time to think too much about it. There was always another one waiting. But the idea of travelling a journey with someone over months or years, and more-often-than-not watching his or her demise was never something I could countenance. It's a great irony, isn't it? She turned to look at the man's face. That I spent six months watching her die.

She'd turned away and leant back against the bogie wheels, just as the younger woman came to join them. It saved Ticky from having to say anything more on the subject.

The driver sought out Ticky to discuss who and how many should go for help.

—Two, or three at the maximum, was his view. The driver agreed. As to who should go they both agreed that the young twins were the best option but that if they didn't send at least some of the group of miners they would have trouble. Ticky suggested some of the miners be sent towards the highway.

31

—There's a better than even chance that they'd end up dead. Can we countenance that?

—It's the shortest distance, a viable option. It could very well be the solution.

—And we haven't yet asked the twins.

—No. But there's no doubt that they'd do it.

—What about you? Should you go with the twins?

—I've thought about that. I think I'm up to it.

The twins didn't hesitate. Simply nodding their agreement. Immediately understanding the gravity of the task and unlike the miners, not treating it like a boy's-own adventure.

The miners decided among their group which three of them would go south. The driver had explained that their experience living in isolated mining camps in the desert made them the logical choice for the cross-country journey to the south. The men gobbled up the faux compliment.

It was agreed both groups would leave the following evening. The driver explained that they should walk steadily through the night hours and into the morning, finding shade during the hottest hours of the day. They'd be given as much water as they could reasonably carry and a small amount of food.

The miners laughed and talked about the challenge. The twins and Ticky sat quiet saying nothing. The driver didn't mention the possibility of encountering the goods train until after the miners had departed to rest up for the day.

—I'm not sure what it could mean, if it's there, he said to the three. It'll be a matter of seeing what they have on board and how far away you are, or whether it's better that you continue on to the siding.

When they'd gone off to prepare the driver sat quietly by himself looking out across the plain through the glassless window. As much as he respected the Matron's friend, the driver was concerned that they'd agreed too quickly to send the miners off into the desert. They had prayed on the leader's arrogance. He didn't feel good about it. But as much as he didn't like it, he didn't see a better option. If he didn't send them they'd cause trouble. He agreed with Ticky on that. The five miners had the potential to cause trouble on the train, to tip the balance, and they couldn't afford that. But neither did the driver want to send them along the tracks, their best option as he saw it. He wouldn't trust them to act in the best interests of the other passengers. If there was a way out for them he could see them taking it. But of the twins and Ticky, he had no such qualms. No, they were the logical choice. And who knew, the miners might make it across the desert and be back with assistance before the twins and the man even got to the siding.

Whatever the case there was still the issue of what was out there. The driver had sat with Ticky and the Matron, quietly discussing this into the night. The young woman was not there, having taken to sitting with some of the younger passengers at the other end of the train in the evenings but still spending the heat of the day with her two companions against the bogie wheels.

It was a week now with no contact. They agreed that it was something serious and that they were more than likely on their own.

—And where are the planes? The Matron said it, thinking that she hadn't thought about it until now. Even if they haven't been able to drive out or send another train, surely someone could fly over in a plane.

—No, it's something catastrophic, said Ticky.

They talked about who might be worrying after them. The Matron and her friend agreed their lot was similar.

—No, Ticky laughed as he said it, my wife wouldn't have raised the alarm. We don't have a lot to say to each other any more. And I disappear for long periods on business without much explanation. No, it'd be my personal assistant or the board who would be most concerned, worrying that a long absence might send a scare through the shareholders.

—No children?

—An estranged son. We haven't spoken in years.

The Matron said that with her partner gone there was no-one to raise the alarm. She had friends, yes, but they weren't likely to be concerned for a long time.

Ticky asked the driver about his background suggesting that he seemed somewhat overqualified for the job as a train driver.

—I mean no disrespect, but I watch you managing people. How you've taken over management of this mess. You look like you'd be at home in the boardroom.

The driver smiled. No, just a train driver, no secrets. Did my time on ships for most of my life and then married late. I needed to compromise. Couldn't disappear for months on end any longer but had to find something that still gave me that sense of freedom but allowed my marriage to survive. Trains were the answer. The Matron talked a bit about her career, repeating some of the things that the man already knew, about her partner and the long drawn-out death she'd had to confront. It was a good night for all of them. Souls bared, they slept with clean slates that would clear their minds for the days ahead.

5

The young barmaid—Izzy she liked to be called—thought the departure of the two groups a strange event. By now the whole train knew of the plan and most had turned out to bid them farewell. Izzy had an image of pictures she remembered of soldiers heading off to war. Men walking up gang planks to board troop ships, railings draped in streamers, heading off into the unknown. Right on their side, self-belief strong. The atmosphere festive, young men with no idea of the horrors that would befall them, things they'd see scalded into their brains that they would carry for a lifetime.

Her grandfather had been one of these. She knew the war had been a big part of his life. Saw it, not just in his house, but in the way he lived, carried himself. Her strongest memory was of him polishing his boots every night, a habit, he'd told her, that he picked up in the army that had continued throughout his life. He taught her how to set fire to a new tin of polish, let it burn just long enough to soften the polish and then slip on the lid to starve the flames of oxygen. And then he'd use the back of the brush, the small circle of bristles, to spread the polish over his brown riding boots. , The sweet odour. He wouldn't wear black. He'd never told her why.Once the polish was on he'd turn the brush over and work it into the leather with firm and quick strokes, his hand piston-like. And then he'd spit onto the surface. Spit shine, he'd called it. He'd let her spit on his boots, she loved it. Loved him. She loved the smell of the boots, the mirrored finish. It was the smell of her Pa. Pipe smoke, polish and Old Spice.

She could see that the two groups were very different. The brothers, she'd spoken to only in passing, were serious-looking, uncomfortable under the attention. No smile. They stood in their outback hats, saying little. Them and the man looked ready.

The miners were loud and excited. She'd seen them over previous days, knew from experience to avoid them. These were the types who came to watch her pour beer in her undies. She could see it in her mind, they'd stand at the bar, quietly, almost respectful. But as the evening progressed so would the behaviour change. She sometimes thought that she should write a paper about it or whatever university types called it. It was mostly comments, cheeky to start and then dirty. But then, occasionally nasty. She was good at handling them, those men. She'd laugh most of it off, was quick with a witty response, make one of them the butt of her joke in front of his mates. It would work more often than not, even earn her a bit of respect in front of them. But then there'd be one, always one. Too drunk, too insecure? He'd get offended at a refusal, get angry at a joke, get embarrassed in front of his mates. Who knew? But she'd been around long enough to recognise the moment, the type. She never hesitated, she'd push the button and the security boys would be there in a flash.

They didn't muck about those boys. Pacific islanders mostly. Big men. They'd encourage the person to leave, frog-march him if necessary. Firmly but with respect. There were cameras now. And they knew the job. The owner didn't tolerate bullies in his employ. They'd call cabs or the police if necessary.

Some of the women only lasted a shift or two. She'd seen it more than a few times. Off in tears, men cheering, a childish victory. They could smell the fear. It was primal, she could see that. Figured that was what made her good at her job. It reminded her of school, when they would have a substitute teacher. A few quick tests to see how the teacher reacted, particularly young women.

The boss would send new starters to speak to her, paid her a bit extra to do it. She'd give them a bit of advice, what to wear, what to expect, how to cope, how to react. She'd know after one shift if someone was going to cut it. And there wasn't much point in saying anything else to them. Some would hang on, usually because the money was good, but hating it. But they usually didn't make good workers. They'd be cold and unfriendly to the patrons, their way of coping. It wasn't good for business, wasn't why they were there. She'd never say anything to the boss, and he didn't expect her to. But he'd know pretty quickly and they'd be sent on their way, often turning up in another place down the street. And there was always someone new.

She sometimes wondered what it said about her. That she could survive the work, do it well, even like it to an extent. Did it mean she was a sell-out to her sex. She'd grown up in a blue-collar household. She was pragmatic. She liked that word, liked the way it felt in her mouth. She knew how to work, had always done well in whatever she turned her hand to, waitressing, factory work with her mum, whatever. But she could see how things were for women. And in her own quiet way would say what she thought to her friends, look out for other women. One of her mates had once called her a rebel, asked if she was a lesbian.

So how did she countenance standing around for five or six hours in skimpy underwear, providing a show for horny miners. The best

37

she could come up with was that she did the job on her terms, that she went home each night with her self-respect intact. And that if men wanted to stand around spending their hard-earned watching her then it was more of a reflection on them than her. But she did think about it.

She could see it in the leader, had a look about him, a chip on his shoulder. One of the nasty ones.

There'd not been any speeches. The Captain—as Ticky was now calling him—didn't want it to turn into an event. It wouldn't have been if those miners hadn't made such a fuss. He could tell the twins were embarrassed by the attention, the approbation. Ticky took it in his stride. But the twins, like everything they'd done since the train had stopped, they just wanted to get on with it, without fuss.

The Captain knew he'd be the same. Who knew what was out there, what would confront them? Death was a possibility. Mind you, he thought, that's what awaits us all in a couple of weeks if this doesn't work. The two groups were at least doing something. He'd thought on more than a few occasions that he'd be happy to go with them. Rather die making an effort than sitting and waiting. Waiting on the actions of others. But he couldn't go. He knew that. He'd created the role for himself. Not intentionally. He didn't really know how it had happened. Both then and throughout his life. Like when he'd started in maritime college. He wasn't the smartest in his group, but the others were drawn to him, he could see even at a young age. Pushing him forward when they needed a leader. And it had repeated itself throughout his life, often in times of crisis. Like the time in Biscay, working as a first officer, when he'd had to take over from a frightened captain. He never gave it a lot of thought, didn't think it made him special but he did recognise it within himself.

And it had happened here, on the train. He'd taken over, largely out of frustration with the manager. And because he could see that the manager didn't want to do it. He liked him well enough. It was obvious the man wasn't afraid of work but he was a poor judge of people, and a situation. The Captain shook his head when he thought of the company pushing a man like this into such an important role, disaster aside.

He watched as the twins and Ticky hefted their packs. The twins sported large, sensible travel packs belonging to a Dutch couple, who had gladly handed them over. The boys gave a final shy wave and turned away from the rear of the train. Ticky hugged the Matron and Izzy and joined them, giving a final nod to the driver. A round of applause broke out as they moved away. The moon was still bright across the plain and the three were lit in its glow for a long time as they moved steadily away along the tracks.

But then the focus shifted to the miners. The five stood in a circle making jokes, the two remaining behind doing lots of back slapping. The three making pointed comments about the manhood of the two. They drew a bigger crowd than the twins.

The Captain frowned. He walked to stand next to the Matron and Izzy who were watching from the periphery.

—Did we do the right thing, sending these three? He said it for himself but loud enough for the Matron to hear.

—I'm not sure you had a choice.

The three hefted packs. They carried a similar load with the addition of a compass that had belonged to the Dutch couple. The Captain had discussed it with the leader of the miners, showing him on the map the simplest way was for them to head due south. He'd tried briefly to explain how he could navigate at night using the Southern Cross, in case anything went wrong with the compass, but he wasn't confident the leader really understood, despite his nods of agreement.

The Captain had talked about the country they would cross and how it wouldn't change significantly along the way, maybe just some thicker patches of scrub here and there, which he said would be crucial for sitting out the worst of the midday heat. He reiterated the importance of this, with the support of the Matron. At the urging of the Captain the Matron attempted to throw a scare into the miners about what would happen if they tried to walk through the worst of the heat.

The three headed off, jibes ringing out across the plain as their friends continued the banter. But then they were gone.

The three heading west walked the rail-bed, one behind the other, the going even but noisy, the blue metal between the concrete sleepers crunching like new-season apples under their feet. They walked without speaking, largely because of the noise of their tread but also because they were three who did not feel the need to fill the quiet with words. They would speak when they needed to. They had talked to the Captain and the Matron about conserving energy, walking a steady but easy pace. Limit their water loss, sip at their water supply. The twins would've done this anyway, but they weren't offended to have it explained to them.

They'd listened to others talk about what had caused the train to stop. Had been asked for their opinion. They had little to offer on the subject. It didn't much matter what had caused it, one of them had said, we need to focus on what we're going to do about it.

They were happy in their own company. But it wasn't as if they were averse to friendships with others. They'd had different friends during their schooling, especially during the final years of boarding school. They'd both brought different mates home to the farm for holidays. The train journey was a final holiday of sorts, together. They'd gone across the continent to look at the university where the younger one was heading—younger by a few minutes. The trip, an excuse, largely, to spend some time together before they lived separately for the first time in their lives.

The other would stay on the farm. Maybe go off to the city at some point and do some agriculture-related study but mostly just work the farm. All that he had ever wanted to do. For him school was an impediment, a test of patience, holding him back from the things he loved. He'd been a good student, not as good as his brother, but solid. But his thoughts went to machinery and cropping, the huge headers they used to harvest the wheat. And to tonnes per acre, rainfall patterns, market demand, wheat rust, storage, transport.

He'd given a lot of thought to buying a contracting outfit to supplement the farm income, buying a machine and heading around the state to harvest the crops of others. He and his father could do that, the two of them could manage a harvesting outfit and their farm between them. But he'd have to convince the old man. Knew that he wasn't keen on the idea of so much debt at his time of life, and with the price of wheat and weather so changeable.

His brother was just as sure of his own future. Sure that it lay anywhere other than on the farm. From an early age he knew that the farm was the last place he wanted to be. He felt constricted by it, to the point that he felt fear that he might be trapped there, like hands around his neck, slowly choking him. That's how he'd explained it to his brother. His brother had said that he should talk to their parents about it, that they'd understand. But he was frightened. Frightened of what his father would say. He could hear his father's voice talking about how his own father had worked the farm. Lineage and generations were words he liked to use. And he talked about his sons taking over when he was too old to climb on a tractor or knock in a steel picket. Their mother would chide him, saying that maybe the boys didn't want to be farmers. Of course they do, he'd respond.

So the boy fretted, until the day he had bucked up the courage to say, during one of his breaks from school, that he didn't know if he wanted to farm. His father had burst out laughing.

—We figured as much, we were just wondering when you were going to say something.

The boy had never felt such relief. They'd suspected for years, had laughed about it, his father had said.

—Why didn't you say something, he'd asked?

—It had to be your decision, his mother had said. It's your life.

And so, he was university bound. Though he wouldn't say it, he was sad to be leaving his brother, to be going so far away, but as twins do, he never questioned the bond that would remain between them. But that was then and this was now. They'd talked about what lay ahead. Were in no doubt as to the seriousness of the situation they were in.

The dingo watched them. He heard them before he saw them. The crunching of boots in the rail-bed, a sound that carried miles in the still night of the desert. He was out in the salt-bush, sniffing out rabbits. He'd stayed close to the train but after the initial gorging on the buried meat there hadn't been much more, apart from buried shit. So when he heard the twins he moved closer to investigate, trailing them, slightly behind and out across the plain a distance, watching them walk steadily away from the train.

It was shit that caused one of the biggest problems on the train. The toilets were already being flushed with dippers of water—the vacuum flushing had stopped working when the train rolled to a halt. As the days had progressed it had become one toilet per carriage, with lessons provided by the staff on how to flush the waste away with a minimum of water. But now that they had agreed the water needed to last two more weeks, the water could not be spared for flushing. And that meant that those that could would need to walk into the marked-off area in the scrub to do their business. But worse, it meant that the elderly and infirm, those who couldn't leave the train would have to use a bucket and then staff would have to empty them. This was the decision that the Captain and the manager made. It wasn't well received.

It was some of the staff who made the first fuss.

—There's nothing in my contract that talks about me carrying other people's shit, a young woman had said.

An argument had ensued. The Captain had left the issue to the manager but then had heard the ruckus in the carriage dining area. He'd walked in and slapped a big palm onto the table. The hubbub had ceased. He'd asked the manager to explain what was going on. It caught him by surprise and he was somewhat annoyed that he'd not thought about the train staff.

Until this point they'd largely accepted the changing roles without complaint. It was the one area where he thought the manager had done a good job. He had a largely loyal and hardworking crew who had been flexible in their dealing with the situation. Working hard to assist the passengers where they could, especially the elderly.

But he'd not thought about when that goodwill might evaporate, and only now did he consider that there might come a time when the staff decided that given the situation, it was everyone for themselves.

He hoped that it wasn't now. It was the next comment that worried him most.

—Who decided that you're in charge anyway? It was the same young woman.

He didn't know her name, knew very few of their names. He had very little to do with the train staff. He and his assistant largely kept to themselves during a journey, taking over from another crew at one of the cities along the route and then handing over further down the line. They spent their time in the cab of the huge diesel-electric engine, one driving and pushing the deadman every ninety seconds, the other spotting, making the coffee and serving up the food. Any communication with the crew was usually via the train's intercom.

The Captain loved the job. It was reminiscent of his time at sea. He'd loved the night-watch shift on a darkened bridge on a gentle sea, a coffee in hand. The only interruption the occasional crackle of the radio with chatter from a passing ship. Someone on a similar watch looking to pass a few minutes in companionable discussion with a brother officer. And he'd found the train not dissimilar. His new bridge might not have been so grand but it was hard to find fault with the magnificence of the changing vista. And unlike the ocean this view would change by the hour, sometimes markedly, depending on what part of the country he was operating in. But it was the desert he loved most. Perhaps it was the closest to his gentle seas. There was something about the sparse openness that was so peaceful, the changes subtle. And the wild-life. Big mobs of red kangaroos, the odd dingo and even a few camels. He was never bored. And then he would be home again with his wife, his need for movement and adventure sated until his next shift.

He'd wondered over the years, often when sitting on the bridge of a ship at night, whether he would ever marry. It wasn't something he wanted to do for the sake of having a wife. Like ticking a box on a list. He'd worked with too many seamen who talked like that. Who were happy to go to sea for months on end to escape the woman at home. No, he didn't want that.

But he wasn't averse to the idea, liking the thought of a companion as he aged. He knew there was a place for someone else in his life but that it had to be a good fit. He knew he could give up the sea. There were other jobs. Ferries, coastal shipping. So he wasn't concerned about giving up the ocean. But when the time came it caught him by surprise. It was as he had hoped. That it had snuck up on him without him realising it. They had married in their fifties, she a widower, with grown children, and he the bachelor. He'd never had a second's hesitation walking off his final ship. It had seemed to be part of a natural process, and a new career had come quickly. When he'd gone to ask about ferries and coastal shipping someone had asked whether he'd thought about trains.

He stared at the young woman briefly, trying to get a read on her, before responding.

—We're all just doing our bit. He ignored the question about his authority. I'm sorry that these jobs have to be done. But we have a responsibility to our guests.

—Easy for you to say. You don't have to carry people's filth around.

A chorus of supportive murmuring told the Captain that things had reached a critical juncture. But it was the Matron who responded.

—Can I say something? The Captain hadn't realised that she'd followed him into the dining car. She didn't wait for permission.

—It's not about us and them any longer. She looked directly at the young woman who protested. I'm carrying shit, I'm climbing out

45

of my bed at all hours of the night, I'm sharing my expertise with anyone who needs it. You're the lucky ones. She looked around the group as she said it. You're young and healthy. If anyone is going to survive this ordeal it's you. Try to imagine how it must be for these older people. Yes, they might be rude sometimes. But I guarantee you it's fear that's driving them. Imagine being too scared to climb off the train to sit in the shade. That you'd rather sit inside this insidious oven, slowly baking yourself because the alternative is to risk a broken hip or leg or arm. Frankly I'm a little ashamed we're even having this conversation. This isn't about your jobs, it's about compassion.

It hung in the air with the smell of their unwashed bodies. No-one wanted to be the first to say anything. The Captain was careful not to show any emotion, or even move. He wanted it to hang as long as possible. The longer it hung the better would seem the impact that the Matron had made. She was good, that woman. But he knew that this kind of approach would only work a couple of times at best. There must be reams of stuff written about this kind of situation, he thought. About how people interacted with each other in times of crisis. Taken out of their normal lives. Hell, there were whole television networks dedicated to it now. He'd never watched reality television. It made him cringe. But he wondered now whether he might have learned something more of human nature. About who prospered and who suffered and how he could better manage the situation.

He waited a few seconds more.

—Right, let's be about it then.

The meeting broke up and the staff moved off, most not wanting to make eye contact with anyone else.

—Thanks, was all the Captain could think to say when he was alone with the Matron.

—You're welcome, was all she had to say on the subject.

6

There were three more deaths in the next two days. One was the wife of the man who had already died. Their friends thought it appropriate, even somewhat romantic. One not being able to survive without the other. The Matron had heard them talking. But she held no truck with such notions.

—It was heat stroke that killed that woman. Too much stress on a heart that was already being supported by beta blockers and statins. I'm sure that the death of her husband was a factor but it was the added load, despair if you like, that sent her into arrest, not some random notion of love.

—Aren't they the same thing? It was Izzy. They were back against the bogey wheels. Just two of them now. I mean isn't the load, as you call it, brought about by despair, just another way of describing love? It's like we're describing the same thing but using different words. The poor old woman suddenly realised what her life was going to be without him, what it had been with him. That without him she was only a part person. Some might call that love.

The Matron smiled as she looked across the salt-bush, waving at the flies with her whisk—she'd pulled a small branch of leaves from an acacia. She liked Izzy's forthright ways. Saying what she thought, respectfully, but making her point.

—But if that's the case, why didn't I die when my partner passed away. I defy that woman to have loved her mate any more than I did mine. Based on your argument I should have passed away as well. Or are you saying I loved her less?

Izzy didn't know how to answer. It was the Matron who spoke first.

—Sorry. That wasn't very fair. And I didn't mean it. It was more for the sake of winning the argument than making a valid point. It's a bad habit of mine. Comes from a lifetime of dealing with men. Doctors and surgeons mostly. And trying to hold one's own in that world of arrogance and privilege. But it's also in my nature to look for the science in something. Being able to measure and test something.

—Like faith, religion? Izzy had re-gathered herself.

—Are you religious?

—Fuck no. Sorry. No. Not at all. I hate that stuff.

The Matron laughed. Don't apologise for swearing. I was a nurse my whole working life.

—I really hate religion, especially Christianity. She looked around to see if anyone was sitting close. I was raised a catholic. A good catholic girl. First communion, all that stuff, church every Sunday, went to a convent school in the country. The way the nuns treated the kids from the old-money families, the ones that gave to the church, and the way they treated us. Made me sick. And then all this shit with priests. The one place that kids should have been safe, the one person they should've been able to trust. Monsters. The ultimate betrayal. Disgusting.

49

—The ultimate betrayal. I like that, sounds like a good name for a movie or book. Yes, you'll get no argument from me on that subject.

—Do you think we'll die here?

The Matron thought about the question for some seconds.

—I can't say that I've given it a lot of thought. Been too busy for that. But I believe there's a good chance we will.

—You know what I hate about it? We're in the hands of others. I've always looked out for myself. Never had much support from my parents. So I'm pretty independent. And now, here I sit, totally in the hands of those two groups. I wondered about asking if I could go, but there didn't seem a lot of point. Our mate and the twins will do a good job for us, that's the only consolation I feel.

—What about the miners? You don't have much faith in them?

—Nope. Not much. Seen too much of their like. Especially the leader.

—Well, I think you're a pretty good judge of character. Let's send a prayer to our friend and those twins.

Izzy swivelled her head to look at the smiling Matron.

Five mounds. By the time number five was in ground the number of mourners had dropped considerably. The older people had given up on the idea of de-training so regularly and the younger passengers had lost interest.

The Captain was concerned about finding more volunteers to dig graves with one having been stung by a scorpion the previous evening. He'd heard the scream from the train and had run over to find the man rolling on the ground, one hand clutching the other in pain.

—Fuckin' scorpion, his friend had said, looking at the Captain, the tone accusatory. He'll probably die. You can dig your own fuckin' holes. He'd kicked the shovel down into the mostly completed grave and then gathered up the injured man and headed back to the train calling out for the Matron.

The Captain looked along the line of graves. He was annoyed that it wasn't in line with the others. It sat slightly above and on a slight angle. And for no reason that he could see. The area was clear of scrub, the same digging conditions as for the previous four. No, it was just incompetence and laziness. It really annoyed him.

The Dutch couple had walked over and the Captain asked the man to help him climb out of the grave once he had retrieved the shovel. He tidied up around the site, ready for the next morning's burial and then walked back to find the Matron.

—There's not a lot I could do. They're not deadly, it'll just sting for a while, a burning sensation. Could only wash the area clean and give him a couple of Panadol. The Matron looked around to see that they were alone. He was a bit of a sook.

The Captain laughed. Yes, I think we'll need to find some new grave diggers. We're going to miss those twins and our friend.

There were only four of them to lower the body the next morning, the Captain, his assistant, the manager and the Dutch man. The day was a clone of the previous nine. The sun began its climb in the north-east, the soft deep red light washing through the salt-bush, casting long shadows across the bare loam, the ochre tones like the rock art of the country's original inhabitants.

The Dutch man looked out towards the sun.

—Strange, isn't it, he said in the lispy Dutch way, that if this hadn't happened, and we were looking at this scene before climbing back into our air-conditioning that we would admire the beauty of this nature. But now all we see is what lies ahead for the day. That burning sun and those buggering flies.

—Perspective, said the Captain, it's called perspective.

They lowered the body without fuss. They were experts now, four was more than enough for the task. Izzy and one of her friends were there to witness, but no others. The Matron had excused herself to do her early rounds of the elderly.

The earth received the offering without fuss, the body eased onto the bottom of the hole, the cords pulled out.

—A shame he couldn't be buried next to his wife, said Izzy to no-one in particular.

The manager looked at the Captain and then around at the small number in attendance.

—Not much point is there?

The Captain agreed.

Izzy's friend headed back to the train but she stayed with the men while the grave was filled. The four men all took a turn with the shovel. The Captain wondered if anyone else felt uncomfortable about using the same shovel that they used to bury their shit. He'd considered keeping it solely for grave digging but then had thought the notion pointless.

The Captain had already made the cross, and hammered it into place at the head of the grave, again feeling the frustration of the graves not being in line.

—I don't wish to be buried. It was the Dutch man who said it. These burials just confirm it to me.

The Captain looked at the tall spare man. The Dutch man laughed.

—I don't mean that I will die here. I mean that when I die eventually. I always felt a profound sense of claustrophobia at the thought of being buried and looking into those holes and being covered with dirt only makes the feeling worse.

The Captain laughed.

—I didn't know what you were telling me for a moment.

—But maybe it's not so stupid to talk about it happening in this place. Maybe we all die here.

The two men were walking back to the train, the others ahead. The Captain had the shovel over his shoulder. He knew people on the train would be looking for it already. Early mornings and late evenings, before dark, were the popular times for shitting. And the fact that the grave digger had been stung by a scorpion the previous evening only reinforced that people would not go out in the hours of darkness for their business.

—I don't think we'll die, rescue will be on the way.

—I think you say this because you are working for the company, the train. But I can see in your face that you do not believe it.

The Captain looked at the tall man, summing him up.

—What do you do?

—I teach in a university here. My wife and I have come for a year. He laughed. Our friends warned us about the dangers of your country. The snakes, the sharks. But nobody mentioned the trains.

—We can speak again later, the Dutch man said. Maybe the truth, between us.

The Captain watched him go, and then went off to find the Matron.

—Have you seen our scorpion-bitten patient?

The Matron smiled.

—Yes. He complained that he didn't get much sleep but the pain has largely gone this morning. He'll be with us for a while yet. And they sting, they don't bite.

The Captain laughed. Ever the pedant, he said.

—Indeed. I remember my father telling me the same about bees, they don't bite, he'd say. They have no teeth.

—You would get along famously with my wife. I hope you can meet her one day.

—I'd like that.

It was during the breakfast sitting that the first serious fight erupted. There were only two dining cars being used to serve the passengers, the cars were next to each other. During normal operations passengers would not be able to move between them, it was the dividing line. But now it meant that one kitchen could be employed for both.

The manager had worked with his staff to transfer all useable food items to one car where stocks could be managed, monitored and rationed. Two dining areas were used to get through the passenger numbers as quickly as possible.

The manager and the Captain had come to an agreement with the carriage representatives that there would be only two meals served each day. A breakfast served in the cool of the morning and a dinner in the early evening. It hadn't caused many issues, with most people having little appetite in the baking heat.

Water was the big issue. The manager ensured that the process for distribution was carefully managed. He understood the potential for problems.

The Captain had begun to revise his opinion of the manager. While people management might not have been his strongest attribute the Captain could see the man was methodical and practical. The manager kept a list of each passenger's name. Every passenger was required to collect their water ration and initial for it each day.

Some of his staff complained of the laboriousness of the process but the Captain saw the sense in it.

Each passenger had been issued with a large plastic water bottle. These were part of the supplies for off-train excursions. The ruckus began when a bottle was dropped, its precious contents spilling through the cracked plastic, to spread across the dining car floor.

By the time the Captain and the manager arrived the violence had started. It was one of the miners. He held one of the older men by the throat, pushing him backwards over the edge of a table. The old man looked more furious than frightened. His eyes were open wide, the veiny whites held the gaze of his attacker, as he breathed heavily from flared nostrils. The loose skin of his neck was pushed up under his unshaven jaw. The area between thumb and index finger of the hand that held him was covered in a spider-web tattoo. Snakes curled around the muscled forearm. The miner was speaking through clenched teeth.

—You old fuck, watch your mouth, or I'll end you. His friend stood behind him facing the audience, fists bunched, a warning to several other older men who might have considered helping their friend.

The manager went forward, but the Captain grabbed his arm.

—No, don't grab him. It won't help.

The manager looked at the Captain. The Captain knew the old man, it was the one who had made the comments about steerage.

—Let him go. It came as a roar from the leonine head.

The miner did not release and the old man grasped the arm that held him.

—I said, let him go.

The miner looked around at the Captain.

—Or what?

—There is no or what. I want you to release that old man who you are hurting.

—Tell him to let go of my arm.

—Sir, let go of his arm.

The old man released the arm and the miner released his grip on the man's neck. The old man grabbed down at the table edge to stop himself from falling backwards.

The Captain raised a hand before anyone could speak. Right, I'll hear from both of you. You, he said to the miner.

—This old fucker.

The Captain interrupted.

—We'll keep this civil.

—He dropped a bottle of water, and then wanted another. Well fuck that. We're all dying of thirst and this old prick wants to waste it, that's his problem.

The Captain shifted his gaze to the old man.

—Sir?

The Captain could see that the old man was building to a crescendo but before he could say anything he pitched forward onto the wet floor.

—Quick, get the Matron.

The Captain rolled the man over. He didn't look to be breathing. And then the Matron was there.

—Out of my way. She came forward and took one look at the man on the floor. Right, all of you out of here. She put her hand to the man's face.

—Not breathing, she said to no-one in particular. She shook her head. Ten minutes later she pulled away, the sweat running off her brow. Another one, was all she said. There was a crowd standing behind her, most had moved back but stayed in the dining car, including the two miners who were watching from the periphery. The dead man lay in the pool of water he had spilled.

—He killed him. Another of the old men pointed to the young miner.

The miner flipped the bird at the man.

—You want some as well?

The Captain stood from where he'd been squatting opposite the Matron.

—Stop it, he yelled. It's enough. We don't need more of this. The room was quiet.

—He should be arrested. It was another of the old men who stood with his bottle of water. It's murder. He can't get away with it. At the least it's some form of grievous assault.

The miner moved towards the old man who took a step backwards bumping into another man standing behind him.

—He can't hurt all of us. Let's arrest him. It was the man behind.

—Stop, it was the Matron this time.

She stood. Isn't one enough? Show some respect. All of you out now. She shooed them like flies waving the backs of both hands towards them. Out now.

—Not you two, said the Captain to the miners. You go that way, he said, pointing at the other end of the carriage. And this isn't finished. He added.

—Yeah, fuck you, said the second miner, walking away.

When the room was clear the Captain looked at the Matron.

—And so it begins.

The Matron bit her bottom lip.

—Indeed. We need to tell his wife. She's very frail. The shock will probably do for her as well.

—And we need another grave.

57

7

The waning moon was still bright enough that the three miners cast a shadow as they went on their way. Sparse vegetation and hard-packed, calcareous soils made for good walking, with little deviation required from their southerly heading.

For all his bluster the leader was nervous. He checked the compass every couple of minutes, correcting the slightest deviation from their prescribed course. His nervousness made him walk fast, chiding his off-siders for their lack of pace.

—They said we should walk steadily.

—Just fuckin' keep up. We'll rest when the sun's up. We can make good miles while it's cool.

—Yeah but we're still losing water. The old girl said that. Just because you're not sweating doesn't mean we're not losing water.

—Don't be a pussy.

The Captain sat with the Matron and the manager in the cab of the engine.

—I'm flummoxed. What do I do with that miner? At a minimum he assaulted the old man.

—But you're not the law, said the Matron, you can't arrest him. All we can do is try to stop this kind of breakdown and if we get out of this we leave it to the appropriate authorities.

—Maybe we should write some sort of report. It was the manager. You know, just some notes, while it's still fresh, and we can pass them on. I saw it all, I'm happy to write something.

—Thanks, said the Captain, do that then. I'd better get back out there. I just hope the old men don't do anything silly.

Another advantage that the track walkers had over the miners was the presence of culverts, the boxed concrete sleeves that run under the rails at intervals where creeks and rivulets occasionally ran. They made an ideal place to sit out the worst of the heat.

The three had walked steadily through the first night and into the morning, taking short breaks every hour as agreed. The man still felt relatively fresh. They'd agreed to stop an hour before noon and wait for four or five hours, sleeping as much as possible. The culvert proved a pleasant surprise. While the bottom was filled with dried out clay it was otherwise clear with plenty of room for the three to sit with their backs against the side or to lie down and sleep. And the temperature was the coolest of anywhere he'd sat since they'd become marooned.

—We should have found one of these close to the train.

The twins both agreed. Ticky was glad they were wearing different coloured shirts, otherwise he wouldn't be able to tell them apart. He'd started calling them elder and younger. They'd explained that they were fraternal twins, but, even so, were so similar in looks that even their parents made mistakes. And yes, of course, they'd had fun with the fact over the years, especially at school.

They talked that first morning. Their relative freshness and the excitement for the adventure enough to keep them from sleep for some time. But tiredness eventually won out and all three men slept through until the late afternoon.

The three miners had not been so lucky. They sat in the stingy shade of an acacia tree.

They had walked far longer than was prudent, but through no fault of theirs. There was no shade to be found. They'd passed some trees not long after sunrise. A copse that would have brought them some reprieve from the sun and the heat later in the day. But it'd been too early to stop. That's what they decided. They were still feeling fresh, sipping at their water. The leader had slowed to a sensible pace. They were confident. As much appeal as the trees held for the men they decided to keep going.

But that was hours before. They had walked on. The sun climbing and the temperature rising almost in commensurate degrees. All three wore caps, ignoring advice to take wide brimmed hats from other passengers. One fiddled incessantly with his collar trying to lessen the burning he felt on the back of his neck.

Their tread grew heavy. The walking conditions had not changed. The chalky loam was still firm under foot, barely offering up a print in their wake. The salt-bush grew sparsely and rarely impeded their progress. But the heat gobbled their vigour.

The leader saw the tree through the swimming haze just as he began to entertain an idea that they were in serious trouble.

—Thank fuck. It was the first word that had been spoken for over an hour. But any sense of excitement dissipated when the tree revealed itself to them, the trunk tall and rangy, long thin branches, a dearth of foliage, like a map of the heart's intricate veins and arteries. The shade was thin at best.

—It'll have to do, said the leader, I'm rooted.

They'd thrown themselves down gratefully. The leader sat with his back to the trunk. The striated bark lumpy against his spine.

—Easy on the water boys. Small sips. Rinse and swallow. No gulping. The situation had taken away some of his bravado, replacing it with a sense of the seriousness for the situation.

—I wonder where those other bastards are sitting right now?

—Probably not having any more luck than us, I reckon.

The Captain had a feeling that the problem with the two miners—the death of the old man and the spilled water—wouldn't end there. Only that he'd misread how it would manifest. The first he heard was when the manager came running up to him, puffing with the effort. The Captain had been sitting in the shade of the engine with the junior driver, talking about nothing much, trains and ships mostly. It was the hottest part of the day, the time when things were quietest, the time when no-one wanted to move. The older people, who didn't leave the train, were trying to sleep, many having taken to lying on the couches of the dining cars or on mattresses dragged there, rather than inside their own sauna-like cabins. Most of the remainder were either leaning against the shaded side of the train or under it in the rail-bed. Some of these too had dragged mattresses from the train. It was days since the manager cared about the treatment of company property.

—They've taken over the water. The manager almost skidded to a halt such was his haste to get to the Captain. He realised what he'd said probably didn't make a lot of sense. The Captain stared, waiting for the manager to say something more.

The manager drew a couple of breaths.

—The two miners and a couple of others are in the kitchen. They

61

say that they're taking responsibility for water distribution. Chased out my staff.

The Captain climbed to his feet. He was annoyed that he hadn't considered this. Their most precious commodity, he should have put a plan in place. It wouldn't have been hard. With the power gone there were only two hand pumps on the entire train where water could be raised from the massive tanks, one in each of the two kitchens. He'd ordered the other pump removed to ensure that there was only one source to manage, and now here was the problem that he'd created.

He thought as he walked. He knew there were drain cocks under the train where the tanks could be completely emptied but they were difficult to access, guarded by protective plating. An onerous task but an option if necessary.

The Captain hauled himself up the steps and into the dining car moving along to where a doorway lead into the kitchen. The kitchen door had a round glass panel and he could see the red-haired miner standing on the other side. The miner saw him approaching and smiled.

—What are you doing? He said it loudly.

—Pretty obvious I'd say. We don't trust you fuckers, so we've taken over. The face was twisted into a snarl, the words delivered with venom. Too many old rich pricks on that side.

The Captain took a moment, swallowing his anger. He needed to manage this. No room for misplaced words.

—Can we sit and talk about this. You and me, and not through a doorway.

Word had already spread along the train. Several of the older passengers sleeping in the dining area came forward to stand behind the Captain.

—They can't do this. It was another of the older men. It's piracy.

The Captain turned. Please, this won't help, please move away so I can speak with this young man.

—Young man? He's a criminal. He's murdered our friend and now they're trying to take over. We told you to arrest him.

—And that's why we've done it, the one with the red hair yelled at them. These old rich pricks think they control things. Who knows how much of the water you're giving them. And it's not just us four in here. Don't worry about that. We've got plenty more from our carriage who agree and will help us. So don't think about rushing in here, not unless you want a bloodbath on your hands.

The Captain knew he'd lost control.

—You need to move back and give me time to speak to him. He'd turned his back on the miner to face the group of older passengers.

—No, this is our water too. Murmurs of agreement came from behind the old man as more people came to stand in the group.

The Captain heard the door open at the far end of the kitchen and saw one of the four running out. It wasn't long before the kitchen was full of the younger men and a few of the younger women.

The one with the red hair smiled through the glass.

—See. As he said it he held up a glass and took a long pull at the water it contained. He smiled again, wiping the back of the hand across his mouth. The group behind the Captain began yelling, almost as one. The Matron pushed through the crowd to stand beside the Captain.

—Can you get them out of here? It wasn't pleading, more of a challenge the Captain set down for the Matron. The Matron turned to the older passengers.

—Please, let's move back.

The group quietened. It was an awkward moment. The Matron

had something to say. The man at the front who had spoken already looked around at his cohort and, as if taking strength from their proximity and numbers, turned back to the Matron shaking his head.

—I'm sorry Matron, but this is our water as well. Our lives at stake here. Look at that idiot. The Matron turned towards where the old man gesticulated. Red hair was still smiling through the glass, taking another sip of water.

—Look. We won't get anywhere if both groups stand here like this. She touched the Captain on the shoulder. You need to trust that this man will act in our best interests. She'd deliberately used the word 'our', wanting the group to know that it was her water and her life as well.

—It won't be in our best interests if these people have power over our water supply. It was one of the older women.

—Do you trust me?

The question made the older passengers uncomfortable. They quietened.

—Well do you? the Matron repeated. She looked directly at the woman.

The woman felt compelled to respond.

—Yes, we trust you. She said it quietly.

—Then please move back out of the carriage while we work this out. I promise we will update you as soon as we have spoken to this young man.

The group milled momentarily like confused livestock. The Matron looked to the old man who had started the discussion.

—Please, lead them out. It was another strategy, anointing the man with a leadership role. The Captain could see what the Matron had done. The man looked at the Matron and then made a decision.

—Come on everyone, let's give them some time. He shepherded them forward and out the end of the dining car.

The Captain, mouthing 'well done' out of the corner of his mouth, turned towards red hair.

—Please, come out here so we don't need to yell through the door. He was tempted to ask some of the others who now filled the kitchen to leave but changed his mind, not wanting to give the miner a chance to refuse. The Captain and the Matron stepped back. The miner pushed the two-way swing door outward and stepped forward.

—Do you really think you'll need that? The Matron said it, looking at the carving knife in the man's hand. Red hair looked sheepish and pushed back through the door. When he returned the knife was gone but a young woman accompanied him.

—Let's sit, said the Captain, moving to a seating banquette, sliding in behind the table. The Matron followed him. The miner balked momentarily. He wanted to maintain control. He already felt that he was giving things up.

—No, we'll stand.

—As you will. What is it you want?

The miner paused, the young woman took the opportunity to speak.

—We're going to control the water from here on.

—Why do you think you need to do that? We have a system, a roster. You're welcome to monitor it. It's very clear and orderly. It works well.

—Who knows what goes on, said red hair. We don't know that you're not giving more water to those old bastards. They like to tell us they paid more to be here, so who's to say you're not giving them more when we're not around?

—I'm no different to you two. It was the Matron. I'm just a passenger. I sit at the front of the train. I don't get any extra water and I trust that no-one else is getting more than their share. It's a good and accurate system. Why make this more difficult than it needs to be?

—Look Matron, it was the young woman. Let's look at it this way. We want to do our bit for everyone on the train. And that bit is managing the water supply. How about that? Tell the oldies that's the job we've taken, to help out. Frankly, I don't care what you tell them, I'll leave it up to you. But we're taking over. It was spoken with conviction. The tone was matter-of-fact, little emotion. This one worried the Captain more than red hair.

—Why don't you just have a couple of volunteers join the crew in the distribution. That way you can keep an eye on the process but without having to organise a system among yourselves.

The young woman smiled and spoke before red hair could say anything. She could see that he was struggling to process what the Matron had said, maybe saw sense in it. She didn't want him to weaken.

It'd been a quick decision after the water was spilled and the old man had died. Red hair and the other miner had returned to their carriage and told the young woman. He was ruffled, she could see that. But then she had talked quietly to the pair and brought in some of the others from their group.

—No, that's okay. We'll take it from here.

The Captain's concern forced him to try another tack.

—What worries me, is that when rescue comes and people begin talking about what happened here, the authorities may reach a conclusion about force and fear being used to take over this process. He hadn't wanted to take the conversation in this direction. Wanted to keep things calm. But he could see that the young woman was set on her path.

She smirked. Is that a threat?

—Just reality. Management of the train and its resources falls to the crew. My concern is how your actions are going to be construed in the wash-up. What do you think? The Captain looked into the face of red hair when he said this.

—I just…look…it's. He struggled, and then turned, wordless, to the young woman.

—We're okay with this. She smiled again. It'll only be an issue if you make it into one. She looked firstly at the Captain and then into the eyes of the Matron. Leave us to manage it and there won't be a problem. Just passengers wanting to help.

—But you saw what the older passengers said already, how do you think they're going to react to you managing the water distribution?

—Well Matron, to be blunt, we don't really care. And you need to understand, we'll be monitoring the preparation of meals as well. Red hair turned to stare at her. She put a hand on his arm. She knew she'd thrown him. They hadn't discussed this. It had just come to her.

—We'll come back to you both in a while with a revised eating and water distribution plan.

The Captain attempted to respond but the young woman held up a hand.

—No, that's enough for now. As I said. We'll come back to you.

The Matron looked at the Captain, raising her eyebrows, saying nothing. They were alone in the dining area.

—A point well made Matron, said the Captain with a wry smile. Buggered if I know, to use the vernacular.

—And what are we going to tell the older passengers?

—I guess the truth. View?

—Agreed. Not much else for it. Perhaps just say that nothing changes. Everyone eats and everyone drinks.

—Let's hope that's the truth.

8

The dingo had followed the three men for several hours on the first night, seen them to the edge of his territory. He sat in the rail-bed for some minutes, tongue lolling, watching after them before pissing on both rails and turning back.

The tap on the shoulder woke Ticky in the late afternoon. He'd slept well. Probably better than the whole time since the train had stopped. He felt refreshed and ready to move on. He'd been slightly worried about how the walking might affect him, considered not going at one point. But the thought of not being in control of his destiny, to some extent at least, outweighed any doubts he held about his ability to cope in the conditions.

He had a reasonable base of fitness. He'd always been a runner. But then his knees had let him down and finally he'd had to admit that there was no future in it for him. He'd subscribed to the view that one of his friends had put to him, that every human had a certain amount of running steps in them and once they'd been used up there was nothing for it but to give it away. Only pain and surgery awaited those refusing to stop. So he had given it away. He'd shifted his focus to the gym, hated it at first. Had always held disdain for gym junkies, reckoning that it was as much about being seen to do something as actually doing it. And he didn't see the point of spending all day in an office and then not getting out to breathe some fresh air. No, he'd loved his running. He'd tried walking and then cycling. But the lycra image didn't do much for him. And walking frustrated him, knowing he could be moving faster. Patience was never one of his virtues. So it was the gym. And while he yearned for the solitary road of the runner, and the simplicity of a pair of shorts and running shoes, he had accepted his lot and got on with it.

They each took a swig of their water and ate some of the rations.

—Time to go?

The boys both nodded, the three rising as one. The sun was low in the north-west. Even the low salt-bush cast a long shadow in the soft red light. Ticky reckoned they had an hour or so of light left to them and then darkness until the waning moon came up. Though they would never know it, they saw the snake at about the same time as the miners found another. It was moving across the road in front of them.

—Gwardar, said one of the twins, barely breaking stride.

—Poisonous? He didn't like snakes.

—Very. Gwardar is Aboriginal for 'go the long way around'. The boy, younger, smiled as he said it.

As they got closer the snake sensed their presence, twisting in tighter 's' patterns to increase it's speed through the loose loam and into the nearby salt-bush.

—Not very aggressive, said the other twin. It's the dugite you've gotta watch.

It was a dugite that the miner stood on. The three had risen at around

70

the same time as the other group. But unlike the other group the miners were sunburned, tired and hot. The limited and moving shade meant they grabbed only snatches of sleep.

It was the smallest of the three who stood on the snake. He'd led the group off and away from the tree after the leader had pointed the way south. The snake was hidden beside a fallen branch. It was a couple of metres long. The tired miner had stepped over the branch and onto the middle of it. It bucked like a crazed rodeo horse, hitting the man twice before he had even registered what had happened. He was unlucky that he'd stepped onto it, stopping its escape. The snake rarely envenomated humans but the black-spotted, pale yellow serpent couldn't get away so the second strike sent venom into the man's calf.

He screamed and fell backwards. With the weight off, the snake rose. The other two saw it, waited. It was still within striking distance of the man. He pushed himself backwards, scrabbling like a scorpion in the dirt. The snake struck again, this time hitting the man's raised boot. It swayed momentarily and then turned and moved quickly out into the salt-bush.

—It got me. Three panicked words.

The leader ran up to the man, watching the snake move away. He paused to make sure it was long gone before squatting next to the victim. They pulled the man's pants down. The tell-tale twin puncture marks were clear on the milky white skin of the man's calf.

—How do you feel?

—Not sure.

—Maybe there was no venom.

—We need to wrap it, said the victim. Stop it spreading.

—Get the bandage.

The Matron had given the two groups a small medical kit each. The leader pulled out a bandage.

—What do I do?

—You have to wrap it tight. Quick. It's fucking venom's in me. He looked at the leader, face white as a sheet, fear etched. And then he vomited onto his chest. The leader stepped back like it might be contagious.

The third miner snatched the bandage and wrapped the leg. The victim moaned. The man turned him onto his side so he wouldn't choke. He looked up at the leader who stood above him.

—What do we do?

—We can't move him. It'll make it worse if he's got poison in him.

—You have to get me back to the Matron, or get her here. The victim rolled onto his back. My head's starting to hurt. That shit is in me. I can feel it. You have to do something. Can't you suck it out?

—We have to get the Matron. It's all we can do, said the third man. We can't move him, it'll make it worse.

The leader waggled his fingers at waist level, beckoning the man to follow. They moved out of earshot.

—Look, he's fucked. We can't move him. There's no point staying with him.

—Then we need to get the Matron.

—It's too far. She couldn't walk this far. And then we'd be stuffed, we couldn't go on. The work we've done will've been wasted. And it looks like he won't survive that long anyway.

—You're a prick. How do you know how long he'll survive? We don't even know what sort of snake it was. What if it only makes him a little bit sick for a while and then he gets better?

The two men looked at each other for long seconds.

—Well, you go back. I'm going on. It's about a whole train full of people not just him.

The other man slowly shook his head from side to side. Yeah, sure. It's about the greater good. That's what you're thinking about. Mister fucking selfless.

The leader took a step towards the man, his face twisted into a sneer. It was a loud moan from the victim that stopped any violence.

—Ah, my fuckin' head. He held his hands over his ears like he was trying to block out a noise, his face a grimacing rictus. He thrashed suddenly, vomited again, a trickle of bile and precious water running through the long bristles on his chin. The man farted, his bowels voiding. Flies swarmed.

The other two were transfixed, statue-like. The leader turned towards the other man.

—Right. What now?

—Alright. But we have to wait with him a bit.

—Half an hour, and then we go. We're wasting time.

The man was dead twenty minutes later. In the twilight it was easy to see the darker disturbed earth around him where he had thrashed as the venom seeped through his lymphatic system to the major arteries and veins, like the soft red light of the sunset washing through the salt-bush. There was no slowing to a final laboured breath. The end was sudden, brutal, like the bite of the snake. One final seizure of pain pulling the man's knees upwards, rolling him partially onto his side, fingers clenching, mouth a maniacal grin. And then nothing. He rolled softly onto his back, limbs relaxing. His friend was stunned. It seemed like any evidence of the man had suddenly been plucked away. He didn't even look like himself. Just a husk of the life that had been.

His friend knelt over him clutching the moistened strip of cloth he

73

had torn from his spare shirt using precious water to mop the man's brow. The leader had stood at a distance, watching. He'd considered warning him against wasting the water.

They divvied up the dead man's supplies and left him where he lay. His friend wanted to do something, say something. But in the end he had nothing, just a final look back as they walked into the south.

The Captain went in search of red hair later in the afternoon. They'd not talked since the initial confrontation and he wanted to know what they'd decided. He was also hoping he might be able to get the miner to see sense. The young woman worried him. The Matron's views had supported his own. That the miner might be made to see sense and might carry enough sway in their group to do something to amend the situation.

He asked the older passengers to stay away from the kitchen and the water tap. He hoped he'd convinced them that there was nothing to be gained by instigating a confrontation. He'd asked the Matron and the manager to keep an eye on them until he'd had a chance to speak to red hair.

He'd walked past the kitchen and could see several others sitting around, clearly guarding the water tap. He found red hair sitting in the shade at the rear of the train with twenty or so others. The young woman was there.

She worried him. She was obviously smart and wasn't phased by confrontation. He wondered what she wanted out of the situation. Did she truly believe they were being cheated out of their share of the food and water. No, she was too smart for that, he thought. It was about power.

He knew better than try and speak to red hair without her. It would only antagonise her and probably the group, so he waived to the pair of them. He felt a slight worry that she might want him to address the group. But he reckoned if she was serious about the power game, that she'd want to have any communication in private. And then she'd hold the power in her group. Information was power, as they said. He was right. She quickly jumped up, moving towards the Captain.

She was happy enough when the dopey miner went with her. She knew she could control him and he still had that one thing that she might need to call on at some point. Physical strength. That and male friends. So she was happy to present as a united pair for now.

—We need to start getting ready for the evening meal. The chef and staff are waiting.

The woman made no pretence at letting red hair speak and he seemed to have ceded any final remnants of authority to her. The woman had been ready to make a stand against the Captain. It hadn't taken much convincing within the group to agree that force could be employed if necessary. It didn't take much convincing that the older, more wealthy passengers were likely receiving special treatment. That all they were doing was ensuring that everyone got their share. She had most of the younger passengers, particularly the males, on side. They didn't represent the majority in numbers but there were more than enough of them to intimidate the remainder if necessary.

She loved the thrill it gave her. She'd show those rich fuckers. She'd been wanting to do it her whole life. And so she'd been prepared for a confrontation with the old mongrel. Had expected one. Was almost disappointed that it hadn't come.

—Yep. I'll get my people to the kitchen. I've got a crew ready. She turned and waived to the group. Several rose and followed her as she walked along the side of the rail-bed, the train shadow long across the plain.

The three made steady progress during the night. They'd stayed on the service road, preferring the uneven surface to the noise of the rail-bed. The boys had assured their older companion that they would keep an eye out for snakes.

He was beginning to flag in the dawn when they saw it ahead. It was the first time he'd started to feel that he didn't have the stamina of the brothers. He'd felt it worst in the dark hours before the dawn. The moon had set. He was at his lowest ebb. He'd tried to look into the faces of his companions, convinced that they looked as fresh as the moment they had departed the train. His face surely must look hagged and drawn. His eyes hurt, felt like they'd been taken out and rolled through the loam and put back in. And his legs were heavy. He wasn't dragging his feet, but he felt like it wasn't long before he would. He didn't want to be the weak link. Didn't want to ask them to stop before the agreed time. He thought back to his running days. The times when he went in a group. Once he discovered there was someone slower than he, he could relax and enjoy it. He didn't need to be the fastest, just not the slowest. He wondered what this said about him.

But then one of the twins had spotted it in the distance. The goods train. Ticky had to lift up his sun glasses and squint to see it in the early morning light, and even then he was doubtful that he was looking at it. It took another twenty minutes of walking to reach it. It grew out of the plain as they approached. Prehistoric, he thought. He'd not wandered far enough from his train to get perspective on how it disrupted the simple lines of the plain. But now, even in his tired state, it seemed to him almost offensive in the way the unnatural shape played against the scene in which it was encapsulated. Maybe an artist would call it a juxtapose. If it was a movie, he thought, it would rear up about now and chase us across the scrubland.

They were still walking the service road, the oblique angle giving them enough perspective to reveal a train about the same length as their own. His fatigue had evaporated. He felt light, wanting to break into a run to cover the final distance. He suddenly felt elation. It was awesome. Two hundred souls sat around in their filth, wondering whether death would take them. And here he was, he and the indefatigable twins. They'd done something miraculous. It was the way he felt with his business. When he pulled off a new deal. Guaranteed the future for while. But it wasn't the security he might have garnered from such a result that exhilarated him. It was the rush he got from knowing that he'd gotten what he wanted, that he'd taken something from someone else. And that's what this was like, he realised. He'd bested the plain with its fearsome heat and poisonous snakes. But he was under no illusion he'd only survived the first round.

They climbed up the rail-bed, approaching the train from between the rails.

—Ahoy the train. His tone was almost jovial. They were close enough now to see into the huge twin windows of the drivers' cab that gave the train a considered, furrowed-brow appearance. It made Ticky think of one of the engines from *Thomas and Friends*, books his son had loved. He couldn't remember the name.

—Swing up there and see if anyone's home. One of the twins went forward to the ladder behind the cab and climbed up to the footway that ran from the cab, back along beside the engine housing. He pulled open the door, not even stepping through before turning to confirm that there was no-one there.

77

The three moved along the rail-bed, past the engine, beside the first of the carriages. It was eerily quiet. Ticky found himself stepping lightly. The situation had changed.

The first carriages were goods wagons with sliding doors, locked.

—Hello. Nothing. The goods wagons gave way to flat beds carrying shipping containers, all locked up tight. Towards the rear of the train was a double decker vehicle wagon full of cars and behind that two final wagons carrying big yellow road-building machines.

The three walked around the end of the train and started up the other side.

—Hello? This time it came out as a question. This time there was a reaction. Three dingoes looked up from the salt-bush. They were a distance out from the train. They paused in their heads-up position briefly and as if a silent command had been spoken, headed away to the north in a dignified trot.

The three men began the return journey beside the train, arriving at the point where they'd seen the dingoes. Still no sign of anyone. Beyond the helloes, none of them had spoken. It was as if any mention of the obvious would bring it to fruition, that the drivers were gone. The man wondered why this was important, that the drivers should be there. What would they be able to do that two hundred others couldn't? They could talk about their train and their experience but that was all.

The smell stopped them, jerked the man from his reverie. It was a faint odour but rank, a cloying sweetness that was not welcome in the heat of the desert.

—Must be what the dogs were eating, said one of the twins.

They continued walking, past the containers, out of the zone of the smell, and back to the goods wagons. The door of both wagons were closed but not locked. Ticky could reach the bottom of the door but couldn't get the purchase required to make it slide.

—Let me. One of the twins scrambled up the side of the wagon, level with the base of the door. He clung to the door jamb and lifted his feet, bracing them against the door and shoved. The door moved. It created enough space for the twin to swing inside from where he was able to shove the door wide.

—Looks like they slept here, he said coming back to the doorway. He helped the man up into the wagon, ignoring his brother who managed the climb on his own. There wasn't much to see. Two piles of cardboard cartons had been flattened on the floor. Half a dozen empty plastic water bottles were lined neatly along the rear wall.

—Someone's a clean freak, said one of the twins.

Both cardboard beds sported pillows. The other twin picked one up and shook it out to reveal a polar fleece sweater, a company logo prominent.

—They must have headed to find the family at the siding, said Ticky. Let's check the other goods wagon and the cab.

They climbed down into the rail-bed and moved along to the next wagon. The twin repeated his manoeuvre and then swore as he swung inside. He came back carrying three water bottles. They were full.

—There's a ton of them in here. Hundreds. Full.

The others climbed up and gazed. Three pallets of bottles sat along the back wall covered in a clear plastic. One had been ripped open. The man turned. Along the front wall of the wagon were the empties.

—Our friend again, he said, pointing.

—Cheers, said one of the twins, upending a bottle and draining half

79

of the contents, before spluttering and coughing, water coming from his nose.

—Easy tiger, Ticky said with a laugh. His brother laughed as well. All three managed to drain a large bottle each. The man asked for the empties, stacking them with the others.

—Seems only right.

—Let's try the cab.

The twins enjoyed the cab, Ticky could see that. It made him smile. They both took a turn to sit in the driver's seat. They didn't go as far as making train noises but he could see that the desire didn't lurk too far below the surface. They touched all the controls, occasionally making a call to the other on what a particular lever or dial might do.

There wasn't much else to do, other than watch the boys enjoy the experience. The cab had not much to offer. He rifled through some notes on a clipboard but it revealed nothing more than the name of the recipients of the goods.

—Shit. It doesn't even tell us what's in the containers.

He pulled open the small fridge at the back of the cab, but there was nothing inside other than an empty water jug. Two white hard hats sat atop two safety vests on a shelf above a hotplate and electric kettle. An empty International Roast tin stood beside the kettle. A rubbish bin revealed empty sugar packets and single-serve UHT milk containers.

—Thoughts?

—No food, said elder. Opposite problem to us. Plenty of water but no food. They've headed west, to the siding I reckon.

—Sounds fair. What do we do?

—Not much we can do other than follow them. Not like we can lug the water back to our train.

—Shame we can't get a vehicle off this thing, said Ticky.

—Electronics are probably shot anyway, same as the trains.

Ticky pursed his lips. Nothing to add to that, he thought. He looked at his expensive watch.

—We're still early for stopping but let's rest up for the day, drink some water, and head off tonight.

It was as if once he said it that his tiredness came flooding back. He wanted to lie down at once. The twins passed down the cardboard and a carton of water bottles and the three made a nest in the rail-bed under the train. The man thought about finding a culvert but didn't want to walk another step, prepared to put up with the extra heat.

He was asleep quickly. It felt like only a few minutes when the twin shook him awake. But once his senses had cleared he looked at his watch and realised it was early afternoon already. He was slightly annoyed that he'd been woken earlier than necessary but the look on the twin's face stalled any comment he might have made.

—You should see this.

They climbed from under the train. The man could see the other twin standing off in the salt-bush, further along the train. The twin lead the way and as they neared his brother he spoke.

—It's what the dingoes were feeding on.

The man stopped. He wasn't sure whether it was the smell that made him want to gag or the sight of what he was looking at. It was a human form. Or what was left of one.

9

I can't remember water tasting this good. It's tepid, but it tastes so good. Just putting the mouth of the bottle to my dry lips and letting a drop spill across is so wonderful. I'm doing what the Matron said—she's a wonderful woman. Swilling it around my mouth before I swallow it. It's not until I swallow it that I realise that I just want to drink the lot. But I won't. I've been good.

It's funny. Everyone's clutching bottles, carrying it with them the whole day. Is it a trust thing, or is that it's just so precious, especially after the ruckus in the dining car? I see people's eyes drawn to each other's bottles when they meet, looking to see how much someone's drunk. I do the same.

It reminds me of my sister. She's long dead. Almost thirty years. Cancer. I miss her. She was a hoarder when we were kids. We might get lollies or chocolate on some special occasion. It didn't happen often, so when it did it was a real treat. We had an old uncle who'd come to visit, my father's brother. He died when I was still young, but I do remember this impossibly tall, thin man in a dark heavy suit handing over a pile of copper coins when he came to visit. Probably wasn't a lot of money but more than enough to fill a white paper bag full of lollies at the cafe.

My sister and I would stand there, agonising over each choice, like it was
a life or death decision. Must have driven the cafe owner mad. I can still see
the smudge marks on the glass of the lolly case where we'd push our fingers,
making sure we got our cobbers and milk bottles. Mine would barely survive
the drive home. I ate them like I knew that if I didn't someone was going to
snatch them away. I would happily make myself ill in the process. But my
sister, she was just the opposite. She was younger than me. She'd eat one or
two and then put them away. Hide them somewhere. I knew she hid them,
because I tried to find them. But I never did. I sometimes wonder whether I
would have eaten them if I'd found them. Yes. I reckon I would've.

So there she'd be. Weeks later, walking around chewing in front of me. At
the time I used to accuse her of doing it deliberately, teasing me, showing me
that she still had them. But I reckon it wasn't the case. It was just the way
she was. I reckon she'd be proud of me now, being careful with my water.

The woman didn't sit and eat with the others. She moved between
the tables, talking to the various groups. The Captain watched her.
She was reinforcing her status, he could see it. He had to admit that
she was good. The red-haired miner sat and ate with the others. He
either didn't understand what she was doing or didn't care. Probably
the former, he thought. Whatever, she'd slipped seamlessly into the
role of leader. Unquestioned, unchallenged.

She'd changed the dinner seating plan for no other reason than
to show control. That was obvious. It was all running relatively
smoothly, so he was happy enough to let things run their course.
There wasn't much he could do about it. He'd told his new friend,
the Dutchman, not to make a fuss when the tall academic had raised
it with him. Just sit and eat and leave it for now, he'd said to him.
We'll see how things pan out.

And they had another body to bury—the old man who'd died after the confrontation with the miner. The Captain asked the Dutchman to help him dig the hole. He didn't bother speaking to the woman about it, or ask any of the younger men in the group, knowing he'd likely be told to do it himself. Especially as it was one of their number who'd been stung by the scorpion.

—I asked several of the younger men from my carriage to help us but they weren't interested, said the Dutchman.

The Captain drove the shovel into the soil for the first time in the new grave. He had started a second row, was able to line it up neatly with the first one that had been dug. He'd walked past the final one in the first row, its slightly askew alignment still annoying him.

They dug slowly, each taking care to sip water and sit and rest between efforts. The Captain could see that he and the Dutchman were of a similar age. He frowned, thinking that they shouldn't have been doing this alone, or even at all.

He laughed out loud.

—What's funny? The Dutchman kept digging as he said it.

—Two old buggers like us, digging in the desert, when there's a carriage full of young people. That's what's funny.

—No respect for the older generation. The same in my country. It's hard for our generation. The shift has been bigger than any other I think.

—What do you mean?

—Well, for one, we gave respect. I'm sure it would be the same for you. My father would have hit me if I showed disrespect. Maybe it's not a good thing. But it meant we gave respect.

—Maybe I should smack them.

The Dutchman stopped. The hole was knee deep. He leaned on the shovel handle, sweat running down his face.

—We may have to do more than that about this water issue. I have a feeling this is going to turn worse.

The Captain didn't reply. He pursed his lips and looked out across the salt-bush into the red light, waving at the flies around his face. The Dutchman returned to his digging. The Captain knew the man was right. It wasn't going to stop here. And what happens in a few days, he thought. If help doesn't come.

He'd already talked to the Matron about it. They'd planned for the water to last for another week. But if either of the walking groups had not returned in two or three days he thought that they should cut the water ration again to stretch it out for another few days. But now what. He'd need to try and speak with the woman again. Tattoo he called her. He'd caught a glimpse of the blue scrawl at the back of her neck.

The two worked steadily into the twilight. When the hole was done they carried out the body from the train and buried it. There would be no ceremony for this man. His wife was too frail to make the effort. He'd gone with the Matron to speak with her. The Matron was worried that she might not survive the effort. So they had both spoken gently with her. The Captain could see that the woman thought the same. Said as much.

Only Izzy came back with them in the dark, offering to help fill in the hole. The Matron had stayed with the dead man's wife. None of the other older passengers were there. The Captain had approached a group, inviting them to come along. They'd looked at each other. As angry as they'd been over his death in the ruckus with the miner it was obvious to the Captain that none of them wanted to climb down from the train and walk in the dark. And so they'd lowered the old man into the ground in the quiet of the twilight, Izzy throwing the first shovel-full of dirt on top of him. The sound of the dry soil hitting the blanket almost imperceptible.

The dingo watched, as he had the other times. He'd gone forward when they left, going about his ritual, sniffing around the site, pissing on the dirt heap and in the hole. But then they'd come back and he'd run back into cover, stopping, crouching, watching from the salt-bush. When they'd gone again he went forward, sniffing around the mound, pissing on it before heading off in search of prey.

The miner stumbled on a salt-bush branch, nearly going down in the dark. As tired as he was the fear of the snake and the agonising death of his friend gave him the energy to fight to keep his feet. He'd thought about not much else since it had happened. He knew the image of his friend convulsing on the ground would stay with him for life. The striations in the busted soil where his dying friend had kicked out in his agony were etched in his mind. That and the final breath. How many breaths do you take in a lifetime, even one this short? Billions he thought. How can there be a final one? It was fucking with him. He couldn't get his head around it.

They'd stopped at midnight for a short rest that had ended up being more than an hour. He could've so easily fallen asleep like his companion. He could almost taste it, that delicious feeling of closing his eyes when he was so tired. Sleep wrapping itself around him like his down-filled doona. But he wouldn't succumb. It was as much about the need to drive that fucker, to make him live up to what he'd said about the greater good, as it was about seeing the job done. What a pile of shit, he thought. Didn't believe a word of it. So he'd push him, that was about all he could do to honour his dead mate.

He thought about how little he knew of his companion. He

realised that he didn't even think of him as a friend, especially after what had happened. They'd met when he and his mate had been transferred to the same mine site, only a couple of weeks back. The five of them had smoked a bit of dope together and the idea to do the train trip had come up. They'd all done Bali, too many times, one of them said. He wasn't sure about it, but his mate had convinced him. It'd been a bit of a laugh. They'd hit it fairly hard, as they always did in their down time. But even among the laughs he sensed something about the bloke he didn't like. His need to be followed. Like he was trying to force respect. He hadn't warmed to him. But with five of them it'd been easy enough to keep a distance. But now, he knew he was full of shit.

He poked a knuckle into the man's ribs, waking him with a grunt. Forcing him up, grumbling, and onwards. He asked to take a turn with the compass. The other refused. The man knew they could navigate at night using the Southern Cross, he just didn't know how it worked. But he saw it as they walked, could see that it was always slightly to the left of their compass bearing so he kept an eye on it. It gave him some degree of comfort. He had a sudden urge to know more about the stars. When he got back he'd smoke less dope, drink less. Look about more.

They stumbled on, barely a word exchanged between them. They stopped again. It was three o'clock. He sat upright with nothing to lean against. He didn't remember falling asleep, didn't remember lying down. He sat up with a start. It was dark. The moon had gone.

—Come on, we have to… He realised he was talking to himself. His companion was gone, and so was his backpack.

He wanted to look away but couldn't. The dingoes had chewed away the face. It was a saucer of rotting meat. No nose or eyes. The mouth was a hole. Maggots spewed out, like live rice. No lips, and the tongue was gone. The shirt with the crest of the train company was ripped open, lacerations covering the stomach where they had tried to force an entry. The man's cap sat someway off as if one of the dogs had carried it away before realising that there was better eating to be had.

—I'll go look for a shovel. It was one of the twins.

Ticky and the other twin discussed what had likely killed him.

—Hard to tell if he's old and maybe just died like the others on our train. I can't imagine what else it would have been. Can't have been a fight over water.

They walked back to the train to help look for something to dig a grave. It was a fruitless search. The best they could find was a board from the pallet that held the water bottles. The twins were prepared to do the work but Ticky told them to save their energy.

They climbed back under the train to see out another couple of hours before they'd leave.

—I actually wouldn't mind going that way, said younger, after a period of quiet.

—What?

—I mean, if I go, I wouldn't mind being left out in the desert.

His brother scoffed. What, having your face eaten off by a dingo?

—Yeah, why not. I hate the idea of a coffin and a hole. Burning's just a waste of gas and wood. Just drag me out and leave me somewhere quiet. I like the idea of giving back to the ground.

—I guess that's what'll make you a good farmer.

—No, that's me, said the other brother. Bugger that.

The three laughed. They saw out another hour or so and then loaded up their packs with water. Ticky was nervous about how he was going to feel. He'd been thinking about it. Scared that he might suddenly realise he was wasn't up to it. He was stiff when he rose, his legs sore. It wasn't a good sign.

They were carrying more weight than when they started. They could take as much water as they wanted and had discussed the optimal amount. Weight versus thirst, the temptation to take too much. Every litre weighed a kilo one of the boys had said.

—We should reach the siding tomorrow, said Ticky, we don't need to carry too much.

They crossed around the front of the train heading to the service road. There was no smell from the dead driver as they walked along the length of the train,. Ticky wondered how long it would be before the dogs were back. He turned once when they were past the end of the final carriage. He thought the twin might be right. Maybe being left in the desert wouldn't be so bad.

They hadn't gone far when one of the twins pointed out the footprints. They were faint and only occasional on the hard ground in among old vehicle and motorcycle tracks, but they were there. The sun was now low in the north-west. The rail-bed threw a shadow across part of the service road. Ticky was relieved that the soreness in his legs was easing. It seemed that his body was building into the effort. He'd already lost weight. He could feel it. He was up to the last hole on his belt. Hadn't been this thin in years. It felt good. And he wasn't hungry. The heat meant he'd eaten sparingly from his supplies, like the twins had. But even eating sparingly they'd need to find food soon.

They ploughed on through the night. The moon only a sliver now, the way ahead dark, the walking good. They stopped at midnight. The man felt much stronger than the previous nights. He looked about him, enjoying the night sky, the cooler air. He was tired but knew he could go on.

The siding revealed itself as the red fingers of dawn reached across the plain. It was the old water tanks that they saw first, standing highest. But then the incongruity of the buildings against the landscape revealed itself. Squares corners, straight lines.

No-one said anything, but Ticky, walking between the brothers, reached out both hands patting each on the back. They smiled. Round two, he thought. He wanted to skip. What a rush.

—Let's see who's home, shall we?

Not much of a place, he thought, like a ghost town. The trio walked past ramshackle buildings, roofing iron loose and rusting, windows broken, straggly grass growing along the walls. The man could see old machinery inside, piled higgledy piggledy. A home for snakes and scorpions he thought with a smile. He caught the faint whiff of old oil and rubber, reminding him of the garage from the small town where he'd spent his youth.

They headed for what looked like a store. It was the only building with a fence. The man pushed open the metal gate. A path cut its way through what passed for a front yard to a white door with dirty panes of glass and a few tired stickers, faded and lifting at the edges, advertising the virtues of Coca-Cola and a few other products likely dispatched at some point. The path was cracked and rough. A fat skink darted away into the dry grass. Paint flakes hung from the fibro-cement sheeting walls like the skin of a peeling, summer back.

Ticky felt the same as he had when they'd approached the goods train, like he should walk quietly, that he was disturbing something. But it wasn't peace, he thought, decay more likely. The man peered through the glass, a hand above his eyes to shield the glare. He could see a counter and shelves through the grimy window. He tried the door and pushed it open.

—Hello, he yelled as he stepped inside. It took a moment until his

90

eyes adjusted to the gloom to see the man pointing the shotgun at him.

10

—Half a bottle? The old woman's look was one of incredulity as the young woman handed back her water bottle. The old woman left it sitting on the counter top. She was the first in the queue for the day's ration, the others lined up out through the swing door. She turned to the woman behind her but couldn't find any words.

It was Tattoo who spoke. She was watching proceedings, standing back with three of the younger men with her.

—If you don't want it, leave it there for the next person and move on. The voice was calm, almost soothing. She came forward as she said it giving the old woman a half-mouth smile.

The old woman turned again to the those behind in the queue. It's half she pleaded. The murmuring started to build in the queue.

—Who made this decision? It was another of the women. Where's the Matron and the driver?

Tattoo smiled again walking towards the queue. Two of the men walked behind her. Her hand darted out snatching the bottle from the old woman who had just spoken.

—We'll save a bit today boys. They keep complaining and pretty soon we'll have plenty.

—Can I have a word? It was the Captain. He'd come in through the kitchen, standing behind Tattoo and the men. Tattoo turned and looked the Captain up and down. She paused before smiling again. Sure, she said, what is it?

—In private, if you don't mind. He watched Tattoo ruminate briefly over his request. He could see she was weighing up the idea of calling out his concerns here in public. Reinforcing her control. But then she abruptly moved out of the kitchen's rear door forcing the Captain to follow. One of the young men went with her. They stopped in the carriage entry area.

The Captain looked from the man to Tattoo with a frown. What are you doing?

—Our job.

—Why are you only giving everyone half their ration?

—Oh, it's not everyone. The tone was flippant.

—What do you mean?

—Well, it's pretty obvious that you've been favouring the old farts. She raised a hand to stop the Captain's retort. We're just evening things up a bit. They're all dying anyway, there's no point wasting good water.

The Captain was stunned, briefly speechless. He stood, slowly shaking his head from side to side.

—You're going to cause a riot.

—Well, we're ready for that. Now you need to move out of my way. We've got work to do. She moved towards the kitchen but the Captain stepped in front of her. The arm grabbed him around the neck, reefing him off his feet momentarily.

—I wouldn't old fella, the man behind him said. Tattoo walked past without a glance, the man released his grip and the Captain grabbed at the wall to stop himself from falling. Once he had regained his feet he brushed at the front of his shirt. A chill of fear ran through him.

Tattoo returned to the kitchen. The woman at the front of the queue stood there, her bottle waiting on the counter top, an expectant look on her face. She tried to look past Tattoo, seeking out the Captain. He hadn't returned. Tattoo smiled.

—You've got until I count to three to take that bottle. This time the tone was cold, the words clipped.

—One. The old woman didn't wait for two. She grabbed the bottle, almost tipping it over, giving Tattoo a venomous stare before walking back along the queue.

—I don't know what to do. The Captain had gathered the Matron, his Dutch friend and the manager in the early morning shade of the engine.

—Well, they're only doing what we were thinking. She turned towards the Dutchman and the manager. We were considering reducing the water ration given we've not yet heard anything from the walking groups.

—I accept that, but you understand that they're only cutting the ration to the older passengers, or maybe those in the forward carriages. Who knows what they're going to do.

—What options do we have? It was the Dutchman. She seems to be organised. Has most of the younger men on side. We don't have the force to take over. And what good would that do. People are still getting water and eating. Maybe it's best left as it is. They were silent for a moment, digesting this comment when someone called along the train for the Matron. She looked to the group, pursed her lips, and then moved along the shaded rail-bed.

They'd laid the old man on one of the couches in the dining area. Blood streamed from his nose and his split lip. He held his hands over his chest and winced.

Ribs, thought the Matron, beginning her examination before she'd reached her patient. The old man was surrounded by a phalanx of the older passengers.

—Let the Matron through someone said.

—Get the backpack from my cabin she said to no-one in particular, as she carefully probed the old man's front. When he winced she could see that his top row of teeth were missing.

—I have his teeth, said one of the women.

The old man's breathing was laboured and wheezy.

—What happened to him, asked the Matron without taking her eyes from her patient?

Several people tried to speak. The Matron turned and looked at the woman with the teeth.

—Please tell me.

—He said something to them about the amount of water and then they just hit him. Animals, they're animals.

The Matron raised a hand, forestalling further discussion. We'll get to the whys and wherefores. But for now I need to know what was actually done to him. Was he hit, kicked? A old man stepped forward.

—One of those little pricks punched him in the face, at least twice. He fell and then another one kicked him in the stomach.

—Thank you. The backpack appeared. Can someone get me a clean cloth and some water. Nothing much happened. Matron turned to see them sheepishly looking at one another. The water, she realised. My bottle is in my cabin, can someone please get it and bring one of my t-shirts. She continued to gently probe the old man's front, knew that he had at least two broken ribs.

The Captain pushed forward through the group and looked at the old man.

—Someone told me, he said to the Matron.

—What are you going to do? The voice came from the group. Aren't you in charge? Isn't this your train? Cries of support came from the group.

The Captain paused for a moment and then turned and walked off without a word.

When he arrived in the kitchen Tattoo's group were busy moving food from one kitchen to the other.

—What's going on?

Tattoo smiled. You can thank the old man who caused the trouble. We're doing what we should have done all along, we're dividing everything. You can use the other kitchen to feed the oldies, and a few others that we send your way. Trouble-makers. We'll use this one and look after the water. Two people can bring all the bottles each morning and we'll fill them. If there's any trouble we won't fill them. She looked unblinkingly into the Captain's eyes as she spoke.

—What's going to happen when we get out of this? Do you realise how much trouble you'll be in for what you're doing?

—There's two sides to a story. You let me worry about that old fella. Now on your way.

The Captain had turned to go when she spoke again.

—One more thing. She walked towards the Captain and stopped with her hands on her hips. I hope you won't be thinking of doing anything silly. Because we're ready for it.

He called a couple of times in the dark knowing that it was pointless. The bastard's gone. Panic rose in him. I'm dead. I'll last a day, maybe,

96

but then I'm dead. His legs felt weak beneath him. He had to squat down. His breathing came in short gasps. He sat on the ground and put his head between his knees. Breath he said out loud. He took several long breaths and lifted his head. Now think, don't panic. More speed less haste, that's what the old boss used to say, wasn't it?

Alright, calm. Need to think. Options. It's too far back, I wouldn't make it. My only option is to catch him. And it has to be before sunrise. If I don't I'm going to get lost. You're my only navigation tool, he said it looking up at the Southern Cross.

—Let's go, he said jumping to his feet. He looked again into the sky and set off at a trot.

—Whoa there, easy, no need for the gun.

—Who are you?

—We're from the passenger train, we've walked here. You're from the goods train? He could see the man more clearly now that his eyes had adjusted to the gloom. He was small, gnome-like, not young. He wore a cap with the name of a rail company on the front. Ticky could see that he looked more frightened than aggressive.

—What do you want?

—The same as you. To be rescued. Please put the gun down. The small man didn't move. The man could see his uncertainty.

—Where is the family that lives here?

—There's no-one here. They're not here. I thought they'd be here and I'd get out of here but they're not here.

—Can you put the gun down. There's no need for it. The small man looked long and hard again at Ticky and then slowly lowered the barrel.

—It's not loaded. I couldn't find the cartridges.

Ticky stepped forward and introduced himself and the twins. The man apologised for pointing the gun. Said that the few days he'd spent at the siding had left him spooked. Couldn't say why that was. Kept thinking he heard things. Would rush out into the road and to the train line expecting something but nothing would happen, no-one there. Just a bit of wind flapping some loose iron on one of the roofs. That was about all he heard, that and a few creaks and groans from the buildings. That ticking noise, he said, you know at night when things cool. The roof would tick as things cooled.

Yes, he was from the goods train. The train had stopped just like theirs. Nothing, no explanation, no communication. Just shut down and rolled to a stop. They'd fiddled for a couple of days. The electrics were shot. They'd tried a few things but nothing worked. And then his mate had died.

—He just dropped dead. Gone off to the toilet. I wondered what had happened, went to look for him. He was just dead. Like he'd never been alive. Like the train. Just stopped working, lying there in the dust and heat. I can't get the image out of my head. And I couldn't bury him or even move him. He was too big, and what was I going to do? Put him in the train. I knew I had to go then. I couldn't stay with him there in the scrub. And we were out of tucker, we'd had bugger-all on the train, just the meals for our shift. Plenty of water but the food was gone. So I had to go. I waited 'til sunset and then walked. Figured I could at least make it here.

—But no-one here when I got here. I hadn't seen them when we passed through on the train. I'd usually sound the horn for the kids, but I didn't see them. Spooked me, walking around, calling out. All these sheds and buildings and no-one. A dingo, that's all I've seen, that and one of those bloody brown snakes. And then you walked in here. I heard you. I should've been happy but something made me scared, I almost hid but I had the gun, knew I could bluff you. Not sure why I did it.

It had all come out in one long burst. Ticky realised that the little driver was traumatised. The whole thing, on his own, had been too much for him. He could tell that the twins sensed it as well. Good boys, those boys, he thought. They sat quietly while the small man ran through his story.

He stopped abruptly. There was no natural ending to it, more like he'd used all the nervous energy that he'd built up and then stopped. It was quiet for a moment.

—Well, we're pleased to be here with you. It was one of the twins breaking the awkward pause.

The little driver looked at the twin, his embarrassment obvious to the others. He invited them into the back of the store. It was a house of sorts, neat and tidy, three bedrooms.

—Don't open the fridge, stinks. I threw some stuff out but it still stinks.

He showed them through. All the beds were made except for the bottom bunk in the children's room. The man looked embarrassed again.

—I didn't feel right sleeping in the big bed. Slept here.

Ticky looked at the poster of the Hulk on the wall.

—There's no power. Like the trains. They've got a gen set, but won't work either. I tried to get it going. Nothing. There's plenty of water, big tank out back is almost full. There's a bit of food in the pantry. Enough for a while, for all of us, but then what? He looked at the three.

—There is the kalamazoo.

He took them out to one of the workshops, a big green shed with a concrete floor. It was the newest building in the place. There were various pieces of rail equipment spaced around the floor and some old framed photos lining the hot walls.

—A museum of sorts, said one of the twins.

—Yep, said the little driver. The passenger trains stop here, you lot I guess. Get a chance to get off the train and have a look around.

He walked to the rear of the building where a small machine sat on the bare floor. It had four rail wheels and a platform with a double-sided handle in the middle.

—A Kalamazoo. It was the brightest he'd been since they arrived. It's a hand-car, runs on the rails. Looks to be in good order. Working condition. I was thinking that I'd try and move it out to the rails. Was wondering if I could do it by myself.

He watched as the others walked about the old machine.

—So you reckon it'll work?

—Best as a I can tell. All the rods and gears seem to function. I moved it a bit yesterday. I even found a grease gun in the one of the other sheds and gave it a hit. They used it up until a couple of years ago. I remember seeing it a couple of times on the siding when I passed through. They do about ten or fifteen miles an hour. Get us somewhere I reckon.

The man turned to the twins. Thoughts?

—No vehicles in any of these other sheds.

—No, nothing. Looked through them all. This is it.

—Nothing much else for it then.

—Where are we going?

—Well let's get it on the rails and try it before we get excited about destinations.

The hand-car was heavy but the four were able to push it easily enough along the concrete floor, the metal wheels crunching their way outside and onto the dirt. The handle moved up and down as it moved. It took twenty minutes of grunting and pushing to get the machine to the rails. The three were lathered in sweat. The small driver stood behind them.

—This'll be the hard bit. Lifting it on.

The three walkers gathered at one end and heaved the rear of the machine across and into the rail-bed, then repeated the action with the front. Then they lifted the front and rear onto the rails. Ticky sat down onto the platform of the cart. It moved forward slightly, easily. He laughed. It's all about environment. The small man came forward and climbed up to stand beside the man. He was keen to help now Ticky noted.

—One of you on the other side, the driver said to the twins.

One jumped up.

—Now you give us a bit of a push. The other twin stood behind the machine between the rails and got the machine moving. The pump handle began moving up and down. Right, let's go. The man stayed sitting, lifting up his legs so they didn't drag along the ground. The little driver and the twin started working the handle. The cart increased it's speed, gears clanking, squeaking its way along the rail, moving out of the siding and heading into the desert.

—Easy boys, let's not let younger think we've left him behind. They stopped the cart. Ticky pushed it back the other way and then jumped on. The little driver laughed. When they rolled into the siding the driver switched the rails.

—You never know what might come through.

The others laughed.

—Let's go have a drink, said Tricky, and something to eat and decide where we should go with it.

The miner kept going through the rest of the night. He walked quickly, jogging when he could. Early on he passed unawares by his empty backpack, missing it in the moonless darkness. It didn't much matter, the food and water were gone. The only thing it might've provided was some comfort that he was heading in the right direction.

He thought he had him at one stage. Saw something in the distance sticking up out of the plain. Something solid. It wasn't a tree or bush, he could see that. He moved stealthily, slowing. It was the first time he'd thought about what he was going to do if he caught up with him. He'd probably have to fight him. He didn't know how that would go. The guy was a gym junkie. Pumped iron when he wasn't pissed or stoned. He wasn't a fighter himself. Had never had a fight since he was a kid at primary school. Would he reason with him? Would the prick listen? Maybe he'd agree to a truce. He didn't know how he'd feel. He was angry, he knew that. Catch him first.

When the shape began to materialise he realised it wasn't his former companion. There was a scuffle ahead of him and three camels stood and bolted. They were quickly out of sight but he caught snatches of noise as they careened away in their panic, the soft pads of their feet slapping down into the chalky soil, the occasional rustle of disturbed salt-bush. And then nothing. He walked to the area where they'd been sleeping. The dirt was disturbed and he smelt before he saw a couple of piles of drying shit. He touched the ground where they'd laid feeling the warmth their bodies had generated. He felt an urge to lie down.

He looked around him and could see the faint red in the east. Don't give up, he thought. He kept moving, the Southern Cross growing faint as the dawn tide rolled across the plain. He took a final look into the sky and stopped. He dragged a line in the dirt with the heal of his boot. That's my south. And then he sat. I'll wait for the sun. And look for some sort of landmark to head for. Surely there'll be a tree, or something. He said these things out loud, searching for a confidence he didn't feel.

The miner didn't know what had woken him. He'd jerked awake. Probably dreaming about that fucking snake, he thought. He was still tired. Could've slept more, thought about it. But they had to keep moving. He grunted to his feet and walked up to his companion, expecting him to wake. Had been about to toe him in the ribs, return the favour, when it came to him. He'd not thought about it until now. It hadn't occurred to him. But now it did. He reached down and hefted the man's pack. It rustled in the dark. Surely he'll wake. Not a problem if he does. But the man continued to breathe the regular soft rhythm of the sleeper. The man stood there for a moment. Think about it. How much further, how much water?

They'd been sensible with it but even so he reckoned they were running behind the distance they still had to cover. Enough for one. Fuck it. Fuck him. He walked quietly backwards watching the sleeping form before turning and striding out into the dark. He took a bearing off the compass and moved quickly away.

—They've got most of the food. The manager said it as he walked along the rail-bed to where the Captain sat with the Matron and Izzy. The look on his face was one of pain. They haven't left us much and we have to feed most of the crew as well, the ones they've chased out of their group. And god knows how much water they'll let us have tomorrow. And they've locked the doors between the two dining cars so we can't move between them inside the train.

It was the Captain's turn to look pained. No-one spoke for a minute or so.

—We've still got the other pump tap, haven't we? asked the Captain. Where did you put it when I pulled it out?

—Of course. I'd forgotten about that. It's in the baggage car. But I can get it.

—No, no. I'll get it. I want you to get as many empty bottles as you can. But don't let anybody see what you're doing. Get them into the storage area in the kitchen. Keep everyone away. The Captain looked at Izzy. Maybe you can keep an eye on Tattoo and her cronies. Izzy nodded.

—Let's wait an hour or so until things quieten down and people head for the shade.

Izzy moved down to the further dining car. She felt nervous and that made her more nervous. She didn't want it to show, especially in front of Tattoo. That woman frightened her and she'd notice. Even before the trouble had started she was wary of her. She'd told the Matron.

She has a way about her. She seems friendly but you get that feeling that she's analysing you, summing you up. Wondering if you have something that she might want or need. I caught her looking at me a couple of times. She never said anything to me but I could tell she didn't like the way I hung out with them, her posse, and then came back up to be with you guys.

This was what she worried about now. Now that everything had gone to a new level. Gone to shit, she thought. She'll be watching me more than ever. But I want to do my bit. The others are doing so much. I love the Matron. She's amazing and the Captain is a good guy as well. They're both doing so much. I need to do something.

She thought this as she crunched along the rail-bed to climb up the steps into the entry area of the second dining car. She'd agreed with the Captain that she'd go to the closest point between the dining carriages. Hopefully she could stand there and look casual. Someone would be looking through the glass partition from the other carriage. If she sensed that anyone was going to check on them she was to put both hands behind her head and stretch.

Thankfully, she thought with relief, there were enough of the gang spread around the dining car that she wouldn't look out of place sitting around at the end of the carriage. And more importantly Tattoo was nowhere in sight. They lounged around in the dining area and the kitchen, a couple of them trying to sleep on the banquettes in the growing morning heat, a couple on mattresses on the floor.

What sent a shiver up her spine were the weapons. It was the first time that she'd seen any evidence of them. There were a couple of carving knives lying on the tables and one of those big barbecue spatulas, a cutting edge along one side and the spiky rear side. In any other environment or time it would look like someone had simply left them there. Innocuous. But not now. She knew why they were there.

One man was sitting there with a smaller knife working on a branch from a mulga tree, chipping pieces of wood away, onto the floor. He gave her a wave and a smile as she walked in. She smiled back. She thought she should. She'd spoken to him a couple of times, had caught him looking at her when she'd sat with the group during the evenings in the rail-bed behind the train. She knew nothing about him other than he was in the army or something and was going home for a holiday. He was younger than she was. She hadn't thought him a bad type, but watching him now fashioning a weapon out of wood she had a change of heart.

She sat at the other end of the banquette near the rear door of the carriage resisting the urge to look through to see if anyone was standing in the next carriage. When she looked up she saw Tattoo standing in the doorway staring at her.

11

—Options lads, what are our options? Ticky stood and paced as the other three sat watching him. We've got three as I see it. We can stay here and see what happens, we can head west on the hand-car towards civilisation or we can go back to our train, also on the hand-car. Now as tempted as I am to go west, it'd be many days from what I can see. Many more days than it took us to get here. If we did that, we'd be killing everyone on the train. Their water just wouldn't last that long. And there's not much point staying here. If no-one comes we'd end up running out of food. No, as I see it, the best option is to load up with as much water as the hand-car can take and head back to our train.

They talked on for the next hour or so and then had some lunch agreeing that the hand-car would leave in the late evening.

It was Tricky and younger who cranked the handle to bring the hand-car up to speed. They'd agreed that only two of them would go, saving space for carrying precious water. Behind them they pulled the small wagon that had been in the museum, a simple design of four rail wheels and a flat top. The man knew the wagon would slow them, especially when it was loaded but it increased massively the amount of water they could carry.

The two had moved the hand-car off the rails at the siding, pushing it along the ground and then lifting it back on. They had to be able to do it, just the two of them, to get past the goods train. Lifting it on and off proved much easier than the man had thought. But he knew it was going to be a big job pushing it the length of the train.

They'd eaten a final meal. On the way out of the house the twin gestured towards the shotgun, where it sat on the counter-top in the store front, next to the box of cartridges they'd found.

—We should take it.

Ticky looked at it and at the twin.

—They'll be getting low on food now. What if we stop everyone from dying of thirst only to have them die from starvation? We can hunt with it.

Ticky smiled.

—Good idea. He gathered up the weapon and ammunition and headed out to the rail where the little cart and wagon stood waiting, looking like a test model of something larger and grander.

The two men staying behind gave them a shove. The twin looked back towards his brother slowly disappearing into the distance. They worked the handle easily, settling into a rhythm, heading into the eastern darkness, looking for a pace that they could sustain for the hours that lay ahead. They'd left late figuring that the journey to the goods train would take no more than a few hours. They'd move the cart ahead of the train and load it the next morning, spending the day at the train before heading off in the late afternoon. They agreed that the next night would be long and tiring and maybe would not see them at their destination.

The steel of the handle was smooth and shiny. The man wondered at the calloused hands that had gone before him. Men who had swung ten pound sledge hammers to drive spikes into wooden sleepers, carried long lengths of railway track with pincer-like tools. Hard graft, he thought to himself. Hard yakka. The early days when the hand-car would've been an integral part of maintaining a railway line in the desert.

—You'll tell me if you see a train coming, won't you, Ticky said with a grin in the fading light. Younger offered a grin in return.

Ticky quickly settled into the cadence produced by the rods and pulleys of the car's gearing. It didn't take him long to recognise the four-beat metallic rhythm on each depression of the handle. He liked it. It made him think about the garage band he and his mates had formed in high school. He smiled. *The Rodents*. It'd been a largely inglorious rock career. A couple of gigs at school assembly with mixed reviews. But they didn't care. They had their groupies and he had his axe. He still had it somewhere. Had promised himself that he would get back into playing when his business settled down and he could take things more slowly but that'd never happened. Always something around the corner. It was his drug of choice. He'd never bothered with stimulants other than the odd glass of shiraz or a good single malt. No, for him, the buzz came from the boardroom. It wasn't the money or the prestige, it was only ever about the next deal.

He knew it had killed his marriage. They shared the same bed when he was home but, when he thought about it, they'd not had sex in months. He'd half expect his wife to tell him one day that there was someone else, that she was leaving. He'd wondered how he'd feel about that. He hoped that he wouldn't be angry of jealous, not wanting to share her with someone else. But he wasn't sure.

It was his son who saddened him. It was classic cats-in-the-cradle–stuff. He hadn't been there. And he'd paid for it, realised too late, didn't listen to his wife's entreaties. Wondered now whether he'd get another chance. He wanted one. He wondered whether that was what drew him to the twins.

He asked the younger to stop after a couple of hours. They'd not discussed a break schedule and even though he felt he was working well within himself he thought it prudent to have a break. The wiry young man opposite him was indefatigable, would match and long surpass any effort that he might dictate. It had to be common-sense over pride.

They sat at either end of the Kalamazoo facing different directions. It had been full-dark for hours now. There was no moon. The desert looked like a guarded secret, the slightest hint of darker patches where the salt-bush dominated the landscape. The man looked up, finding the Southern Cross. He thought about the boys walking south, wondering how they might be faring. They might be back at train when we get there. With help. But he didn't believe it.

—Time to push on I reckon.

The miner was already thirsty. His tongue felt rough and dry along its edges as he rubbed it along the corner of his mouth. He'd found a pebble to suck. He'd read that somewhere. It did help him to make saliva. He'd swish it along his tongue and then swallow it. He could already feel the dryness in his throat. It frightened him.

He watched the day erupt in front of him. One minute it had seemed to be too dark to see and now the plain revealed itself before him. He stood and looked around, wanting to see the bouncing head of that bastard nearby, making his way south. But there was no-one, nothing. Just him and the flies already buzzing his eyes and mouth. He looked along the line he'd scraped in the dirt and looked up but there was nothing to guide him, nothing more than anything else that he looked at. I can stay here 'til night, navigate by the Southern Cross, or risk it in the daylight. Use the sun. I can't sit here. Might as well die trying as doing nothing. He took a final look along his boot scrape, glanced at the sun and started walking.

He saw the dingo an hour or so later. He'd tried to keep the sun on his left but he struggled. It was behind him in the north-east and would pass behind him to the north-west. Even though it was still early in the day it was already difficult to navigate by it, not like watching the Southern Cross, there in front of him the whole time in the clear night sky. And it was hot. His back felt like it must surely catch on fire such was the heat he felt through his shirt. He could feel the strength draining from his legs. He wasn't stumbling but he knew it wasn't far off. There was no more moisture to be had from sucking on the pebble. He'd spat it away. He realised that he wouldn't last the day. He wondered how it would end for him. He figured he'd just stop eventually, able to go no further, sit down and not get up again. He wondered what would actually kill him, which part of his body would fail. Obviously my heart will stop beating at some point, but what makes that happen?

He thought he should start thinking about the things that were important to him. Be prepared to go. Think about family, his mum, that sort of thing.

The dingo was close. He stopped and watched it. It hadn't seen him, struggling with something it was carrying. The man blinked in the heat, waving feebly at the flies around his face. He must be closer to death than he thought. The dog looked like it it was dragging a human leg. He could see the black shoe on the foot, the sock, the rest of the leg bare. He shook his head. That was when the dog saw him. It changed direction, bolting, but dragging its load. He figured this was what happened when you died from thirst, you saw things. He cut the dingo's track and could see the drag mark in the soil.

He saw the sun glinting off something ahead before he saw the other dingoes. And then he could see something black in the distance. He heard the dingoes before he saw them. They were everywhere, fighting, growling, snapping at each other.

And then came the smell. He believed it then, believed what his eyes were seeing. As if smell couldn't be imagined but visions could. It was putrid, rotting, a deep cloying odour. He gagged before he was amongst the cause. The dingoes saw him. Some ran, others didn't, emboldened by the feast on offer. He passed by one. It had it's snout in the cavity of a corpse. It looked up and growled as he passed.

Death was everywhere. Pieces, bits, chunks, of dead people, smashed through the wreckage. Some of it cooked. The black he saw was the damage caused by fire. Some of the wreckage had burned. But had burned itself out. The fuselage was broken up, only several small sections had stayed together to provide any sort of evidence as to what it might have been. He saw the airline's logo on the tailplane lying in a patch of salt-bush. There was baggage strewn all over, and seats. Rows of seats still intact.

It was the trunk of a child that stopped him. Hit him like a hammer. Still strapped into her seat. It was, had been—he wasn't sure of the definition—a little girl. He could see the colourful dress, blues and yellows, primary colours, a floral pattern. But there was no head or arms, just legs. Bits plucked off in the massive deceleration. He stared, transfixed. A teddy bear was tucked into the seat belt with her. He sobbed. It came in a gasp. He lunged at some of the dingoes, yelling. His voice came as a croak. He realised he hadn't spoken for hours. The dogs circled, came back, feasting. A frenzy. He ran again but then was too tired. He collapsed to his knees, folding forward, prostrate, but he had no god. And seeing this, only reinforced that there couldn't be one.

He continued to sob. He wanted to lie there, to die among the dead, but the smell drove him to his feet. The dingoes ignored him. He watched two worrying an arm, growling at each other through clenched teeth, refusing to relinquish a hold on either end. The arm still sported a watch. It was like two puppies playing with a toy. He had to get away. Decided he couldn't die here, like this.

He glanced at the sun. It was overhead, no use to him. But he knew which direction he'd come from, the wreckage had given him that at least, so he ploughed through, stumbling over baggage, around rows of seats, trying not to look at whether they still held passengers. A wing, landing gear. And then he saw a bottle. A small plastic water bottle. He fell to his knees in front of it, fear surging through him that it might be a trick. There was a mouthful in the bottom. His hands shook as he unscrewed the cap. He barely felt it on his lips and tongue. They were so dry that all feeling seemed to have gone, like pumice stone. He gagged when he swallowed, spitting some out onto the baking earth. And then it was gone. But it spurred him. It was life. He circled back, kicking his way through the detritus. Trying to ignore the gore that was everywhere. It was the heads that would haunt him. Faces stared, accusing. Flesh rotting and torn by the dingoes. But he found more water.

The second drink was the best one. He could feel this one. His lips had moistened and his throat less parched. And the bottle was full. New. Seal unbroken. He wept as he upended it. He could feel the energy return to his limbs. He found another, and another and then he found some soft drinks, Coke, Fanta. Even hot the sugar was a tonic. He slugged them down until he was sated. He knew he should be frugal but he didn't care. There was plenty. And even food.

113

Packets of peanuts and chips. He hadn't realised he was craving salt so much. He gathered them, found a row of empty seats, sat, and ate, and drank some more.

Once his feeding frenzy had stopped he thought about what he needed. He spent twenty minutes or so searching baggage, hoping to find a compass, but didn't. He found phones, lots and lots of phones. And many had been turned off, rather than flight mode, so they had battery life. There was no reception. He wondered if people downloaded compasses. But they all had screen-locks, so he didn't waste his time for long. He wasn't much of a tech geek.

He took a backpack, filling it with water bottles, a couple of soft drinks, and snack foods and some useful clothing. And a wide-brimmed hat he'd found in the luggage. He stepped over the aluminium walking stick before stopping and going back to retrieve it. He gave it a few satisfying swishes through the air. He though he might need a weapon.

And then he was suddenly very tired. He needed to rest, to sleep. He could afford to sit down now, knew he'd be able to get up again. But it wouldn't be here. Amongst the carnage, the feeding, the putrid smell. So he headed off, without a backwards glance, the image of the little girl and her teddy bear traveling with him.

They were almost at the rear of the goods train before they saw it. Ticky felt a thrill. Another victory. He still felt good and it had taken about as much time as they'd figured.

—Should we move the hand-car now, while it's cool? asked younger.

—Yes. Definitely. Let's have a drink and then do that, and then we can rest.

They unhooked the wagon from the hand-car and then lifted the front wheels off the rails letting the car run down off the rail-bed and onto the service road, the handle wildly cranking with the spurt of speed. And then they pushed from the rear, both stretched out low to the ground, like sprinters coming out of the crouch.

It was hard work. Slow work. Inching forwards with their toes. But not impossible. By the time they were done with both machines the red dawn was flooding across the plain. The two men sat in the goods carriage, behind the engine, legs dangling over the side, sipping from large bottles.

—Well, this time tomorrow, we'll hopefully be back at the train. Should give them a surprise.

12

I feel pretty useless. I should be doing more. I know that. I hated the Captain at first but now I have nothing but respect for him. I thought he was trying to take over but it made me realise that he needed to. I'm just not cut out for it. I should never of taken the promotion. I tried to convince myself that I was up to the job, but even then I knew I wasn't. It's always been like that. I seem to do okay, get noticed. I'm always well-liked. But I reckon it's more about me wanting to please everyone rather than any sort of ability. And that seems to do the trick a lot of the time. People confuse it with skill. So I get pushed forward for things, I start to believe my own press, you know, the things that others think about me, say about me. It's not that I'm useless. It just seems that when push comes to shove I just don't seem to have it. You know, that ability to make the important decision or the quick one. But funny, the way things are heading here I wonder whether it would've been much different if I'd stayed in charge. It couldn't be much worse than it is now, so I do think a bit about whether I might have done okay, you know, being in charge. But probably not.

Izzy felt a cold shiver when Tattoo smiled at her. It wasn't a friendly smile. It was more of a warning, a knowing look that told her she was being watched. Tattoo held her gaze long enough that Izzy didn't know what to do, to look away or hold on. In the end she looked away making an inane comment to the soldier, carving his stick. He called it a knob-kerrie, said it was a fighting stick used by tribes in South Africa.

She glanced up from under hooded brows to see if Tattoo was still staring, but she'd gone into the kitchen, she could see her through the round glass pane.

—Why are you making that?

The soldier looked at her. He suddenly looked unsure of himself, like he'd been caught doing something naughty. He blinked a couple of times.

—Just something to do. Always wanted to make one. Good wood this. Hard-wood. Tough, like the stuff they use to make them in Africa. I don't imagine I'll need to use it on anyone. He tried to laugh as he said it.

The Captain worked quickly to re-install the pump tap in the kitchen. But he was a bit panicked, crossing the thread twice on the connecting nut before he managed to get it right. He'd told himself to calm down a number of times already.

—Will this be enough bottles?

The Captain looked at them stacked together on the counter.

—There'd be more along the train but I didn't want to go looking. You know, raise suspicion.

—No, you were right to think that. This will have to do. It's just insurance. If they cut our supplies it means we'll have a bit up our sleeves.

The Captain began to pump. It was a slow process, lifting the water from the belly tanks of the train. They'd filled three-quarters of the bottles when the water stopped running. The Captain looked at the manager, unsure of himself. He pumped again, could hear the air coming from the tap.

—There should've been way more. More than enough to fill all the bottles. I checked the tank gauge this morning.

—Could the gauge be wrong?

—It must be. It's probably always been wrong but it never mattered in the past, there'd always be way more than we needed for a single crossing. Filled again before the train came back. Shit.

—What do we do with it? We've got it all.

—Bugger. I didn't want all of it. Now they'll know. We need to put some of it back.

As the Captain turned the Matron called from along the carriage.

—She's sent the signal. Someone must be coming.

Tattoo stormed out of the kitchen, the door swinging back and slamming against its stopper.

—What have you done, you little bitch? Watch her she said to one of the men, don't let her out of here. She turned to the soldier. Come with me.

Izzy felt the rush of fear in her chest but had the presence of mind to stand near the door and put her hands behind her head. It was an incongruous gesture given the situation. Izzy felt it. And she could see that the man sensed something as well. He stood and looked around her, could see the Matron through the glass, heading away from the door in the farther carriage.

—What are you up to?

Tattoo stormed along the rail-bed, kicking outstretched legs before turning up the stairs into the other dining carriage, the soldier behind her. She pushed open the kitchen door. The room was empty. The stainless steel counter was bare. She turned away but then turned back and walked forward, looking into the sink. She reached out to touch the water droplets in the bottom. She looked into the empty socket where the tap would have been. Water in there as well.

—Fuckers. She yelled it and slapped the counter top. The noise reverberated around the empty kitchen.

—Get all the boys. Wake them, get them up. They've got the water. She paused. Bring that fucking barmaid to me as well.

They'd taken the water out the other side of the carriage, the sunny side, the hot side. It was slightly after the noon, close to the hottest part of the day. The sun beat down on them. The distance was short but the Matron could feel the ferocity of the rays on the pale flesh of her unprotected arms. She was focussed on not dropping any of the bottles. Five of them had all that was left of the train's water. It made her very nervous. The Captain put his bottles down onto the track side and climbed the ladder up to the platform near the cab.

—Quick, pass them all up. As it was done he moved them through the door and into the cab, stacking along the back wall, locking the door, before climbing back down into the rail-bed.

The group walked around the front of the train and settled themselves in the shade of engine at the urging of the Captain. It was only a matter of seconds before the group came towards them. Tattoo was in the vanguard, along with the soldier who had a claw-like grip digging into Izzy's upper arm. Tattoo stopped at the feet of the Captain, glaring down at him.

—Where is it?

The Captain didn't have a chance to answer before Tattoo turned

119

and slapped Izzy across the face. Izzy let out a cry and the soldier looked at Tattoo but said nothing. She turned to her group.

—They've taken all the water. There's nothing left. They'd let us die. She turned back. Where is it?

The Captain tried to stand.

—No. Stay down old man. The soldier stepped forward following Tattoo's command raising a boot heal.

—Uh uh, was all he needed to say.

Tattoo looked around and saw that the soldier was holding his stick in his other hand. She beckoned for it with an index finger and he passed it over. She pointed the knobbed end at Izzy's stomach and then swung back, the stick gripped in both hands.

—NO. It came out as a roar from the Captain. It's in the cab.

Tattoo never paused in her stroke. She drove the knob-end of the stick deep into Izzy's stomach. The soldier was caught off balance and couldn't hold her. She dropped to the ground, writhing in the foetal position, moaning, her breath ragged.

Tattoo turned to her off-siders. Get it.

—You'll need these. The Captain held out a set of keys.

Tattoo waited until the group returned, quietly tapping the knob of the stick into the palm of her other hand, the soldier by her side. Izzy sat up and slipped back against the wheels of the engine with the others. Tattoo looked at her and smiled. You can blame him for that, she said gesturing with the stick. That and the fact that you were spying on us, you little prick. She suddenly swung the stick back like she was wielding a squash racket. Izzy's hands shot up to protect her face. But the blow never came. Tattoo smiled again. Not yet she said.

—There's not much. It was one of the miners.

Tattoo turned and raised the stick, this time over her head, Izzy again her target.

—NO, NO. It was the Matron who screamed it loudest. There's no more. That's all there was. I was there.

Tattoo halted the blow.

—And why should I trust you, you old cow? You're as bad as them.

—Because it's the truth. We were only going to move a bit of the water. Just in case. And then it ran out. Everyone was surprised. The gauge on the tank was unreliable. Not a true reading. That's all there is.

Tattoo looked back at the Captain.

—It's true. The gauge must be faulty.

Tattoo stared for a moment and then turned to the miners.

—Go with him, get him to show you how to check the tanks. She turned back. Get up, you old bastard. You better be telling the truth. Let's go, she said to the others. Bring her, she said to the soldier, pointing towards Izzy.

The two men loaded the wagon and the hand-car in the late afternoon. They couldn't take all the water. It wouldn't fit. They tried various amounts, cranking the hand-car up and down the track in front of the train until they were satisfied with their load.

—Anyway, someone can come back and get the rest, straight away if necessary.

—Yes, no point busting ourselves.

They ate a final meal before mounting the little cart. Younger gave the wagon a shove to get the cars moving in the right direction before jumping up opposite the man to begin working the handle. They headed off towards towards the east, the sun low in the sky off the northern side of the track behind them.

The dingo was forced to move away from the train in the night to

121

hunt. The food smells had diminished but still lingered, so he was loathe to move away completely. It was a compromise. He hunted his rabbits at night and then spent his day's curled in the sandy cool of the culvert, barely a kilometre from the train. He still circled the train on occasion, had been spooked a couple of times by encounters with people. But he was getting used to them now and did little more than trot off a safe distance before turning back to look.

He'd found some shade not far from the plane. A clump of acacia, thick enough to give him succour through the long afternoon hours. He woke in the early evening. He couldn't remember having fallen asleep. The sun was just under the horizon. He felt a sudden elation. I'm fucking alive, he yelled at the plain, laughing. And now, where are you, my friend, he said looking into the sky for his guiding stars.

He drank and ate and scraped a line in the dirt, judging the direction from which he'd come, and to where he had headed. When the night was dark enough he found his constellation. He'd been heading a bit too far east from what he could tell but hopefully not too far. He shrugged into his pack, retrieving his walking stick and headed into the night.

Ticky asked to stop somewhere just after midnight. He need to rest. His pride had given him half an hour longer but his common-sense prevailed. They stopped cranking on the handle, stepped back, let the cars ease to a halt.

He sat on his end of the hand-car, his feet planted between the rails, elbows on his knees, staring back along the rails where they disappeared into the night. For the first time he thought about them as a connection to where he'd been going, where his journey should've ended.

—What do you reckon is back there at the end?

He couldn't see the twin. He was in the mirror-opposite position on the cart, sitting, facing east, sipping from a water bottle. Not a little tired himself. He didn't get to answer before they both jumped to their feet, fatigue gone. It was an aircraft, somewhere to the south of them.

13

They all heard it. Elder and the goods-train driver heard it first, then the men on the hand-car. The passengers on the train heard it at around the same time as the two men walking south, who were much closer to the flight path, so that it seemed almost to pass above them. Even the dingo gave a curious glance into the sky as he trotted through the salt-bush searching out a meal.

The noise woke the miner. It freaked him out. It flew low, low enough that it was an intrusive noise rather than something far off, white noise. He jumped up, still half asleep, not knowing where he was. He stood still, swaying, his breath coming in short gasps, like he'd woken from a nightmare. He could hear the aircraft in the distance but then the sound was gone.

His first thoughts were for his companion that he'd left behind. It didn't bother him much. And then he had a sip of water, checked his compass and headed south, always south. It was an hour or so later that he walked through the table drain, going slightly down and up again without noticing. He was half-way across the highway before he realised that he was there. He stopped as if waking from a dream, his head snapping up. He tapped a foot onto the flat, macadamised surface and then he laughed, dancing a few steps, pumping his fists.

—Well fuck me, he said it loud He sobbed. I've done it, I've fuckin' done it. And then he wanted to sit, to sleep again. He looked east and west along the roadway, wishing for headlights, saw nothing. He stepped back to the road edge, lying down in the table drain, smiling at the thought of being run down before he could tell his story. He looked up into the sky, could see the Southern Cross before falling into a heavy sleep.

Izzy was forced to sit at the very end of the train in a passenger seat.

Tattoo sneered. You can see how the other half live.

Izzy resisted the urge to respond. She was scared. She was made to sit there the whole night, let out only once to pee. Not that she had much to pee, she'd left the remnants of her water in her cabin in the front of the train and her request for a drink had been met with a laugh from more than a few of Tattoo's group.

She tried to sleep in the uncomfortable seat, sweating and slipping against a surface designed for longevity not comfort. When she did nod off she woke after short spells as people talked and moved around. She could tell they were operating in shifts. Tattoo had them standing guard outside the train. The others slept on mattresses pilfered from the cabins, some in the same carriage as Izzy but many, she suspected, in the dining car.

The Dutchman and his wife had attempted to speak with her but they were forced away before they'd had any chance to say anything. Izzy felt nervous for them hoping they wouldn't be in any sort of trouble. It wasn't the plane that woke her but the talk from others who had heard it first. But she could hear it now. It sounded low to her, but off in the distance. Was help coming?

—Why didn't it fly over us? The Matron asked it of herself. It doesn't make sense. She sat with the Captain in the cab of the engine. Neither had wanted to go back to sleep after the plane passed and to avoid keeping others awake they'd gone to the engine to talk.

—I don't know. Maybe they were flying along the highway, checking that first. I don't know.

—They must know we're here.

—Yes, they must.

—We've had another two deaths in the night. A man and a woman. The Matron delivered the statement to the Captain as the sun peaked over the salt-bush. The pair had eventually gone back to their mattresses to snatch some sleep but had still woken early.

—There'll be more pretty soon with the water gone.

—Do you think they'll share it?

The Captain looked at her, pursing his lips. Come with me, let's go find out.

The two walked through the train. The smell of shit, piss and unwashed bodies. They were met by older passengers along the way who asked about water. The Matron could see the fear on the faces, could sense it in the tone they used. Gone was the anger against the others. It was like death was now a reality for them. Before, even with people dying around them, there was no reason to doubt they might survive. But water was life. They knew that, had it drummed into them by the Matron. Gone was the aggression and demands. It was pleading now.

They found Tattoo in the dining car. She and some of her

companions were eating and drinking. The Matron noticed that the soldier was now never very far from Tattoo's side.

She turned in her seat to look at the two arrivals.

—Wait there. Sit down.

They did as they were bid and Tattoo turned back to her meal.

—What do you want? She didn't bother turning towards them to ask.

—Water for the passengers. It was the Matron who said it.

—Sorry. There's not enough.

—That's murder. There were two dead overnight and without water today you'll kill many more. She had deliberately used the word kill to hopefully make this monster see some sense or at least understand the ramification of her actions. Didn't you hear that plane. There'll be rescue. Have you thought about what will happen when people come?

Tattoo smiled.

—Finished? Good, now piss off.

—Can you let our friend go please.

—Ah, the skanky little stripper. No, I think not. She might stay with us a while. For security. You know how it is. You can't be trusted. She waved to the soldier who came forward forcing the pair from the carriage.

They climbed back into the further dining car and were met again by a group of older passengers.

—I'm sorry, but there'll be no water this morning.

The Matron added, let's pool what we have left and make sure everyone gets some today. The reaction from the group was astounding, the Matron said later to the Captain. I could see it on their faces, the ones that still had some water and those that had finished theirs. It was like the group suddenly split in two, cleaved in half. Went from being a united force to one that despised the other.

They'd gone to the shade on the south side of the train, were sitting alone leaning against the bogey wheels.

—I'm not sure I can spare the energy to dig a grave tonight. And no-one is going to help, I wouldn't expect them to. As he said it, he turned his head to see the Dutchman and his wife walked along the rail-bed. They sat beside them. The woman clutched a full water bottle.

—Looks like we're out of the gang. The tall man said it with a smile. Fraternising with the enemy I think it's called. Told us to go.

—Here, have a drink. His wife held out her bottle towards the Matron. The Matron could see it was full.

—It was our parting gift. She said there'd be no more.

The Matron thought briefly before taking the proffered bottle and taking a sip. It was fantastic. She'd not had water since early the previous afternoon after having shared her final few mouthfuls with one of the older passengers. The Dutchman offered his bottle to the Captain, who also gratefully took a swig.

—Have you seen Izzy?

—She seems okay. I saw her before I left. But I'm not sure if they've given her any water. She doesn't look very comfortable, they won't let her outside the train.

The Captain felt an anger burning deep inside him. Wasn't sure it was anger or frustration at not being able to control the situation. No doubt a bit of both he thought.

—I don't know what to do. We can't attack them. There's more of us but I doubt our elder friends are up for the challenge.

—It's stupid, said the Matron, the small amount of water that's left will only keep them alive for a few days more at best. It'll make no real difference if nothing changes.

—I guess that's what happens in these kinds of situations, said the Dutchman's wife, people take hold of whatever they can to survive.

—I wonder will it remain harmonious in their group when it becomes late and the water is almost gone? asked the Dutchman.

The question hung. No-one spoke, the four stared out across the plain as the heat gathered itself to assault them in the hours ahead. The waves danced and the light against the dry, dun-coloured earth became unbearable to look at.

Izzy wondered that she still had any sweat left to give. She'd not had water since the previous afternoon. She thought of the bottle in her cabin. A few tepid mouthfuls that would taste like nectar right now. One of Tattoo's gang, a woman, had tried to give her a drink but Tattoo had intervened.

—No, she's a fucking spy. Nothing for her.

The dry tongue in her mouth had swollen. She found it hard to swallow the little saliva she managed to muster. It frightened her, realising that death could come so quickly. She'd never given any thought that she wouldn't come through this. Not really. Sitting with the Matron and the Captain she'd taken comfort from their confidence and experience. They'd never directly told her not to worry but that had been her take-away.

She was drawn to the Matron. She felt a little foolish about it but she'd never had much of a relationship with her own mother. Her mother had fed and clothed her, made sure she went to school, cleaned her teeth, went to bed. More like addressing a list of obligations rather than something driven by love. There'd been little encouragement to excel or to think about a direction in life. And no affection. She could count the cuddles on one hand. She remembered a day, she must be have been five or six, grabbing her mother's hand to hold as they walked into a shopping centre. Her mother swatted the hand away like it had been an annoying fly, told her not to do that.

There'd been other experiences like that but nothing that stayed with her as that had. She couldn't remember what she thought at the time. Sadness certainly, tears maybe. But she wondered whether the younger her had thought about her self-worth, deeper emotions. What she may have perceived that it said about her, that she somehow she wasn't worth the effort. She hoped not.

She left home at a young age and rarely returned. Her calls home had been less and less frequent as the years passed. And then it was just awkward. She'd wondered at times that her mother might seek her out as she aged but it hadn't been the case.

She smiled to herself. Didn't people make resolutions in this kind of situation. That, if I ever get out of here… No, she thought, I won't be so dramatic. She looked around. The others were all outside at the far end of the carriage, beside and under the train. One man sat in the doorway, tasked with keeping an eye on her. He seemed to sense her looking, turned his head and smiled. She dropped her gaze and looked away. She heard him rise and walk towards her. Shit.

He casually swung a water bottle at his side. She could hear the splashing sound it made against the inside of the bottle. It made the saliva run in her mouth. Oh, she could taste it, couldn't help herself looking at it.

—You'd like some, wouldn't you. He held the bottle forward but not within her reach. How badly do you want it?

Her spirits fell. Anyone but this one she thought. She'd noticed him looking at her a number of times. It wasn't like she wasn't used to being ogled, working in her underwear. But this was a bit different, she thought. Furtive glances, not wanting to get caught. A bit creepy. But still, nothing too serious, nothing more than that. But she suddenly realised that she was vulnerable. There was no-one close by.

—We could come to an arrangement.

—No, that's okay. I'm okay. It came as a croak.

—No, come on, you must be thirsty. Aren't you?

—Yes, I'm thirsty.

—Well maybe if I let you suck on my bottle…

She looked into his eyes the first time.

—You're kidding right? You disgusting animal.

He hadn't needed more than that. He lunged forward clamping her mouth with his hand. She hadn't expected it. Expected a mouthful of filthy language, maybe a smack across the face, but not this. She could taste the salt on the skin of his hot hand. She tried to scream, tried to bite. He was a big man, fat. He pushed her down, backwards, against the bench seat. She was so horrified that it had gone this way so quickly that she found it hard to respond. But then something snapped in her. She wriggled, kicked, freed an arm, went for his eyes, raking nails across his cheek. She was struggling for breath, getting snatches of air when his hand moved slightly away from her nostrils, the air sucking in violently.

He squashed himself on top her to stop being kicked and pushed her legs out straight beneath him. He was so heavy, so strong. It was the smell of his body odour that she would remember afterwards. He stopped briefly but kept his hand across her mouth. He turned to look sideways. Izzy followed his gaze. Tattoo stood in the aisle between the seats. Her face held no expression. The man on top

131

of her remained still, as if waiting for a response from Tattoo. Her expression didn't change, and then she turned and walked away.

He hit the highway just as the dawn broke, several hours after his former travelling companion. He looked into the east, the sun lighting up the long, straight road rising and falling over the swales of the land like lazy swells on a calm sea.

He hadn't been surprised by his arrival like his ex-companion. He'd seen the semi-trailer parked on the road from a distance in the growing light. A road-train, not a semi he thought, two trailers. It sat half-on, half-off the road, the driver given no opportunity to find a more suitable stopping place and too cautious to take the huge rig any further from the bitumen. The bonnet was open.

He found the driver beneath beneath his rig on a foam mattress. It looked more like birds that had been at him, rather than dingoes. His eyes were gone and small pieces of flesh were missing from his face but he was otherwise largely intact. His sunglasses sat on the ground beside him. The man kicked the water jug sitting on the ground. It sloshed. He was surprised. He picked it up and opened it, peering inside. He could smell something industrial, couldn't see through it. He tipped it out and dropped the container on the ground. He looked again at the man and could see the stain on his shirt front where he'd vomited.

The man hauled himself up into the cab and looked around, checking the sleeping area behind the seats and inside the little fridge. He saw several radios and a mobile phone. The mobile was dead. He tried the ignition key. No lights came on, no power. He checked the doors on the trailers, both were locked with huge shielded padlocks. He went back to the cab and checked the ignition key ring. Nothing resembling a padlock key. He had a brief look around the cab. The driver would've opened it up if he had a key or if there'd been anything useful in there.

He climbed down and stood in the middle of the highway in the centre of a long white line. He looked into the east, the sun rising just above the horizon, slightly to his left. He turned one hundred and eighty degrees, an almost military grade turn and stared to the west.

—Well, here I am, he said out loud. Now what. He laughed, thinking about what he'd done, what he'd seen and for what. To die here. Might as well have stayed where the bastard abandoned me, would've saved myself a long walk and not have that girl in my head.

He thought about his options. He was tired but the water supply and the food from the plane had given him a new strength. He knew he could go further, but to what, to where? The train driver had told them that there was nothing on the highway in either direction, not for a long way. Probably about the same distance as the others had to walk to the siding, a couple of days. Have I got enough water?

Or do I wait here, wait for someone to come? Didn't do this guy much good he thought, turning to look at the truck driver. Might as well die doing something as sitting on my arse. West, go west young man, he said to a couple of crows hopping in the roadway.

—Keeping you from a feed am I? And with that he hefted his pack and started walking on the smooth surface, the sun warming his back.

The man woke in the table drain, a fly up the nostril the cause. He sat up, brushing furiously at his nose. He'd had a long sleep, the most he'd managed in three or four days. He had a swig of water, frowning at the half bottle he had left. He stood, unzipped his fly and pissed into the dry grass, then hefted his pack and headed west.

He'd been walking for some hours when he saw the caravan in the distance. In the shimmering heatwaves he could make out its outline on the top of a swale in the road. When he was closer he could see that it was two caravans and cars, one parked behind the other. He could make out people sitting in their lawn chairs under an awning on the southern side. They'd not seen him until he stepped into the gravel on the roadside, the crunching beneath his boot causing the woman's head to dart around and stare at him open-mouthed.

—Oh my, look. She dragged on the man's arm. There were three of them there, they all jumped to their feet to watch the man walk the final few metres.

He collapsed into an empty fourth chair. Morning, he said with a smile, got any water?

They plied him with water, as much as he could drink and then offered him food, apologising for the meagre fare. He told them where he'd come from and how long he'd been walking.

The old man explained that like the train their cars had simply stopped. They'd been travelling in convoy, the trip of a lifetime. Been planning it for years. And then the cars had simply stopped working. Nothing they could do. The man had explained that he was a bit of a dab hand with an engine, or things electrical. But over days he'd gradually realised that nothing was going to work. And worse, that no-one was coming.

They'd sat and waited, one of the women said. They had plenty of water, topped up the tanks a ways back and plenty of food. But when more than a week passed her husband had decided to go for help. She explained that he was quite fit for his age and was sick of sitting about. Wished he'd brought his bike with him. But then off he went, into the west. That was four days ago. They'd not heard anything since. She was very worried about him. They told the man that he was welcome to stay, to share what they had. Or they could give him some water and a bit of food if he wanted to go on.

134

He thanked them for their kindness and said he would see how he felt after a rest.

The man had sat out the worst of the heat in the stingy shade of some road-side scrub. He hadn't slept much, just a few snatches. The sun, the flies and the image of the little girl making it impossible, and so he walked earlier than he might have. Like his former companion he saw the caravans from some distance.

14

The two men waited out the day's heat in the relative comfort of a culvert. They thought they might have reached the train before the morning. But the breaks during the later part of the night had become more and more frequent. Both of them were feeling the workload, and said as much. The skin on the man's hands had broken. He wished he'd looked for some gloves at the siding. There would have been a pair there somewhere. But as it was the skin had opened and he found himself trying to alter his grip on the smooth steel of the pump bar to ease the pain. Nothing helped. The twin glanced over from time to time. He could see that the man was in pain and felt bad that he could do nothing for him.

During one of their breaks the twin tipped antiseptic—from the kit that the Matron had given them—onto the man's hands. The skin was broken and rucked-up in places, white striations. Neither man said anything about it. There was no point, they both realised it was what it was. And while the antiseptic would help with avoiding infection it didn't assist with the pain of holding the bar. The man wrapped his hands in his spare shirt. It helped. But they had lost some of their speed, and as the sun rose the man looked at the fatigue on the face of his companion, and figuring that he would have looked worse, called an end to their effort.

The culvert was sublime. Cool and clean. The box-shaped ends framed the view across the plain. The bottom was covered in a loose sandy loam. It was easy enough to dig through the crusty surface to create a hole for his hip. And using his backpack for a pillow the man curled into the foetal position and was quickly asleep. His companion not far behind.

The Captain walked the length of the train in the middle of the afternoon. People were spread along the side of the rail-bed and beneath the carriages. Nothing and no-one moved. He could feel death around him. A couple tried to speak to him but he ignored them and kept moving.

He found Tattoo with her group at the rear. She was laying back on a mattress but not asleep. He stopped at the edge of the group. She spoke to the soldier. He and another of the men rose, walking menacingly towards the Captain.

—What?

—I'd like to speak with her.

The soldier looked back. Tattoo watched but didn't move or change her expression. The soldier turned back. Go, or you're going to get hurt.

—You're killing everyone.

—Well, we're all going to die. Just some sooner than later, he added with a sneer.

—Can't you let our friend go. There's no point keeping her here. Let her come and die with us.

The soldier turned back to look at Tattoo. She pursed her lips.

—Sure, tell the little bitch she can go.

The Captain turned and walked quickly up into the carriage before Tattoo had a change of heart. The soldier followed and told the guard to let Izzy leave. Izzy looked up when she heard the voices. The Captain beckoned, his urgency apparent. And then he saw the look on her face. He turned to the guard.

—You bastard, what did you do?

—Wasn't me man, the guy before me.

The Captain moved forward and draped a protective arm around the small woman. He had to half-lift her to her feet.

— C'mon, lets get you back to the Matron. Izzy said nothing. They walked through the train carriages the whole way. The doors between the dining cars were now open. The Captain knew why. All the food and water was at the rear of the train, he'd seen it. They passed several of the older passengers lying on mattresses. The atmosphere felt different to the Captain. It looked no different to previous days, bodies lying all over on fetid mattresses, but he could feel the loss of hope, sense approaching death. And now this, he thought, glancing down at Izzy who crabbed along beside him.

The Matron didn't need to be told when she saw Izzy. She could see the look in her eyes, on her face, the carriage of her shoulders. She'd seen it before. She came forward quickly to take her from the Captain. Please bring your water, she said to the Dutch woman. Together the three of them went to the Matron's cabin.

The dingo stood on the tracks, the train in the distance, his nose raised above him. The odour was stronger but the same as the one he smelt from beneath the mounds. It was death. It would ensure he didn't wander too far in the night, drawing him. But for now he crept down the side of the rail-bed and into the relative cool of the culvert, curling himself into his hole in the sandy loam, surrounded by the bones of many kills.

It was the blow from the aluminium walking stick across the bridge of his nose that woke the miner. He'd been dozing in the camp chair. The couple were inside the van and the other woman had returned to her van.

The man fell over backwards in his chair and wasn't quick enough to ward of the second blow that struck him across the mouth, his face now a bloody mess. His nose pumped and his lips were split where they had been forced against his teeth. His screamed after the second blow, blinking, realising who it was standing over him. He was lucky that the stick wasn't solid wood or he might have been in worse shape. The man above stood with the weapon poised over his head for a third blow. The man on the ground covered his face with an arm.

—Please, no. No more.

The blow came, striking the man across the forearm. The man screamed and tried to roll but was trapped by the sides of his upended chair. He begged again. The couple came out of the van. The woman screaming for him to stop.

He turned to look at the old couple. He left me for dead. He turned back, aiming another blow. Paused it. He waited until I was asleep, and then snuck away with all the water and food. Left me to die in the desert.

—I'm sorry. The words were smothered in the blood of his broken lips.

The man had raised the stick again.

—Please, no more. It was the old man. He'd stepped forward and held out a hand between the man on the ground and the poised walking stick. Enough now, it won't help.

The miner shook with rage. He hadn't felt it until he'd seen him, sitting there, comfortable in his chair, a bottle of water at his side. And then it had boiled up inside him. He didn't see himself as an angry person, and he was certainly no fighter. But it made him realise something about himself, that when the time came he was capable of almost anything.

But a look at the old man's face, remarkably rational and calm, given the circumstances, and the abject fear on the face of his wife, it was enough to snap him out of his rage. He stood, breathing hard. He lowered the stick but didn't drop it. Even with the shift in emotions inside him, he knew he'd have to watch this bastard.

—Come, please, sit. Have some water and something to eat..

The old man had reached out a hand to help the man off the ground. The man winced from the pain in his injured arm as he tried to use it to stabilise himself to rise. But he didn't dare show any anger or say anything. That would come, he thought.

The old man led the injured miner to the awning of the other van, thinking it prudent to separate the two men. He sat the man down on the step and handed him a wet cloth and some antiseptic which he dabbed gingerly against the broken skin of his lips and nose.

The other miner hooked the handle of the walking stick over the arm of his chair and collapsed gratefully into it. It was like a hug. So comfortable, he thought. Didn't realise how tired he really was. He drank the proffered water and ate the food that the woman brought to him.

The three caravaners sat and listened as he told his story. Feeling, now that he'd calmed, that he needed to justify his violent reaction. He apologised for scaring them, feeling a little embarrassed.

140

—But don't trust him, were his final words on the matter. He looked across to where the other man sat, holding a hand on the growing welt on his forearm and staring back.

—He raped her. It was delivered without emotion. She sat down with the Captain and the Dutchman. I've left your wife with her. Said she'd done some counselling in your country.

The Dutchman nodded. Yes, she's very good.

The Captain stood. He yelled, swore and kicked at the ground. Fuck, fuck, fuck. And then he sat again. Sorry.

Before anyone had a chance to say anything a voice called for the Matron. She raised herself. The Captain watched. It was the first time that he thought she looked tired. Tired and worn. No water, no food.

The Matron came back shortly after.

—Another one gone. And the other two are beginning to smell. At the least we need to drag them away from the train. It's not healthy.

The Captain looked at the Dutchman, who nodded. They rose and followed the Matron along the rail-bed. They dragged the three corpses out into the bush near the site of the graves. The third one almost did for them both. The Dutchman offered the Captain a last mouthful of water before his bottle was empty. They walked back to the train. The Captain steadied himself with a hand on the Dutchman's shoulder. He was just shy of passing out. The Dutchman sat him in the shade and collapsed beside him.

It was the man who woke first in the late afternoon. His fingers had formed claws and he could feel the skin crackling as he straightened them, the pain making him wince. My kingdom for some gardening gloves, he thought. His movement enough to wake his companion.

141

—Sorry.

Younger smiled. Time to rise I suspect.

He helped the man bathe his hands and rub on some more of the antiseptic cream. The man thought the wounds were still clear of infection but he knew he would be susceptible in the days to come in this climate and with those flies around. But what worried him more at this stage was how he was going to hang on to that bloody handle.

They waited until the sun was low before starting out. The twin's shove barely got them moving and both groaned with the first push on the bar. They both laughed. The speed built slightly but never came close to matching what they'd managed when they'd left the siding. But it would be enough to get them there sometime in the night thought Ticky.

The miner listened as the woman explained that her husband had gone off along the road towards the west some days previous. The miner decided that he would follow in the evening. When it cooled, and if they could spare a little water and food.

—And what about… the old man nodded towards the second caravan.

—I don't know what to say about him, to be honest. I don't want him with me. But I don't want him here with you. I'm not sure what to tell you. Maybe send him off much later tonight. Give me some hours head-start. Can you spare the water?

The man explained that they were being careful and that with only three of them they still had enough for a week or more. They agreed on the strategy. It was already late in the afternoon. The man filled his bottles and took some of the offered food, promising that he would look out for the woman's husband along the road.

He didn't even spare a glance for the other man as he walked off up the road into the softening light. He felt healthy but he was tired.

He hadn't walked far when he started thinking about that bastard heading off after him. He realised that he'd now be looking over his shoulder the whole time, scared to sleep. He made a decision. He waited until he topped the next swale in the road, moving into the salt-bush, waiting. It was barely an hour before he heard the man's tread.

He stepped out of the scrub hefting the branch he'd found for the purpose. He still had the walking stick but knew that the light metal would make it much harder to do what he wanted. The bastard heard him at the last second, turning to face him before the knotty, tight grain of the mulga branch caught him across the forearm he raised in defence. The same forearm he'd struck with the walking stick. The snapping bone was clear to both men, one screaming. It softened the blow but it still caught the man across the top of his head,enough to drop him to his knees. He looked up at his attacker, blood streaming from the cut, flowing down across the swollen nose and masticated lips.

He didn't have time to plead before the next blow caved his skull and he collapsed forward, limp and lifeless. The man didn't bother to check a pulse, the collapsed skull enough to convince him that the other wasn't getting up again. He dragged the body deep into the roadside scrub and then sorted the contents of both packs into one and then set out on his way.

He figured that the guilt would come. But for now it was a kind of elation. Freedom. That he could continue on his mission unmolested and confident. He had water and food. It was good.

He walked for another hour or so before stepping off the road and rolling out the blanket that the woman had given him, falling into a deep sleep in the security of the salt-bush.

15

When Ticky saw the front of the train it was after midnight. Had he the energy he might've burst into tears, such was the relief he felt. The effort had been immense for both of them. Their speed had dropped almost to a walking pace for the final hours. They'd encouraged each other with an occasional word but then, towards the end, couldn't even muster the strength for that.

The man had seriously considered the idea that the train had moved, that they must be way beyond where it had been stalled and that they were simply heading further and further into the desert.

But then it had appeared, the huge diesel electric engine there in front of him, watching them, imperiously.

—Mate, it's there. They were within fifty metres of it and stopped immediately, both releasing that bloody handle. Ticky's hands had bled into the shirt he held around them. The twin had resorted to using one as well.

Such was the slowness of their approach the man doubted that anyone would have heard them. They both climbed down from the little cart and then sat on the platform, resting and straightening their spines from the bent-over positions they were forced to adopt to crank the handle.

—What should we do? It was the twin who spoke first.

—Let's go find the Matron and the Captain, no need to wake everyone just yet.

They climbed down from the rail-bed and walked past the engine along the service road. They both smelled death at the same time, the odour hanging in the air.

—That can't be good.

—No.

It felt good to walk. They climbed the rail-bed, legs protesting, and then stepped up and into the first carriage. They could hear the noises of the night inside the train, the sounds of deep breathing, a couple of snorers, moaning. The smell shocked them both.

The man tapped lightly on the wall of the Matron's compartment. She snuffled but didn't wake so he tapped again. He watched her in the dim light, sit up, rubbing her eyes and struggle to see who might be waking her.

—It's me.

It took her a second and then she gasped. She stepped out of her bunk and moved forward, catching the man in an embrace. He squeezed her in return.

—Let's get outside, where we can talk, don't wake anyone. It sounded like a warning to Ticky.

The twin had found the Captain and had woken him. The Captain led them to the front of the train where they stood between the rails, looking up at the hooded brow of the engine.

The Captain and the Matron told them what had been happening in their absence. Explained what it was they were smelling. The Matron saved Izzy's rape until the end.

Even the twin swore, the first time Ticky had heard a bad word out of either of them. They sat and talked. As bone-tired as he was Ticky realised the importance of making decisions right now, while they still had an edge. They agreed on a plan and walked back, quietly, along the service road, taking more care than before not to wake anyone else on the train. They needed to get to the gun. The gun would be the difference, they'd all agreed on that.

The driver woke his Dutch friend and his wife, who had since moved to the front of train. The manager had snorted and sat up abruptly when the driver had tapped his shoulder. He warned them to remain quiet and to follow. They climbed down the rail-bed and along the service road and back to where the two men sat with the Matron on the hand-car.

The man held the shotgun, the stock standing on his thigh, the barrel pointing into the air. The Matron had wanted to attend to his hands but he told her that it could wait. They needed to get things done.

The story was quickly shared. The only sound for some minutes was the swallowing of water. And then sighs of contentment and a couple of giggles.

They set about moving the water into the train. They'd agreed that the dining car was the best place.

It was a pair of quail thrush which woke the miner. The high-pitched piping, a peet-peet sound, carried through the saltbush to where he lay wrapped in the blanket against the relative cool of the dawn. He couldn't see the birds but they were not far away. When he rose, the early morning concert stopped and they took flight. He watched them quickly disappear. Had he known better he would've realised that he'd been treated to a rare experience.

He unzipped and pissed into the chalky loam. He was pleased to be able to piss, that his system carried enough fluid to be able to do that. He hadn't taken a crap in a couple of days but he wasn't surprised. He ate a small amount of his food and then packed and set out on the road.

The low morning sun cast him a long shadow off the roadside as it climbed from the north-east. He walked steadily for several hours before he saw the truck in the distance. Another road train.

He found the old man in the saltbush. If not for the smell he might have passed him by. It was clear that he hadn't died of thirst, the stoved-in skull, a not dissimilar wound to the one he'd so recently inflicted. And if that wasn't conclusive enough, he found the bloodied wheel-brace a bit further out, several hairs pasted to it's knobby end. He figured it was the woman's husband, confirmed it by the wallet he carried in his back pocket.

The miner moved on. He wondered that the smell didn't seem to worry him and figured that his experience at the plane would save him from that forever more. He had a quick look through the cab of the truck but found nothing of use. The containers it carried were locked up tight and he didn't bother searching for keys, figuring—like the previous truck—the driver would've opened them if they offered anything valuable.

He walked on thinking about what had most likely transpired. That the old man had arrived, no doubt feeling happy that he'd encountered someone, that he'd made it to somewhere other than where he'd been, that maybe it gave the old man a sense that he was achieving something. His wife had said he was a man of action. He wondered how long after he'd arrived that the truck driver had bashed in his skull. How had he done it? He could imagine that the old man would've offered the man a drink. Willing and happy to share what he had. The driver would've accepted it gratefully, was probably already long out of water. Would have been desperate. He would have taken the drink and then thought about what lay ahead for him. Maybe the old man had invited him to walk with him. To share his supplies. Selfless. Willing to risk death to help the other. But that wouldn't have been enough for the driver. No, he'd decided that one of them stood a far better chance than two. The miner hoped the old man hadn't seen what was coming. That the driver had been able to catch him by surprise before the old man had any idea. That's what bothered the miner the most. That the old man, just for a moment, might have known what was about to happen. That he would've stared at the truck driver with a look that said he didn't understand. The miner hoped it wasn't the case. One blow and then death. He chose to believe this was the way it happened.

As he headed off up the road, walking the centre line—the tap-tap of his walking stick the only sound—it didn't occur to him to think about the experience of the man he'd killed.

The Captain sat guard in the dining car for the remainder of the night. They'd shifted the water in, waking many of the older passengers who slept there on the mattresses dragged out from their cabins. Some water had been dispensed. It was an exciting time. Now there was hope. It hadn't been there when they went to sleep, the hope. The smell wafting through the empty window holes had been a blunt reminder of what probably awaited them the next day. But now there was some hope.

The Captain double-checked the lock on the door between the two dining cars. There was no way in that way. They'd also locked the exit doors from the carriage. There was no way in without the door being opened from the inside. They could unlock the doors leading to the carriages of the older passengers but for now they would remain locked.

The Matron had seen to Ticky's hands, bathing, cleaning and patching them as best she could. He'd then joined the twin on one of the mattresses and fallen into a deep sleep. The Dutchman had stayed with the Captain and they had discussed options.

What was clear was that they would need the remainder of the water from the goods train, one more load. But they were only buying time. With all the water they might have another week to ten days at best. And now the food was almost gone. That had been the deal, to make the water last as long as the food. There was plenty of water at the siding. Enough to keep them all alive for weeks or months. Maybe they could hunt food. They had the gun and there were kangaroos about, the man had seen them. But how would they get there. They could run a shuttle with the hand-car but it would carry ten or so people at best. The healthier could walk perhaps. It was a logistical nightmare the Captain said to his friend.

—And who gets to share the water? asked the Dutchman. This is the question that no-one has yet asked. Do we share our good fortune with those who would have seen us die?

The Captain nodded. It's the question of our times. Isn't it. He thought about whether he'd be able to pull the trigger if they came for the water. The last thing that Ticky had said before he'd gone off to sleep was that he must. That the gun was the only thing that stood between them and death.

The Captain had nodded his agreement. He thought he could do it. He thought about Izzy, lying there after what had been done to her. This is what the Captain used to sharpen his anger. What he would draw on if he needed to pull the trigger.

The dingo finally had his food source from the train. He'd watched the corpses being dragged through the saltbush, could smell them long before they were moved. He recognised the same smell that had come from beneath the mounds. He was confused at first. He'd never attacked a carcass of this shape before. He chewed briefly on the face and nose. There wasn't much to be gained there, but the clothing flummoxed him. It took some minutes before he worked his way between the shirt buttons and into the soft flesh of the stomach. And then he made progress, stripping away the pale skin and working his way into the stomach cavity. He feasted for several hours. Going away and then coming back to feast again. Finally he moved back to his culvert to sleep, his stomach swinging from side to side. He looked out into the night. The smell would likely invite others.

There was much excitement the next morning. The Matron and the manager had gone between the carriages explaining that they had water, that their saviours had come through for them, but to try and keep the excitement down to where it wouldn't be noticed. Where the group at the rear of the train didn't have any idea about what was going on.

The man wondered how long they could keep up the charade. The twin had taken the hand-car back down the track on his own, out of sight of train. The man had suggested keeping the hand-car's existence a secret. It was their only way out.

The manager quickly organised a distribution system for the water. Despite the fact that another woman had died in the night the atmosphere was festive as they lined up once again. Ticky and the twin were treated as heroes, as they sat close by to monitor proceedings. Many asked how the water had come but the man provided little in the way of information, simply asking people to trust them and be patient. He realised he was probably sowing false hope, they were a long way from saved, but he figured false hope had to be better than giving up.

It didn't take long for Tattoo to hear about the water. A much shorter time than Ticky and his friends would have liked. An old man had waved to one of Tattoo's lieutenants through the window, smiling and brandishing the full bottle of water, before delivering him a two finger salute.

She'd stormed through the train with her supporters in her wake, only to find the doors locked between the dining cars. She stepped down into the rail-bed, walking along the train past the dining cars to find her access barred at all points.

She was feeling foolish as she turned back to the dining car. She stepped down from the rail-bed to better see through the empty hole of the dining car window. The blinds were drawn on the north side of train so she couldn't see anything in the darkened maw.

—Who's in there? Someone speak to me, or there's going to be trouble.

They were all there and heard her spiel. The man, the twin, the Captain, the Matron, Izzy, the Dutchman and his wife, and the manager. They knew this was coming. Had talked about it in the early hours of the morning. But had hoped that it might have taken a little longer.

The discussion had centred around whether or not they would share the good fortune. Ticky, as was his want, had set out the options as he saw them.

—We share it, no problems. We share it and then they take it. We don't share it and they aren't aware. We don't share it and they are aware and attack us. Thoughts?

The conversation had gone round and round with no clear result. The Matron thought they should share, not because they deserved a portion but that it would not be right to deny it to them. That it would make them no better than their adversaries if they didn't. And then there was the issue of collecting the remainder of the water and some people potentially carrying on to the siding and beyond. But that would mean abandoning others, the older people, those who had no ability to walk any distance. It was a discussion that troubled many of them. They were still talking when Tattoo's voice broke through.

They looked at each, most eyes resting on Ticky and the Captain. The Captain stepped towards the glassless window and looked out at the group centred around Tattoo. He said nothing.

—You've got water.

—Really.

—You need to share it.

The Captain didn't see any point denying the water's existence.

—Like you shared?

—How about we come and take it, all of it.

The Captain reached into the gloom and turned back, the long black barrel of the shotgun protruding from the window. He thought about this moment. He pointed the gun at the woman and then raised it up high, not wanting any of the pellets to inadvertently find a target, and squeezed the trigger. The noise was brutal in the desert quiet. Many of the group ducked, including Tattoo. No-one spoke for a moment. The smell of burned gunpowder wafted around the group and inside the carriage.

The Captain looked down at Tattoo. We're still discussing whether we'll share. We'll come back to you. Now off you go. It wasn't delivered with sarcasm. A matter-of-fact tone. Tattoo looked as if she might speak but then turned and walked along the rail-bed, her group in her wake, heads bowed, like protesters who'd been given short shrift at a rally.

It was agreed that they would provide some of the water to the others. The amount was also agreed and the bottles carried down from the train and left in the rail bed in front of the second dining car. It was further agreed that a pair would head back to the goods train to retrieve the remainder of the water. It was the twin who suggested that they could take a number of people with them on the outward journey, who could continue on to the siding on foot.

It was a good plan, thought Ticky. But who would go, who could go? First and foremost it has to be people who can make the journey. It'll be many hours through the night. When he spoke the eyes of the others were drawn to the pristine white of the bandages on his hands. They were a beacon in the dark and fetid atmosphere of the dining car.

—And do we offer to take any of them? It was the Dutch woman, nodding towards the other end of the train.

—No, said Ticky. We can't afford to create any issues at the siding. They cannot be trusted. We'd end up in the same situation there. The group must come from among us. And they should go as soon as possible. Tattoo and her mob will be wondering where the water came from, how it got here. They'll be watching. We should have a diversion.

They talked about who should go, who could go. In the end it was agreed that the Captain, Izzy, the Dutch couple and several of the manager's crew, those that were not at the other end of the train, would leave and not return. The twin and the manager would return with the water and then they could carry some of the older people the full distance to the siding.

—We can look at how many of these trips we can do at a later stage, said Ticky.

It was further agreed that they would leave as soon as it was dark enough and when the Captain provided a diversion.

It was the first time that day that he'd left the train. The only people who'd gone out were a couple of the manager's staff who'd had to empty the fetid ablution buckets. They were tipped onto the thirsty earth where the flies were waiting. Hygiene worried the Matron. She thought about cholera and how it could decimate a population with little water. She hoped it wouldn't come to pass.

The Captain stepped down into the service road, the shotgun at port arms.

The sun was gone for the day but the twilight still provided good vision. He thought about the people leaving as he walked. It was Izzy foremost in his thoughts. She was a shell of her former self. It made him angry, maybe angry enough to shoot someone. Especially the prick who had done it. She'd barely spoken a word since it had happened. Since she was raped. The Matron and the Dutch woman had talked to her each day, watched over her. He was thankful to them, for them. It scared him to think about where Izzy would be without them. Without their support. He himself had no clue what to say or do. The best he could offer was a hug, and he wasn't sure that she wanted that from him, from a man. But she'd seemed to welcome it as he'd said his goodbye and wished the group well.

His was the job of diversion. As long as they remained inside the train then he needn't worry, the group could slip away undetected. But if they were out near the dining car then there was a chance that they might see something. But he needn't have worried. He walked the entire length of the train and it wasn't until he reached the rear that he saw the group on the tracks. It seemed to be all or at least most of them. He thought it looked like a meeting of sorts.

Several people on the perimeter of the group turned to see him.

—What do you want? Tattoo stepped forward, the group parted before her.

—Just checking that you received your water and to let you know that we've given you half of what we had. And that there may be some more coming.

—Just like in the beginning, we don't trust you fuckers. I was right all along, wasn't I? You were keeping things from us. And now you're doing it again. Water suddenly appearing and now this gun. You're trying to control us, to kill us.

The Captain could see that she was building the mood in her group. It happened so quickly, the Captain pulled the trigger before he'd even had a chance to think about it. One of the miners had darted from the edge of the scrum of people. The Captain saw him from the corner of his eye, heard his footfall in the dirt. He swung the long barrel and the gun boomed. The shot took the man in the side, his momentum was halted as he half-pirouetted, his feet swinging out from under him and collapsing onto the hard pan of the road.

The Captain moved backwards, the gun pointing at the group. They stayed frozen in place.

—That was stupid. It came out haltingly. The Captain's pulse raced. I only came to talk. It sounded like an apology. Why did he do that? It was stupid.

The man on the ground moaned.

—I'll get the Matron, but the rest of you will have to move away from him, get back inside the train or we won't come. Just one of you stay with him.

The Captain turned and jogged back along the train, arriving panting and calling for the Matron to grab her medical supplies.

—I heard the shot.

—I had to shoot, he charged at me. I couldn't give up the gun, that would have been the end of things. The Matron could feel that it was more of a justification to himself than an explanation for her.

When they arrived at the rear of the train Tattoo and the soldier stood above the man who had been shot.

—We think he's dead, can you confirm it? It was the soldier who spoke.

—Let's go said the Captain.

—Let me just confirm it. The Matron stepped forward, squatted and checked for signs of life. The soldier read the situation well. He edged sideways slightly, the Matron between him and the Captain, and then lunged forward grabbing the Matron by the arm, reefing her to her feet, spinning her around, grabbing her in a choke hold. The Captain could see the shiny steel of the knife blade pressed into the soft skin of the Matron's throat.

—Drop the gun, said Tattoo. It was obvious to the Captain from Tattoo's tone that she wasn't surprised by what had transpired.

The Captain swivelled the barrel towards Tattoo and then back towards the Matron and the soldier. He was annoyed with himself that he felt uncertain, unsure of what to do. So he made a decision.

—Drop it or she dies. The words were as cold and emotionless as he could make them. He pulled the gun butt into his shoulder and pumped a cartridge into the breach. He was glad he hadn't reloaded earlier, he hoped the sound of the action would give more impetus to his demand.

He swivelled back towards Tattoo, the black eye of the barrel aimed at her face and made a decision, dropping his aim to Tattoo's legs. I'm going to count to three. If you haven't released her by then, then she loses a leg. I can't kill you, but I have no qualms about maiming you. He kept the barrel pointing at Tattoo but turned his head to the solider. And if she's at all harmed, then that will probably push me to do something more serious to you.

—One. No-one spoke. The Captain could hear his own breathing, could feel his heart pounding, nothing else. He looked as menacing as he could into the young woman's eyes. He thought he could see some doubt there. Two. He nestled his cheek against the stock, more for the effect he hoped it might have on the woman. He pulled the stock more firmly into his shoulder, adjusting the pointing elbow for the same reason. He didn't want to do it but knew he had to. If he gave over the gun they were as good as dead. He took up the slack on the trigger. He could feel his finger at the crucial pressure point. An ounce more he thought.

—Let the bitch go. Tattoo turned to the soldier, who hadn't moved, still held on to the Matron. I said let her go. The soldier held on a moment longer and then pulled the knife away and gave the Matron a shove forward. She stumbled but kept her feet. The Captain stepped sideways, exhaling the breath he'd been holding, to take the Matron out of the firing line. He shifted his aim back to Tattoo. Maybe I should shoot them both. Would it stop our problems? Maybe. But he knew he couldn't do it. Not this way.

He stepped backwards taking one hand off the gun, waving the Matron behind him. He walked backwards for several more steps before turning away and walking off into the night holding the Matron's hand.

16

He rested through the worst of the heat under a clump of mulga trees. He rolled onto his stomach, his arms around his head to keep the flies away from his face. Sleep had come easily. He woke in the late afternoon, an hour, maybe two of light left in the day. He climbed to his feet and kept walking. He felt comfortable. He realised that with rest and a steady supply of water and food he was actually building into the effort. He'd lost weight, quite a bit. But he felt strong and ready.

He saw the buildings in the distance just as the twilight was fading into darkness. There were no lights just the straight incongruous lines set against the pink sky. As he closed he could make out several caravans parked in a desolate gravel camping area, still hooked to the vehicles that towed them. He thought they would have been ready for an early departure, the stop, just an overnighter. Nothing to see or do in this wind-swept place. Maybe a shower and a beer. And then bed and an early start.

He headed towards the buildings, walking past the first of the fuel pumps, the diesel pumps not covered by the forecourt roof, the ones used by the big rigs. He was almost at the inner line of pumps under the roofline when the voice rang out.

—STOP. The voice startled him. A man's voice, angry.

He'd done as bid more out of shock at the sound than any obedience he might have felt.

—Hello? He couldn't see anyone. The shopfront was dark, he couldn't even tell if the door was open.

—Keep going. You're not welcome here. I have a gun. It was made in three statements, like they were being read from a list of talking points.

—I don't understand. It was the best the man could do. He didn't understand. He didn't want anything, just wanted to engage, explain where he'd come from, and maybe find out what was going on.

—I said keep going, I won't tell you again. It was quiet for a moment, interrupted by a metallic noise that the man recognised as the bolt of a rifle being worked.

The man stepped back slowly, managing to get one of the fuel pumps between him and where he thought the voice was coming from. He kept moving backwards to the highway to where he knew he could no longer be seen in the moonless night. He sat down on the centre line. He had to think.

He didn't stay there long. He climbed to his feet with the aid of the walking stick and headed back the way he'd come, then turned and cut across through the bush to the edge of the camping area.

He squatted in the low scrub to watch for a while. The only thing that separated it from just being a flat cleared area in the scrub were the handful of short power poles where caravaners could connect to a power supply. There were three rigs in the park, all double axle and pulled by late model SUVs. They were clones of each other. He wondered had they been travelling together.

He waited fifteen minutes. He heard no sound other than the light breeze ruffling the bushes around him. It was eery. He wondered about the voice, thinking whoever it was would be wondering about him. He figured it was worth the risk to approach the caravans. He still had some water and food but he'd need more.

He left his pack but carried his walking stick, stepping out of the scrub, keeping two of the vans between him and building. He frowned at the noise the gravel made beneath his boots. He walked as lightly as he could but the sound seemed loud in his ears.

The doors of the vans were all facing away from him. He figured it gave them morning shade on the door-side. But it meant he had to cross around to the other side. He took the shorter more concealed route across the drawbar between the van and the tow vehicle. He straddled the bar and then stopped to listen again. He waited for a moment and stepped around the front of the van, another rig between him and the building.

The door was open. He changed grip several times on the walking stick, wondering which would be most effective. He glanced into the darkened doorway. Couldn't see anything. He sniffed at the air, looking for that tell-tale odour.

The van dipped slightly beneath his weight, the suspension creaking. He walked to the back into the bedroom area. He felt across the bed. It was neatly made. He could feel the cool of the cotton sheet folded back over the single woollen blanket. He opened the door to the tiny bathroom-toilet cubicle. Likewise it was clean and orderly.

He worked the hand-pump over the sink and held his breath. Four or five pumps brought a stream of water. He opened the cupboard at his head and found a plastic mug and drank as much water as his system could take. Shit, he'd forgotten to bring his water bottles. He pulled open the second drawer, the one beneath the cutlery. And

161

there it was, a torch. He flicked the switch and a beam pierced the darkness. He aimed the beam at the floor, giving himself just enough light to look around. He rifled the cupboards and found two large plastic containers with screw-top lids filling them and placing them on the table. He sat for a moment at the dining table trying to think about what he needed.

He found a shopping bag and filled it with all the canned goods he could find. He also found a can opener. He thought he was being greedy, that he'd need carry it all. He wished he had some sort of cart to put it all in.

He searched the second van and found it held two bikes on a rear carrier. He took the largest of the pair, feeling the air pressure in the tyres. He stepped aboard and rode it back across the gravel to where he'd left his back-pack. He took the pack back across to the first van, filled his bottles, loaded the food and gathered the extra water. He groaned under the weight, trudging back across the scrub.

He laughed out loud at his good fortune. He lifted the bike. It gave him a thrill to feel the handgrips beneath his palms. He wheeled it to the road and then raised the seat to a more satisfactory height and climbed aboard. And then he stopped to think.

The idea of sleeping in one of the caravan beds held a lot of appeal. Clean sheets, a soft mattress. But why risk it. He thought about camping close by and then checking out the building in the daylight. Maybe whoever was there would be more reasonable in the light of day. Where were the people from the caravans he wondered. He couldn't smell anything. If they were dead, then they'd been buried. And why would they be dead, they still had water and food. And where was the truck driver, the one who'd murdered the old man from the caravan?

In the end he decided he had enough to keep him going, especially now that he had the bike. He climbed aboard and headed off down the road to put some distance between himself and the gun-toting person in the garage.

He'd not ridden a bike in many years but he'd ridden a lot in his youth. It'd been his main transport source up until he went off to work in the mines. He didn't own a car, even now. He didn't see the point, he was away for half the year working and when he came home, if he wasn't off on a trip somewhere he could use his mother's car, or hire one if he wanted to travel a distance. He thought about his mother, wondered what she was thinking. Knew she'd be worried about him. But then maybe something had happened there, in the city, as well. Maybe she had her own problems. He'd not thought a lot about what had happened. He was too busy surviving. But now with a cool wind in his face, the pedals turning easily, the quiet hum of the tyres on the macadamised surface, he had time to think about it.

He'd started thinking about stopping to sleep when he went down. The night was so dark that he had enough of a problem keeping the bike on the road. He'd seen something at the last second, way too late to react. He came down hard, the air whooshing from his lungs. The bike was on top of him, his back-pack tangled around the seat. He extricated himself and rifled in his pack for the torch. His elbow was sore, he knew there was blood there, hopefully nothing too serious. He flicked on the beam and pointed back at what had brought him down. With the image came the smell. It was a man. He lay face up, sightless eyes staring up at the Southern Cross.

The dingo knew they were coming. Whether he could smell them, or whether he was drawing on some evolutionary intuition, he knew they were coming. He fidgeted. Couldn't sit still. Walked circles. Stopped. Looked. And it came to pass. There were two at first. They came together. They were bitches, smaller than he, a similar colouring, a tawny brown over most of the body with some darker patches at the end of the tail, around the neck and ears. The area around the nose and eyes was almost white, and then those almond eyes. They were from a neighbouring territory. Outside of mating season he sometimes met members from other packs on his territory or where he might cross over into another territory. There was rarely trouble in this type of situation, almost a treaty of sorts.

But this was different. This was the heart of his domain, and they'd come for his food. He ran at them growling, even gave a bark of sorts. It would have been the first noise the people on the train had heard from him. And they would have heard it, he wasn't far away.

His rush forced the two bitches back, but not so far. They circled near each other, gathering confidence and security from each other, all the while sniffing the air, the smell of rotting flesh goading them into another attempt.

This time they split. The dog ran at one. The other nipped in. Was almost there, at a corpse, when he came back for her. He chased her, snapping at her back legs. She ran with her tail clamped. Had the other bitch been smarter she might have come in now. But he'd scared her enough that she didn't. He turned off his chase and moved back to the food source. The two bitches linked up again, circling back, growling at the dog.

It was going to be a long night.

Younger took first shift on the handle along with one of the manager's staff. He could feel the load was about the same as the journey out, maybe a bit lighter. But at least this time they could rotate the work, a couple of hours on and then rest while others did the work. They'd hopefully get to the goods train sometime in the middle of the next morning. They wouldn't need to stop and rest on the way. The pace should remain fairly steady with changing crews. But the journey back would be hard. Doing it on his own again with the manager. The load would be the same as the last time but he was a little doubtful about the manager's ability to sustain the effort.

He wished Ticky could be with him. He was a tough bugger that one, older than the manager, but driven. But the state of his hands meant he wouldn't be grabbing that bloody handle for a while. He thought he'd probably be better off with one of the younger crew but the manager wouldn't hear of it. Wanted to do his bit. The twin gave him some credit for that.

He was facing west, could see everyone. He watched the manager's face, wondered how he'd go. They had a couple of people on the hand-car with them, one on either side, legs dangling. He warned them about keeping their feet away from the wheels. The others sat around the edge of the little wagon. He thought that they might've squeezed a couple more into the centre, maybe back to back, but it'd be uncomfortable. He looked at Izzy, knew what had happened to her. Ticky had told him. He'd wanted to hurt the bastard who'd done it. As if she could feel his thoughts she turned and looked into his eyes, emotionless, and turned back to staring out into the darkness. He wondered whether the mongrel would face justice. But that would depend on getting out of here, out of this. What is this? He'd not spent a lot of time thinking about it, especially now that his brother wasn't there to talk with. It was all about survival now. But what would happen when it wasn't, when they got somewhere safe, with water and food. What would they find? Would it be safe?

He thought about his parents on the farm. Probably the best place

165

to be. Plenty of water and food for a while. If things had gone the same in the towns they'd be better off out on the farm.

He looked at Ticky. He was easy to spot, the white bandages almost glowing in the dark. He felt his frustration. Knew he wanted to help, needed to be doing things. The twin knew Ticky hadn't wanted to leave the train but the Captain had convinced him they needed a leader at the other end, at the siding. They'd hopefully be sending more people that way and he needed to be there to sort out the next step.

Ticky had seen the sense in it, but had not enjoyed it. He'd wanted to be back at the handle of the hand-car with the twin. He was angry at himself for letting his hands get in the state they were in. Should have been smarter than that he'd said to himself. Hated the idea that he wasn't up to it. But he knew that the Captain was right.

The miner played the beam over the dead man on the road. His shirt was crusty with dried blood along one side. He pulled the shirt open and could see the small hole where the bullet had entered. There was a t-shirt, dried into a rust-coloured ball, that the victim had held against the wound.

He shone the beam at the wording sown over the pocket of the man's shirt. The name of a trucking company. He'd paid the price for what he'd done to the old man. Karma coming back quickly. He wondered at whomever was holding the gun at the roadhouse. Would he get his? The miner thought it was like paying it forward but not in a good way. He wondered about the caravaners camping at the roadhouse. Were they in a shallow grave somewhere?

He went through the man's pack. And then thought that it had probably belonged to the old man. He had one of those bottles, the ones with the pop-up drinking nozzles, full of water. It fitted neatly into the bottle cage on the bike. He couldn't fit any more food into his pack so he moved away a short distance and sat in the middle of the road eating as much as he could from the old man's supplies and finishing another half bottle of water that the truck-driver had been drinking, even squirting a little on his bloody elbow.

He had to straighten the handlebar on the bike, which had moved off-centre in the collision. He stood with his legs either side of the front wheel facing rearwards twisting the bars to re-centre them. The effort didn't help his sore elbow, but he didn't think it was a serious injury. Satisfied with his effort he set off into the west, squinting into the dark night ahead for any more surprises.

17

The Captain locked them inside the train. He knew that Tattoo and the soldier wouldn't leave it there, that they'd use the death of the man in their group to justify some sort of attack. He looked around inside the dark of the dining car. The Matron was already asleep. He could hear her gentle breathing near him on the mattress on the floor.

He'd said no to the Matron when she'd offered to take a shift, staying awake to keep an eye on things. He had a couple of the older men organised to take a turn. It didn't fill him with confidence. He quickly realised the ramifications of sending away the man, and his Dutch friend. He'd drawn no small level of comfort from their proximity and missed that now. And the remaining younger people, the ones who could make the walk to the siding were gone as well. It was just him and the Matron and a bunch of sickly old men and women.

The smell was enough to keep him awake. A gentle night breeze brought the odour of death and decay into the train to mix with the smell of stale sweat, piss and shit. He smiled briefly at the thought of this inside the swanky dining car. A place for the wealthy. The sound of fighting dingoes snapped him from the brief reverie. The thought of what they were doing to the corpses made him shiver.

When his head snapped up and his eyes shot open he hadn't realised he'd been asleep. He looked at his watch, it was way beyond the three hours he'd agreed with the old man. Something had woken him. A noise? Or was it just one of the dreams he'd been having? He looked around, not moving, trying to get himself back in his equilibrium.

But then he heard it. Was sure of it. The noise of a foot pressing down into the blue metal of the rail bed. That scrunching sound. He held his breath, not moving, waiting for another sound. He let the breath go as gently as he could but it came out raspy and he quickly had to draw in another. He thought about the gun, needed to chamber a round. He taken out the cartridge he'd threatened Tattoo with, not wanting to leave the gun loaded, not even with the safety on.

He stood and moved quietly towards the window from which he thought the noise had come. He stood in the centre of the dining car aisle, unblinking, his eyes aching from a lack of sleep and the strain of staring into the dark. He heard it and saw it. The softest of padding noises, a hand coming up and over the bottom of the window sill. And if he doubted what he'd heard the appearance of a silhouetted head confirmed it. He pumped the round into the breach. The head paused.

—I wouldn't if I were you, said the Captain, trying to sound menacing.

The head dropped out of sight. Before the Captain could think what to do next he was punched from behind. It had taken him in the kidneys, the air rushing from his lungs with a whoosh. The gun was snatched from his hands, reversed, the stock jabbed into his face. He was out cold before he hit the floor of the dining car.

He woke with one of the passengers, a woman, dabbing a wet compress into the wound on his eyebrow and waving away the flies. He could feel the stickiness of the dried blood on his face. He tried to sit up but the lunge to do it brought a flood of pain to his head and he sat back again, the urge to vomit very strong.

—Please, don't move, you're badly hurt. We thought you'd died.

—Where's the Matron? The words came out in a voice the Captain didn't recognise.

—She's gone, they took her. Said if we came near them they'd kill her. They took all the water.

He managed to sit up on the second attempt. He was surrounded by a sea of old faces glowing in the darkness on the edge of his sight. It was like a bad dream.

—What are we going to do? They're going to let us die.

An old man chimed in. They know about where the water came from, they were going to hurt me, Matron spoke up, told them what had happened. The Captain needed to sit again. He collapsed into one of the banquettes, a hand to his throbbing forehead. He needed to think. He didn't know what to do.

The two men released the handle of the hand-car to complete its final few cycles unaided, before it pulled up short of the nose of the goods train. The man shepherded them into the shade beneath the goods wagon that held the water, where they would wait out the afternoon heat, loading in the twilight, the two groups then going their separate ways.

The man boosted the twin up into the wagon to retrieve more

cardboard to cover the uncomfortable blue metal underneath the train. The twin also passed down some bottles of water. The afternoon passed quietly, people chatting and snoozing in the heat, batting at the persistent bush flies. The Dutchman's wife sat off to the side with Izzy. Ticky could hear her talking to the young woman from time to time but could not make out what she was saying. He was thankful for the Dutch couple. They brought much more than themselves to the group.

When the sinking sun started to seek them out beneath the wagon the man knew it was time to pack. They passed the water down and loaded it onto the little wagon, keeping enough back to see the walkers through the journey to the siding.

Ticky gave the little wagon a shove, passing on some final words of encouragement to the twin and the manager as they rolled away, slowly working the handle up to speed. Unlike the twin, he had no qualms about the manager's capacity to do his bit. He recognised that while he may not be a decisive man, or a fine physical specimen, he saw in him a resolve and strength to push through to get the job done. It had been a shift for Ticky, but he was glad the manager was on their team. It gave him some disquiet to recognise this. He prided himself on his ability to read his fellow humans. But in this instance he recognised that his first negative impressions of the man had been wrong.

He watched them roll into the distance, listening to the rods clanking against their housings, the two men bobbing up and down like a wind-up toy, disappearing into the twilight.

—Alright, he said, turning on his heel. Let's get this show on the road.

The group gathered up their water and the small packs that they'd been permitted to bring, donning them and stepping down onto the service road and into the west, the sun melting into the saltbush ahead of them.

The dingo was tired. He needed to rest. He lay in the shade of the saltbush licking at a deep wound on his flank. He'd spent the better part of two days fighting with the other dogs that had moved in, the smell of death drawing them from vast distances. There were better than a dozen dingoes in his territory now. He had gone into the early battles with right on his side, his territory, his right. He kept the two bitches at bay most of the first night. They'd not sampled a mouthful of the rotting meat. It was making them frantic. But then others had arrived. It was the big white male that had tipped the balance. His colouring was unique among the group that were there.

He'd come at the resident dingo head on. There was barely a growl. They'd charged and rolled and bitten. The earth of the bare ground scuffed and scraped by their efforts. The fight had gone on for a long time. Both of them suffered. Both bleeding. It had ended in an uncertain draw. Neither dog having the energy to re-enter the fray. Both had moved back and lay down, licking at wounds but keeping a wary eye on the other.

And while this had happened the other dingoes had fed. They snapped and snarled at each other but unlike the resident dog they were more than willing to share the spoils with each other. The resident had run in a couple of times, scattering several dogs off a corpse, but while he did it at one others were feasting on another. It seemed a matter of honour. He hadn't eaten for a day, and showed no sign of doing so, preferring instead to spend his time vainly trying to send the interlopers on their way.

The corpses were torn, barely recognisable as human shapes. Stomach cavities were eviscerated, rib bones, picked clean of their flesh, gleamed white in the night, like they'd been there for months. Heads had been severed with strong teeth tearing firstly at the cartilage and flesh of throats and then pulling apart spinal chords. More than one head had been removed and dropped at a distance, and then discarded when it offered little in the way of nourishment.

The resident watched it all. He'd sat for some hours now. His nemesis had long-ago risen to feed, ignoring him. The resident finally made it to his feet. He walked slowly, gingerly back to the culvert. He walked through the frenzy, dogs darting backwards and forwards, pieces of flesh taken off into the saltbush to be consumed. The resident ignored it all, head down he went to the culvert and lay in his hole in the sand. He tried licking at the wound in his flank. As much to move the flies as anything. He was stiffening and struggled to reach the tear. It was deep, had ripped through into the cavity beneath. Infection had taken hold. He wouldn't rise again.

He kept riding until the sun was well into the morning sky. He thought about stopping. It was hot, but riding was much better than walking. The speed of the bike created a gentle breeze against his face that encouraged him to keep going. He'd ridden past a parked car and another road train, the car pointed east and the truck west. They were directly opposite each other, both off on the verge, like they'd stopped to speak to each other, friends meeting in an unlikely place. But there was no sign of anyone near either vehicle, and no tell-tale smell of death in the air. Both vehicles were locked. He found it amusing, that with all that had gone on these people had considered the security of their property. But when it happened, he thought, they'd have had no idea of what lay ahead.

He wondered where or if he might see them, like the other driver. It was many days now, well over a week, maybe more than two. He'd

173

lost track of days. But one thing he was certain about, if they'd not had water, they wouldn't have made it far.

He considered breaking the windows of the vehicles but then thought better of it. He had about as much as he could carry. And it seemed somehow wrong. In the end he decided to rest in the shade of the big rig. He leaned his bike against the drive wheels, pulled out his blanket, spreading it out over the section of bitumen shaded by the trailer from the midday sun. The flies were annoying and he wasn't overly tired but he thought a few hours rest at this time of day prudent. He pulled the walking stick out of the straps of the pack and lay it by his side. You just never know.

The walking group made good time in the night. Ticky could feel that it wasn't as quick as the pace that he and the twin had followed but not so much slower. He laughed at one point. It was almost pleasant to be stepping out with this group. An adventure. But then he thought about Izzy and he quickly put such notions aside. He could see it in her face every time he glanced at her. Like she wasn't there. Gone was the bubbly happiness and willingness to laugh at their situation. Replaced with something he found hard to describe. He angered quickly when he thought about it. He felt no small measure of guilt.

He'd largely avoided speaking to her since he'd returned with the twin. He didn't know what to say. It was as simple as that. He told her that he was sorry. And she'd given him a wan smile and said nothing. Sorry seemed lame, pointless. Of course he'd be sorry. He'd felt stupid. It wasn't like him to not know what to say in any situation. Words and deals were his business. Or at least he'd thought they were. But now he realised how little it all meant. That it didn't seem real, not real like this was real. He knew he had the lives of

174

people in his hands with the company, or at least their livelihoods. But it wasn't like this. Death was all around him. And it probably waited for him. Maybe not in the days ahead, now that they were on their way to a good supply of water, but then what after that?

How long could they stay at the siding? Especially if they could move some or many of the others. The water would last, they'd checked it. Thousands of litres. But what would they eat? There wasn't nearly enough food for them all.

They could send the hand-car west. That was what they'd talked about. Once they'd moved people to the siding a couple could go on the hand-car. Travel light and fast. It'd be many days, more than a week they'd estimated, before the first town. It could be done. But what would they find? No-one had come for them, so what was awaiting their arrival?

The sun was well into the morning sky when someone saw the siding. They were tired now, Ticky could see that. Conversation had all-but ceased. The enthusiasm for adventure was mostly gone and replaced with fatigue. His friend, the tall Dutchman, had struggled through the final few hours. They brought up the rear of the group, his wife egging him on. Ticky had stopped several times, dropping back to walk beside them. At one point he reached for his friend's pack, wanting to take the extra burden away. The Dutchman pulled away, refusing to release it. He gave Ticky a smile but said nothing. Just kept plodding.

But even the Dutchman's face was beaming as they walked through the buildings of the siding. The twin, elder, had spotted the group, had been out walking through the buildings. He ran to meet them. Shaking hands, showing concern at the man's bandages.

He ushered them into the living quarters, setting water to boil.

175

Making teas and coffees until everyone had been served. The goods driver hovered in the background having made acquaintances.

Ticky explained the situation at the train. How things had gone in the twin's absence. The plan to move people if they could. That he should hope to see his brother in a couple of days. The twin showed the group to a bunkhouse, an old quonset hut that had been used by maintenance crews from years previous.

It had a flat shade roof built over the curving sheet metal to take the worst of the baking sun. It was divided into two rooms. A pile of old wire shearer's stretchers were stacked against one wall next to a pile of foam rubber mattresses. They swept out one of the rooms, and with an hour or so of effort had a serviceable sleeping area for thirty of so people.

It pleased the man to look at the neat rows of stretchers. Here was something practical, tangible. An outcome. He smiled to himself.

While the group recovered from the night of walking, the man spoke with the twin about other details. When the man raised the issue of food with the twin, the twin mentioned the prevalence of kangaroos in the area. That if they had the gun they could kill and butcher them to feed people for a while at least. He just didn't know how long they might stay around once they started hunting them. They could only kill what they could eat for a day or so. The meat wouldn't keep any longer than that, cooked, it might last a couple of days. They agreed it was a temporary measure at best. They needed the hand-car and the gun.

18

The Matron tried not let her fear show. She sat in one of the banquettes, an untouched water bottle in front of her. She knew she was being stubborn, stupid, but she refused to drink. Couldn't bring herself to do it knowing that the others, her friends, had none. And the Captain, she didn't know if he was even still alive. She'd seen the blow. Called out against it. Had seen him go down. The blood had come instantly. That's what head wounds did. She'd seen enough of them in her time. Most often looked far worse than they were. But it wasn't the external injury that she worried about. A blow so brutal could easily kill someone, damaging the inside, crushing bone against the delicate functions of the brain. That's what concerned her. He hadn't moved the whole time they'd threatened the other old man, wanting details about the water. She'd watched the Captain for any sign of movement or life. That bitch wouldn't let her go to him. Wanted information. Threatened to do the same to the old man. Would have. She knew that. So she'd told them. Everything. About the hand-car and the water. That they'd be back in the next day or so.

It was then that she'd been dragged off into the other dining car, no chance to look at her friend and his wound.

But she wouldn't give them the satisfaction of drinking any of their water. She realised that she was likely killing herself. So be it. She couldn't think how this was going to end any other way. They'd lose the water and the hand-car when the pair returned. And they'd have the gun. And then they would go, leave them, without water and head to the siding. And then it would happen again. The remainder of her friends would die.

The younger twin had to admit the manager was plucky. That was the word he had thought of, didn't say it, but thought it. He could see that he'd underestimated the man's determination. The man worked as hard and as long as he did. But he could see that the manager was suffering. They'd talked a little in the beginning, as much as they could over the noise of the clanking of rods and wheels on rails. But then the conversation had stopped coming from the manager, and the twin knew that he was hurting. He couldn't see his face in the dark, could only make out its outline, couldn't see the fatigue or grimacing that it most likely betrayed.

At least his hands are wrapped. One mistake we didn't make again. The twin's hands had hardened already against the work. He figured he could go on for days now. Even his legs and back had grown used to the position, the rhythm. What had Ticky called him, the Kalamazoo Kid.

He asked the manager if he'd mind stopping, that he needed a rest. He thought this a better approach and then avoid the issue of pushing him too hard. Like Ticky had done. While Ticky had far greater endurance and strength he'd gone well into the red zone with his effort and had paid for it in the end. Thankfully they'd made it. He wouldn't make the same mistake with the manager.

They stopped in the night, sitting side-by-side sipping water from their bottles, surrounded by the load of other bottles.

—The Southern Cross, the manager gestured into the sky.

The twin didn't know what made him do it. He'd not discussed it with the manager as they worked but when he caught the first glimpse of the train he told the manager to stop. He'd asked to be on the east-facing side for that reason, had exchanged places during a rest stop.

When he wanted to back the hand-car away from the train the manager had shown emotion for the first time. The twin could see that the man was done. All in. Spent. The twin dismounted and gave the hand-car a push to set it heading in reverse before he responded to the manager.

—I'm sorry. I just think we need to be careful. I just want to get us out of sight. You can wait here, I just want to go forward and check.

The manager nodded his agreement and they moved the unit a few hundred metres back the way they'd come. The train was an almost indiscernible smudge. The twin figured they'd be invisible to anyone looking. Hoped that no-one had been looking when they stopped earlier.

It was approaching midday. The worst time to be doing this. He didn't want to do it. Just wanted to climb into the shade of the train and sleep away the afternoon, sip some water and maybe eat something. But something nagged. He just needed to be sure. Their cargo was life, he needed to check.

He pointed to a stand of acacia off the side of the track, suggesting that the manager make himself at home and that he'd come and wake him in an hour or two but not to move until he came back.

The twin thought about which way to approach the train. The most sheltered option was straight down the track. That he couldn't be seen from any windows, but if there was an issue that's where they'd be, looking along the rail bed. So he'd have to move through the scrub, stay low, very low in the saltbush. He went to the northern side of the train, knowing that all the windows were covered against the prevailing direction of the sun. He moved out from the position of the hand-car, way out in the scrub. He could make out the train clearly enough but he hoped it was far enough that no-one might see him.

It wasn't long before he questioned the wisdom of what he was doing. The sun bore into his back and head, under his hat, beating him into submission. It was far worse than working the hand-car handle. There was no gentle breeze. He stumbled several times over the low bushes. He thought about the gwardar they'd seen on the night so long ago.

He moved to where he was opposite the first couple of train carriages and then began to work his way towards the train, trying to stay as low as possible. But short of crawling on his hands and knees he was never going to be lower than the top of the saltbush.

As he moved across an open space to the next patch of salt-bush he glanced to his left, sensed something. Two dingoes stood in the shade of the scrub watching him with interest, and it seemed to him, with very little fear. He paused for a moment when he reached the security of the salt-bush, looking back. He marvelled at their tawny sleek hides. He had always had a soft-spot for them. But most of the farmers hated them. Losing stock, mainly sheep, to them a common occurrence. It was more often wild dogs that did the damage. Dogs abandoned by owners interbreeding with dingoes. But it was pointless trying to convince an angry farmer to differentiate between pure breeds and mongrels. They were all the same as far as a farmer was concerned. Death the only good outcome. The twin's own father felt the same.

But the twin loved to see them, the pure dingoes. Loved the fluidity and parsimony of their movements, never wasting more energy than required. And that they could survive in this environment amazed him. Out here where water was almost non-existent.

The dogs sniffed at the air, noses slightly raised. He wondered what the smell told them. What smell would present a threat. Obviously his didn't because they dropped their heads again and simply watched him move away.

He knew why they were there. There were no doubt others. And the reason soon assailed him. The smell of rotting human flesh. He gagged slightly, fighting the urge to be sick. He couldn't believe how thick it was, the smell. It was like it had been poured over him. It seemed to hang in the air like a curtain. He wondered that he might actually be able to see it, such was its substance. He came across bones, picked clean, white against the off-white of the chalky loam. He was thankful that the powerful jaws of the dingo had done their work and that most of the bones were unidentifiable as human. But then he saw the head. It'd been picked over but still carried tufts of hair on the scalp. He vomited. He was annoyed. He was wasting precious fluid, and he'd not brought a bottle with him. He wiped the back of his shirt-covered wrist across his mouth and moved forward in a crouch.

He was close enough now that he could make out the details of the carriages, so he dropped to all fours. He moved forwards thinking that this had a been a lot of effort for nothing, that he'd look a bit stupid when he climbed into the carriage, but he'd come this far…

He thought he must look like a prairie dog, his head popping up from time to time. He couldn't see anyone. He moved forward in a half squat and was very close now. He could've tossed a rock and hit the train from here. He couldn't make out anyone under the first carriages. He knew it wasn't unusual, other than the Matron and her friends the others from the front of the train had long-ago stopped leaving their carriages. There'd likely be people beneath carriages further back, the other group. It was the middle of the day so there'd be no-one leaning against the far-side wheels.

He was about to move forward again when movement from the engine caught his eye. He ducked low, looking through the stringy branches of the salt-bush. The glimpses he caught weren't enough to establish an identity but he dared not raise his head. And then he heard the noise of someone pissing into the rail-bed from a height, the stream gushing into the blue metal below. He moved slightly, a gap opening through the scrub. It was the soldier, the shotgun leaning against the rail beside him.

He found the first body towards sunset. He'd seen the dingoes from a distance, suspected what it was they were crowded around. One of the dogs raised his head when he was still a distance away. An inaudible warning, at least to the miner's ear, sent the dogs scurrying into the scrub growing thickly along this stretch of the road.

He didn't stop, but couldn't help but glance across the roadway at the massacred corpse. They'd been at it for a while. It wasn't until he saw the white bra, further along the road that he realised it was a woman. He wasn't sure why he thought that it would be a man. There were plenty of women truck drivers around now, or it could be a woman from the car. He decided it didn't really matter. He kept peddling towards the setting sun.

He found a shoe just on dark, the kind a businessman would wear, three-hole lace-up. Sitting there on the black-top, like a piece of art, laces undone, pointing south-west.

For some reason it made him think about what he'd done, killing the miner. What was he going to do when he got to civilisation? Would he tell anyone? Be dead easy to say he never saw him again after the caravan. The old folk would back him up on that.

I don't feel anything, that's what troubles me. Surely I should feel some sort of guilt about what I've done. He was a prick, and he left me for dead. As good as tried to kill me. But even so, surely I should feel something about taking a human life. It's not like I've done it before, or even thought about it. Sure I'd had those chats with other blokes, you know, about whether you could kill someone defending yourself or your family, or in a war. And I might've said yes, but I'd not really thought about it. And yet I don't feel anything. I don't feel good about it, or bad. I don't feel anything. I made a decision. Had to be done, so I did it. Probably saved him from getting shot at the roadhouse. But you'd think I might feel something. Did he have family? I don't remember him saying much about that. He talked about women, all the time. But I used to tune out of that. I'm pretty sure there was no wife or girlfriend. But nothing about a father or mother or brothers or sisters. And I swatted him with not much more thought than I would've given to squashing a cockroach. Fuck. What does that make me. Sociopath, psychopath? Not sure of the difference.

He found the other shoe a bit further along the road. This one was still on the foot of the owner. He stopped this time. For some reason the dingoes had not fed. Maybe there were none in this area or maybe there was something about the young man they didn't like. He was well-dressed, a neat button-up chambray shirt, dark pants, office pants. Management he thought. He lay face up, the eyes open. Looks like someone enjoying a night of star gazing, he thought. The face was burnt and the lips cracked, blood, dried black, on his chin. But it was the tongue that intrigued the miner. It was two or three times the size of a normal one, hanging out through the bloody lips. Almost comical.

So the woman had been driving the big rig. This guy was certainly no truck driver.

He took a sip of water from the bottle on the bike frame, remounted and headed into the darkness.

The twin had to speak to the Captain, or the Matron, he knew that. The soldier had gone back into the train cab. He figured he could probably continue moving to the train. But then what? If he ran into someone from that bitch's group… But he didn't have a choice. Now was probably the best time he thought. Most people sleeping. No choice.

He moved forward, scanning for signs of life. Nothing. He climbed the rail-bed and into the shade of the first carriage. He looked down the length of the train. No-one. He moved forward to the bogie wheels which signified the end of the carriage before emerging into the sun again. The flies buzzed his face. He thought about where they'd been. Crawling on dead human flesh, or on the shit that had been thrown out by the bucketful, unburied. He didn't know which would be worse.

He moved quickly into the stair-well of the carriage, the door open above him. He stood, tried to act casual and walked into the carriage. All was quiet. He could hear murmuring but couldn't see anyone in the low light. The smell was terrible. Not as bad as the rotting flesh, he thought, but bad enough. Shit, piss, body odour, they were all there. He glanced into the first compartment he came to. An old man lay on his side on the bunk. His knees were slightly drawn up and his hands arranged neatly against his stomach, eyes open staring towards the door. The twin gave a small wave. The man didn't move or acknowledge his gesture. Dead? Hard to tell He didn't have the time to check.

He moved forward past several compartments to the Matron's, glancing in. It was the Captain on her bed. He wasn't asleep. He started when he saw the twin, but quickly waved him in, putting a finger to his lips. The Captain climbed off the bunk, shook his hand, and then gestured for him to follow. They went back the way the twin had come, out of the train and into the shade underneath.

He shook the twin's hand again.

—Well done.

The twin explained his covert approach and seeing the soldier with the shotgun. The Captain told him what had happened.

—People are dying now. No water in our group, most won't see out the next day or so. Some gone already.

The twin told him of the man in the cabin. The Captain nodded but said nothing.

—We need to go, said the twin. It's the only thing we have on our side. That they don't know we're back with the hand-car.

—Either that, or get the gun. The Captain paused before going on. But that's unlikely. I think you're right.

They talked about how many they could take with them, how many could climb down and make the walk. Whether they'd have to go out through the scrub, the way the twin had come in. Neither said anything about those they'd be leaving.

—There's only a couple who'd be up to it. But I'm not going without the Matron.

—Where is she?

—In the second dining car I think. That's their base, where that Tattooed bitch is holding her.

—It'll have to be tonight. Reckon you can get in and get her out while I distract them?

They talked through the twin's idea, agreeing it wasn't great but it was the best they could manage. It was now or never.

The twin knew he had to go back to the hand-car. He worried that the manager might do something silly if he didn't get back there soon. Like bring the hand-car up to the train. The two men shook hands and the twin went out into the heat of the saltbush, glancing first along the train to make sure that no-one was watching. He wished he'd brought some water, as much to give the Captain a drink as himself.

Ticky was edgy. They'd sorted the sleeping quarters to his satisfaction. They'd confirmed that there was plenty of water, enough for each of them to have a wash from a bucket. And they'd confirmed that food was going to be an issue. Rationing was worked out and put into action. And when all this was done there wasn't much to do, other than to wait.

He wondered how long they should or could wait. He talked to the Dutchman and the twin about what they could do if the hand-car didn't return. Would anyone start walking west. There didn't seem to be another option.

The only shining light was Izzy. He'd talked to the Dutch woman. Swallowed his inhibitions and asked her what he might do to help her heal. What to say and how to say it.

—You men, the same in every country. She'd laughed at him and then apologised but still with a twinkle in her blue eyes. And so they'd talked and then the man had talked to Izzy.

186

He admired her. Despite her pain, he could feel the core of steel that ran through her. He made sure he listened as much as he spoke and didn't try to find a solution to everything. It made him think of how he'd not talked to his wife properly in years. She'd be jealous if she saw the way he was talking to Izzy.

The twin explained his plan. He filled a small steel trough with water, that the kangaroos would be attracted. He'd fixed a light steel cable that he found in one of the sheds, to one of the water-tank posts, fashioning the other end into a snare.

Ticky looked dubious but with little else to do he'd sat with the twin in the darkness of a nearby shed in the late afternoon. The kangaroos came. He counted twenty two of them. There'd no doubt be some in the pouch as well, he thought. The twin had been right. He watched a big male, taller than he was, a breast like Chesty Bond. And huge testicles. He was the boss, that much was obvious. He moved around, pushing gently off the huge tail, given plenty of room by the others. They were marvellous creatures he thought. He'd never really sat and studied them before.

He almost laughed out loud at the absurdity of the situation. But he held. Wanted to give his offsider the best chance. He didn't have a lot of faith in his plan. It relied a bit too much on luck for his liking.

They came for the water. The twin was certainly right on that. Zeroed straight in on it. When a group had gathered around it the twin waited briefly and leaped towards them, yelling like a madman and brandishing a length of steel pipe.

It was a female that went down. She caught one leg in the steel noose dragging it forward where it closed tightly against her effort. She went down hard. The thump audible. The twin drove in bringing down the pipe onto her head before she had a chance to

187

struggle against the steel cable. The first blow glanced off her head, jarring his arms as the pipe struck the ground, but the second stilled her. A third was insurance. The rest of the mob were long gone. The man stepped into the light, laughing and shaking his head.

—Remind me, never to make you angry.

The twin reached into the pouch, frowning as he pulled out the young joey.

—Bugger, was all he said. He swung the tiny kangaroo by the legs, smashing the head against the leg of the water tank.

They dragged the carcass into the shade of the shed in which the two men had been hiding. The man looked around for the first time. It was full of rusting tools and machinery. Benches teamed with the detritus of decades of rail maintenance, things the man didn't recognise. The smell was of oil and rust. Not unpleasant thought the man.

—Watch out for snakes in here, said the twin.

That brought Ticky to his senses, snapping him from thoughts of the romance of railway history. His eyes immediately began to dart left and right, scanning the floor around them.

The twin had been busy. Ticky watched as he cut at the back legs with a carving knife, just behind the tendon. He pierced the skin of both legs and then pushed through a steel rod, bent in the middle and hooked on either end, through the incisions. He slipped the rod over a large hook which in turn was connected to one of several heavy chains looping up into pulley wheels suspended in the rafters. He hauled on one of the chains. The female kangaroo lifted from the floor, suspended upside down in front of them.

Once he was happy with the height, the twin went to work, skinning and gutting. The man watched on, impressed with the skills of the young man.

188

—Done this a few times?

—Only on sheep. Never on roos. Principle's the same.

He split the skin and then worked it free of the carcass with the big knife. Pulling it down and away after severing the head. The man was amazed at how white the kangaroo looked without its skin. The twin split the chest cavity, careful not to pierce the gut. Most of the internal organs fell into the dirt at his feet.

—Dingoes will enjoy that.

He wrapped the organs in the skin and dragged them outside and into the scrub and then rinsed his bloody arms in the water that he'd set out for the kangaroos. The man had followed him out and they stood watching the sun disappear into the saltbush, across the plain towards the west.

—We'll let it hang for the night. It'll taste better. I'll butcher it in the morning and then we can make up a big pot of stew. The twin pulled the doors closed on the shed. We don't want our wild dog friends getting at it.

—That was pretty impressive, Ticky said, as they walked back towards the living quarters. I'm sorry I doubted you.

The young man smiled but said nothing.

The miner rode his bike well into the night, stopping at midnight. He was feeling the effort. His legs were tired and his bum was sore. He decided to treat himself to a night sleep, knowing he could make good progress on his bike through most of the daylight hours.

He figured there must be another roadhouse somewhere close-by. He had about a third of his water remaining. He'd need to replenish it soon. He lay in his blanket in the roadside ditch thinking about how tenuous life was in this country. The difference between life and death was a few sips of water. With full bottles I'm impervious. But once they're gone I'm dead. Simple as that. He went to sleep hoping his reception at the next place was better than the last.

19

—Your choice old girl.

The Matron could tell that Tattoo was annoyed that she wouldn't drink the water. It was a small victory but she enjoyed it nevertheless. A bit juvenile she thought with a wry smile to herself, especially as it will likely kill me. She watched Tattoo walk off into the kitchen of the dining car.

The Matron stared at the bottle of water in front of her. She wanted it, badly. Her lips were already dry and she could feel her tongue heading the same way, seemingly growing in size as it dried. She knew, better than any of them, that with the heat inside the train she'd be lucky to last the day tomorrow. Systems in her body would begin shutting down, chiefly the kidneys. She knew what she was doing was stupid and pointless, childish, but what the hell. She wondered what her partner would have said. That she was stubborn. It made the Matron smile again. She took comfort from the thought.

She used the time to think about her life. She ran through the good things that had happened along the way. She narrowed it to two things. Her partner and her work. Her life in five words, she thought. She knew she'd been fortunate in both, less so the work. That was mainly due to her commitment and effort. It hadn't always been plain sailing. Hospitals could be tough environment. Men had been at the root of most of the challenges. She'd thought about it, talked about it with her partner, many times.

She knew she wasn't some rabid, anti-man dyke. She hated the word dyke—it sounded too harsh to her, a word you'd use to describe something that was wrong or inappropriate. And she wasn't one for the lesbian sisterhood. She was a bit of a failure on that front. No mardi gras for her. But she'd been happy and motivated to do her bit for women. While she rarely pushed the gay agenda she worked hard for the women in her world. Nurses mostly. Their lot was tough. She'd been through it. An often thankless profession lorded over by men. There were some great ones, she acknowledged that. But there were a lot of pricks. Arrogance. That was what she'd seen every day of her working life. Men treating their patients and their staff the same way, with indifference couched behind some lame view that you needed to keep people at arm's length, not get personally involved. She'd seen the traits in some women doctors as well. But mostly the men.

But whenever it got her down, no matter the situation, she would always go home to unconditional love. That had been the difference.

She sat with her chin on her hands on the table top. The bottle inches away, a smile on her face.

Tattoo watched the Matron smile from the doorway. The smile wasn't directed at her, she could see that, could tell it was some private thought. But no matter, it made her want to charge back and slap the old bitch across her arrogant face. She wanted her to drink, that was all. And the old cow wouldn't. She was so stupid.

192

When the twin arrived back at the hand-car the manager was nowhere to be seen. Before he set about finding him he drained his water bottle. He hadn't drunk for hours. He knew he'd been stupid to leave without it. Lucky he didn't pass out somewhere in the hot scrub and become dingo food, he thought. Never again.

He found the manager asleep in the shade of a stand of acacia. He didn't wake as the twin approached making no effort to be quiet. The twin smiled knowing that the older man must have been bone-tired. He didn't wake him. There wasn't a lot of point. They didn't need to be about for another few hours, so the twin sat down in the shade, waved briefly at the gathering flies and fell asleep.

His alarm woke him. Woke both of them. The twin explained what had happened, explained the plan. The manager was quiet for a time. The twin could see that he was troubled. Asked him about it.

—Leaving them. It's wrong. This trip, on the hand-car, that was to do something useful. But this. Well, it's wrong. For me, not you. It's my job, my responsibility. I need to think about it.

The twin said nothing in response. He thought it odd, but said nothing. He'd die. Anyone left on the train was going to die. No-one had come from outside. He couldn't see any reason why that would change now. But, if the manager wanted to do that, he wouldn't talk him out of it.

They parted ways hours later, in the dark of the moonless night, the twin reminding the manager to wait until he saw the fire before moving the hand-car towards the train. He'd hopefully meet him there not long after, he and the others.

The twin made the return journey along the rails for a good part of the way knowing that he'd be invisible to anyone looking from

193

the train. He waited until he could make out the dark bulk of the engine set against the slightly lighter night sky before he moved into the scrub.

The dingoes were still busy, the smell prominent. He scared several, a couple growling at him when he came close. He had to deviate, rather than the dingoes running off. It frightened him, he'd never seen them act like this before.

When he was about two-thirds of the way along the train he set to work pulling together what he could find that might burn, mostly dead acacia branches. He pulled together a pile that stood at the height of his head. That'll throw a light he thought. And then it'll be up to the Captain.

He pulled out the box of matches from his pocket. Here goes he said out loud.

The Captain waited in the dark, resting against the bogie wheels. He knew it was early, but he had nothing else to do but wait. He'd spoken to three crew members in the afternoon about what was going to happen. They readily agreed. He didn't speak about it to any of the older passengers. Most wouldn't be able to climb down from the train and none of them would be able to walk any sort of distance. And they couldn't risk losing the hand-car. They'd all die.

He'd walked through the train in the late afternoon. It was his farewell. He felt some guilt about abandoning them to the desert but was too pragmatic to think about going down with his ship. But he knew it was something that would stay with him.

There were three dead bodies. He spent some time with an old woman who lay next to her dead husband. They were in their cabin. The most expensive that the train had to offer. Had their own en-suite.

194

She explained that he'd gone in the last hour or so. She held on to a lifeless liver-spotted hand. There were no tears. She told the Captain that they'd only be apart for some hours, like he'd gone to the shops, that she'd soon be with him. She said matter-of-factly that even if they suddenly had water, that she didn't want it, wouldn't drink it.

He'd warned the three crew to be ready, near the front of the carriage and that he'd collect them. And they'd have to move fast. There were other crew but they'd made their choice, thrown in their lot with Tattoo. He had no sympathy for them. He could probably try to talk to some of them. Knew that they'd readily amend their ways if they were included in the escape. But he couldn't risk it.

They'd leave the water that the twin and the manager had brought with them. Pile it on the tracks where it would be seen from the train. There was no point taking it with them. The Captain knew that none of it would find its way to the older passengers, but he resigned himself to the fact that it didn't really matter, that it was semantics. A matter of a few days.

It was one of Tattoo's men, the remaining miner who saw the flames first. The Captain not long after. The soldier had been sleeping, to be woken in another hour or so to take his turn as one of the look-outs from the engine.

The Captain moved quickly along the rail bed to the steps into the second dining car. He let out a long-held breath when the door pulled open. He stepped into the dark of the entry area, looking into the dining car. He could hear voices outside. One of them Tattoo's. Then the soldier's. He moved into the dining car to the seating area. It was almost black inside.

—Matron.

—Here, she shot back almost immediately.

—Quick, let's go.

She came forward in the dark, colliding with the Captain. He grabbed her arm and pulled.

—We need to move.

—What are we doing?

—Not now.

He knew the fire wouldn't hold their attention for long. And they still needed to get along the rail bed.

He had to help her down the stairs. He could feel that she was shaky on her legs. When she stepped down to the rail bed her legs buckled. He put an arm around her and moved her down onto the service road, heading towards the front of the train.

When the soldier arrived a group of them were standing and looking towards the flames that they could hear crackling into the sky. Tattoo was pointing a torch, the beam on its last legs. She looked to him, uncertainty in her voice.

—What is it?

—Looks like a distraction to me.

The woman turned suddenly. Is anyone with that old bitch. No-one spoke. Shit. The soldier bolted towards the train door, Tattoo in his wake. The torch beam revealed an empty carriage. The soldier didn't hesitate, running forward and down into the rail bed towards the front of the train.

Once he was sure that the fire was not going to go out the twin moved quickly back through the scrub cutting the diagonal to the train engine. He stumbled up the rail bed praying that the fire had drawn away any prying eyes. He rounded the nose of the engine. He heard rather than saw people back towards the first carriage.

He was taking a risk but he had to know. He whispered into the dark.

—It's us came the response.

The twin let out a breath.

—Quick go. Head along the track. Unload the hand-car, everything on the track and be ready to leave. Tell your boss to be ready to go, quickly, when we get there.

As they disappeared into the darkness the twin hoped that the hand-car wasn't too far away.

He turned back, could hear someone coming towards him, heard the Captain's voice, cajoling the Matron. He inserted himself on the other side of the woman and together the two men started moving along the service road. The twin heard voices behind and could hear someone running.

—Keep going, he said, slipping out of the Matron's grasp. The Captain didn't argue, disappearing into the darkness.

The twin felt around on the ground, looking for something, anything to use as a weapon. His hand swept over a fist-sized rock. He picked it up and then squatted down, trying to make himself invisible in the darkness.

He could hear the runner, close now, coming straight at him. He sprang upwards at the last second, catching the soldier in a rugby tackle, driving a shoulder towards the stomach, connecting with the butt of the shotgun. Both men went down in a tangle, wrestling for a time. And then the gun fired.

The shot came as the Captain and the Matron reached the hand-car. Most of the water was stacked between the tracks in front of it. The manager stood beside it.

—Quick, go. I'll give you a push. Just push down on the handle, it's easy. And then he realised the twin wasn't with them.

—He's back there. They froze. No-one knew what to do.

—I'll go, said the manager, I was staying behind anyway. It's okay. I'll try and yell.

The Captain stumbled for a reply but nothing came out.

The manager moved back in the darkness along the service road. He heard someone running towards him.

—Hey, stop.

The shot took the manager in the throat. The soldier was almost on him, had fired on the run, shooting from the hip. He was so close that the pellets had hit the manager in a tight cluster, almost decapitating him. He had no time to yell.

—Go, yelled the Captain. The second shot told him all he needed to know. He shoved the hand-car and leaped up. One of the crew was on the other side, unfamiliar with the operations of the machine.

—What do I do?

—Just fucking crank up and down on that handle. The Captain could hear the steps coming in the darkness. He pushed and pulled as hard as he could. The speed grew. The wheels groaned against the rails, the connecting rods straining in their joints. A shot belched out. He was facing towards it, saw it. The man on the far side of the handle, grunted and folded. The Captain felt something sting his thigh, like he'd been stung by a wasp. The man fell back onto the tracks. The Captain kept cranking, alone now, but the speed had grown. Running speed now. Another shot rang out but from further away. A couple of pellets rattled off the crank housing. The Captain expected to feel more pain but didn't. He kept pushing. Another shot and then another, but too far away.

—One of you get over here, he yelled over his shoulder. One of the crew came forward, stepped over the gap from the wagon and onto the hand-car, careful to avoid the feverishly working Captain. He stepped around the side and into position behind the handle. He watched the motion for a revolution before snatching the handle and contributing to the effort. They kept the pace high for the next hour, before the Captain called for an easing.

The soldier came back to the pile of water bottles, some stacked neatly on the tracks but others scattered beyond, empty, peppered with shot from his gun, the vital fluid greedily swallowed by the blue metal of the rail bed.

He took a full bottle from the pile, draining the contents. He heard someone call out to him from the train. It was that mad bitch. What should he do? He knew. He walked back a ways along the service road. The first bloke was well dead, he could see that. His first kill. He knew it'd come, but thought it'd be in Afghanistan. He kept walking. Heard the moan before he got to the twin. He was bleeding from the stomach. The soldier could see the blood staining the hard-packed earth in front of him.

—Sorry mate, was all he said as he kept going back along the road.

—What happened? asked Tattoo when he met her in front of the engine.

He said nothing but kept walking, to the second dining car. He climbed the steps, grabbed his backpack along with some of the meagre food supplies. Within a minute he was out and walking back to the front of the train, saying nothing in response to the questions thrown at him. The gun and his business-like walking enough to keep the interest to a minimum.

Tattoo grabbed at his arm as he walked past her when she realised that he wasn't going to stop. He reversed the gun and drove the butt into her stomach. She dropped into the dirt, wheezing. The twin was dead when he went past again. He stopped at the pile, loading as much water as he could carry, and then drinking as much as his system could take before setting off into the west in the wake of the hand-car.

The miner had camped within a handful of kilometres of the roadhouse. The sky was barely giving an indication of the coming day when he sighted its outline in the distance. He decided to be much more cautious on this approach. He left his bike in the brush. But this time he took his backpack with him, and his empty water bottles. He brandished the aluminium walking stick.

He cut through the scrub, using the roofline of one of the buildings as a reference point. He carried the metal walking stick in one hand. This was a bigger place than the previous one. There were several buildings that he could see, one of them offering accommodation. Besser blocks by the look of it. Not fancy and not cheap I bet.

Like the previous place there was a hardscrabble camping area. He moved around through the trees and saltbush until he was at the back border of the property, the furthest point from the highway, the camping area in front of him. There were two car-and-caravan units.

He wondered what to do. I could stay and watch and wait, figure out who might be there and whether I'm in for a warm welcome or not. But then I'd lose my early morning element of surprise. I'd like to be in and out quickly. Just get some water and get out, back on the road. I don't need to hang around. I figure I can make a town in two or three days.

He moved towards the caravans, trying to walk lightly on the dry gravel but once again feeling that the crunching sound must have been audible for miles. He clutched the walking stick tightly.

The doors of both vans were closed, shade awnings wound in, like the owners were ready for departure. The inside told a different story. He tried the handle of the first door. The click loud in the morning cool, like his tread. He sniffed the air, out of habit now. Nothing. But the van was chaos inside. Every cupboard and drawer was open. Cooking utensils littered the floor. The camp chairs had been thrown onto the bed. And not a skerrick of food to be found. He tried the sink pump, air, nothing more.

In one of the bedside tables he found a man's wallet, looked at the driver's licence. Another grey nomad on the retirement road.

He stepped out and closed the door behind him moving to the other van. Same result.. Maybe the owners had taken everything, found a way out with their supplies. But he didn't really believe that.

He suddenly felt vulnerable. The first time since the plane that something hadn't gone his way, some sort of reward. But there was still the buildings. He'd have to try them now.

He stepped out of the van and clicked the door closed behind him. The closest building was the besser block accommodation units. He could see five blue doors set into the drab, water-stained, grey concrete blocks. He walked across the camping area until he was behind the building. There was no window, just a blank grey wall. He moved along the wall to peek around the corner, on the side with the doors. Nothing. Nobody. But he'd left the walking stick behind. He looked back, could see it standing against the side of the caravan. Too far, too much time.

He edged along the front wall of the first unit ducking below the window next to the door. He stood when he'd passed the window, reaching for the silver doorknob. He gently turned it, quickly coming up against the resistance of the lock. He looked back to the window. The heavy red curtains were drawn. He moved to the centre putting his eye close to the glass, but there wasn't the slightest hint of a gap.

It wasn't until he got to unit number one that a doorknob turned. He'd reached from the security of the wall, and almost let it go, such was the surprise. He stepped around in front of the door, the silver cursive 'one', screwed on at eye height, slightly askew. He continued turning the knob until he knew that all he had to do was push the door open.

He moved the door just enough to open a crack between the door edge and the jamb. Two things assailed him, the blackness and the smell. The blackness was complete, the smell metallic, coppery. Not a rotten smell like the others. He knew what it was. He didn't want to push the door any further but knew he had to. There'd likely be a tap inside.

He stood in the doorway staring, horrified. Frozen to the spot. There was no furniture in the room, just a rectangle of maroon carpet, a cupboard and sink at the far end. In the middle of the floor a sheet of black heavy plastic. A hole had been punched into the ceiling above it. Suspended from the exposed rafter and over the plastic was a block and tackle, chains hanging, a hook on the end. The hook stained, dark.

He stepped in. The carpet was stained darker along one edge of the plastic where blood had run off. The plastic was indented with a perfect circle off to one side where a heavy receptacle had forced its shape. There was a grey plastic bucket standing on the drying area of the sink. He couldn't see into it from where he was standing. Didn't want to see into it. But he needed water. He had to try the taps. The sink was spotless, he could see that. A bottle of washing-up detergent stood against the wall near the taps, a wash cloth was spread out and hung neatly over the front lip of the sink.

He stepped forward trying not to look at the bucket but then couldn't help himself. He let out the breath he'd been holding. It wasn't good but better than he'd been expecting. Two knives were standing upright inside the clean bucket along with a steel used for sharpening. He'd seen those kinds of knives before, had worked in the local abattoir when he first left school, before the job in the mines—it was why he knew that the smell was blood. Killing knives they were called. Both long blades but one thinner, pointier, the boning knife. Used for cutting meat away from around the skeleton. The other, a carving knife, much wider, a gentle arch of steel, for cutting away the hide or dissecting the boneless pieces or carving slices. He dry-heaved.

He tried both taps. Nothing. That empty feeling of air like the caravan pumps. And there was no bathroom. Must be a shared one. Had to be one. He stepped back across the room, careful to avoid the plastic and the dried blood. Outside he pulled the door quietly closed behind him, the coppery smell in his nostrils. He realised that his pulse was up, his breathing rapid. He took a couple of deep breaths.

And then he heard something, like a whimper. Muted. Faint. It sounded like it'd come from the room next door. And then it struck him. How many people were travelling with the caravans. You wouldn't kill them all at once. It, they, wouldn't keep. He heard nothing more. Maybe it was nothing. Can't risk it, forcing the door or breaking the window.

He crossed the gap to the next building. More besser blocks and a doorway at the far end. Between the top of the blocks and the roofline was a gap of half a metre or more filled with steel mesh. The shower block he figured. He moved to the far end.

A sign next to the door read 'sheilas'. The door was made of steel mesh and was closed, locked up with a silver padlock. He moved to the end of the building. He wanted to check the other side, the men's side, hoping the door would be open. But the need to get away was strong. Knew that the place was wrong. He wanted to run now, back to his bike and keep going. But he calmed himself, knowing that he needed water, that he wouldn't make it with what he had.

He edged along the wall, knowing that the next building was the roadhouse itself. There was a gap of a dozen metres or so but he'd need to pass through it to get to the other side of the shower block. Maybe better to go back and around the building the other way. No, I need to get out of here. He stepped around the corner.

—Hey you, the voice said.

20

The frenzy had faded. Most of the meat was gone. A handful of crows pecked and probed. The bones were picked clean. A young dog nosed at a skull, bunting it around the clearing, pushing his tongue into the holes. He'd not eaten the same as some of the others. He'd come late and because of his youth had run at the first sign of aggression from any of the other dingoes. So he was still hungry.

Many of the other dogs were sleeping, stomachs full, but with no intention of leaving. It was a strange scenario, dingoes from various territories, many enemies of the other but a truce of sorts with so much on offer.

And they'd stay for a while. The smells were there, out in the scrub where they'd eaten. It was still strong. But not as strong as what was coming from the train.

Tattoo stood alone by the pile of water bottles staring off into the darkness, the soldier long since swallowed up by the night. She made a decision. Taking as many bottles as she could carry and hiding them in the scrub.

She started to walk back to the train encountering several from her group.

—Bring the water back to the dining car. She pulled the miner aside, her original accomplice.

—Let's go, let's get out of here.

He looked at her without speaking.

—Whaddya mean?

—I mean, let's get the fuck out of here. I've stashed some bottles in the bush. Let's get back and grab what's left of the food and follow that bastard with the gun. We're gonna die here, there's not enough water.

He hadn't needed much convincing. The two walked quickly back to the dining car, taking most of what was left of the tinned food. They climbed down from the train, the woman leading them out into the bush away from the train and then cutting west. They stopped and listened when they heard voices and waited for them to pass back towards the train. The pair then cut back to the rails. She was thankful the group had left the busted water bottles on the track otherwise she may never have found the stash.

They collected the bottles and set off west in the wake of the soldier.

The Matron could feel the pellet in the Captain's leg, tucked up just under the skin. But she had nothing with her, had run without anything. She'd recovered slightly after a long drink of water. She sat on the little wagon, the breeze from their speed cool against her skin. The Captain sat next to her. Two of the crew working steadily on the handle taking them to the west.

There were only six of them. The Matron thought about that.

—We could have brought more.

The Captain didn't speak for a time. Ruminating, knowing she was right. Angry at her for making him think about what they'd had to go through. He didn't know what to say. Didn't want it to be a problem between them. It was the Matron who spoke.

—I understand. And I'm thankful, more than I can ever say. It's just hard knowing what we've done. We've killed all those people. And the twin and the manager, what happened to them? They've given their lives for us, or worse they're wounded and dying and no-one to look after them. The final words came out in a cry, the tears running down the Matron's cheeks. Say something, she said.

The Captain paused before speaking and when he did, he spoke quietly. I don't know what to say. You're right. About everything. But we can't go back. Otherwise it'll all have been for nothing. He turned and stared into the Matron's eyes, the little wheels clacking merrily on the rails beneath them. I know that sounds like an excuse. Maybe it is. And it's something I'll have to live with. But going back won't fix anything.

The tears ran freely in the dark, the Matron's and the Captain's. They dropped over the edge of the little wagon, the speed generated by the crew on the hand-car making some of them fall into the dry chalky loam by the rail bed.

Tattoo noticed the dingoes before the miner. They'd been walking for an hour or so when she heard something. She stopped, peering into the darkness behind them. A new moon had joined them, sending the smallest amount of light down to bounce off the burnished rail, so that they seemed to faintly glow. The failing light of her torch revealed nothing.

In a short while she turned again. Convinced this time. The sight in the beam gave her a chill. She let out an involuntary yip. A dozen

207

or more red eyes glowed back at her. They were close, standing frozen in the dull beam.

—Haaaaa, yelled the miner, running back along the rail-bed. The dogs scattered, several running off the side and a couple running back the way they'd come. But they didn't go far. They stopped and gathered again, milling around the rails, walking around each other in a huddle, soundless, watching.

—Don't worry, said the miner, they're just wondering what we're doing. Curious.

They started walking again. Tattoo glancing nervously over her shoulder from time to time, the dingoes never far away, close enough that their coats shone under the sliver of moon.

The stew was well received. The twin had risen early, before the dawn and the flies to butcher the kangaroo. The meat had hung well. The moisture had drained from the flesh, he could see that, could feel the dryness and stiffness as he cut away the various pieces. He knew it would make the meat more palatable, less chewy. And the carcass smelled fine, no rotting.

He'd hung the carcass in the bathroom of the bunkhouse later in the night, worried that animals might get at it in the shed. Not ideal and not overly welcome by some of the people, but it had kept the flies away and kept the meat relatively cool. He moved it into into the house while everyone was still asleep. He enjoyed having a task to complete, something useful.

He'd found all he needed in the kitchen. A set of killing knives, a steel and a cleaver. The equipment was old but in good fettle, and sharp. Someone had kept it this way. He wondered how long it had been since someone butchered meat here. Would have been years he thought.

He worked on the long fat tail, severing the complex skeleton in several places so it would fit in the pot. He knew that it contained a lot of fat and would add flavour to the stew.

He'd found a huge cast-iron camp oven in the museum shed, perfect for what he was making and probably used in the past for similar meals. But even so the pile of meat was more than the oven could take, so he found another smaller saucepan in the kitchen that would take the remainder. He needed to cook it all. If he didn't he knew it would be rotten by lunchtime.

Just as he'd finished filling both containers with the meat the man came in and together they set about gathering wood for the fire they'd need. Sunlight was beginning to poke it's way between the buildings as they walked the scrub looking for fallen wood.

They made the fire in the open in front of the store. The twin explained what he wanted. The man more than happy to take orders. The fire took quickly, the dry, hard wood sent flames above their heads. While the fire burned down they added water to the meat, what few vegetables they had, mostly potatoes, along with salt, stock cubes and other spices they'd found in the kitchen.

Satisfied with his pile of hot coals and ashes, the twin and the man, struggling under the weight, lifted and dragged the oven into the edge of the fire. The boy shovelled some of the coals on top of the lid. They put the smaller pot on the opposite side.

—This one'll cook quicker, but won't be as good. We'll let the big one cook most of the day. It'll be nice and tender and tasty. We can eat this one first. I'll add a bit of flour later to thicken up the liquid. Should be good. We can make a couple of dampers to eat with it.

A few of the others had risen by this time and stood around the fire marvelling at the young man's efforts and energy. The man watched, smiling, but thinking about what he and the Dutchman had spoken about the previous night. That staying here could only be a temporary measure, particularly if more arrived from the train. Some would need to keep heading west on the little hand-car. They'd been so focused on survival that they'd not had much time to consider what lay out there to greet them.

But they would need to see. Otherwise they'd all die here eventually. It would take a lot longer than for the people left on the train but it would happen. The water would last a long time but not forever. The food supply would go first. There'd be only so many kangaroos they could kill. And what then?

The Matron demanded to have her turn on the handle of the hand-car. She'd recovered some of her strength. Now she felt like she needed to do her bit. And she figured it might help take her mind off the people they'd left behind. And the death of so many. So she cranked, her and the Captain worked together. She laughed out loud when they had the little machine up to speed. She realised how long it had been since she'd laughed. A long time.

They made good time. The three pairs swapping every half hour. The distance fell away behind them. The moon sliver moved across the sky, starting behind them, slowly catching and passing the team on its way to the western horizon.

They only stopped once, for a toilet break, and then only for a few minutes.

—What a grand adventure this would be, if we weren't in the position we're in. The Captain said it, looking up into the night, waiting for the Matron to finish her business behind some salt-bush.

She smiled to herself. Her partner would be horrified had she known that she was peeing, voluntarily, next to a man in the middle of the desert. She pulled up her pants and they walked back together. She reached for his hand, holding it briefly.

—Thank you.

The Captain looked at her, barely able to make out the familiar features in the dark. He didn't respond. It seemed pointless, inappropriate. She had no reason to thank him. She'd done as much or more than any of them.

—Do you think we'll be good friends if we come through this.

The Matron didn't respond immediately.

—Yes, I should think so. You'd better explain things to your wife first.

The Captain laughed out loud.

—Yes, I'll do that.

They climbed onto the little wagon and the convoy set off once again into the west. The Matron fell asleep at some point, finally succumbing to the stress and sleeplessness of previous days. It was a fly that woke her, crawling on her face. She snatched at it, annoyed. She sat up, almost tipping off the side of the wagon, a hand of the woman from the crew steadying her. She smiled her thanks and looked to the hand-car. The Captain gave a quick wave taking a hand from the handle on an up-stroke. She smiled back.

—It appears I've missed a turn or two.

—He didn't want to wake you.

She smiled, stretching. Well, I'm awake now. She rose to her feet and stepped carefully across the gap to the hand-car, shooing the Captain away from the handle and assuming her position.

The first attack was a probe, the pack not totally confident in what they doing, in relation to both the prey and the approach. Most were from different territories, brought together by the long-travelled smell of rotting flesh on the flukey desert breezes. Some were from larger groups, others had lived a solitary existence. But now they were a pack, under a flag of convenience, one focus.

It wasn't usual for them to hunt humans. There were cases, some famous, but it was rare. But now they had the taste for it, saw the quarry as that, prey. Much easier than running down a kangaroo or even a rabbit.

It was an older bitch who made the first sally. Darting in to nip at the calf of the woman. The scream sent the bitch back to the pack but she'd drawn blood. It was just the beginning.

Tattoo's scream was as much out of fright as it was pain. She hadn't believed the miner's line about curiosity any more than he did. She'd kept glancing back as they walked, catching glimpses of them in the pale light. She knew it was more than curiosity. Her stomach churned with the fear she felt. She pulled up the leg of her pants to see a thin trickle of blood running down from her calf into her sock. While she did it the miner searched frantically along the side of the maintenance road for a weapon. He came back with a fallen branch from an acacia. It was large and heavy, unwieldy.

Tattoo could see the fear in his face.

—Come on. We'd better keep moving. He reached down offering her a hand.

The hand-car crew reached the goods train mid morning. They'd agreed that they'd see out the heat of the day in the shade of the goods wagon.

The Captain had a look around the train while the others made themselves comfortable on the cardboard beds left in place by the previous visitors. The engine was a slightly different model to his own, but largely the same. He hauled himself into the cab. It looked older and less well-maintained. Not ship-shape he thought with a smile. Not like his train. He wondered what his off-siders said about him. Old bastard still thinks he's on a ship. He smiled at the thought. He was never too rough on them, just making sure that the cab was left cleaner than how they'd found it. All the gauge glasses wiped clean, along with every other surface in the cab. He sat in the engineer's seat for a time and looked around him, tapping the dead-man button before he rose.

He moved out of the cab and walked back towards the engine housing, and inside the engine corridor. He flipped the huge switch connecting the batteries to the starter circuit and then back again. Nothing, no power registering anywhere. Out of habit he flipped the myriad of switches on the circuit breaker panel. All systems were dead. When he arrived back at the goods wagon the others had all made themselves comfortable, some already asleep. The Matron had saved him a spot next to her and he lay down and they talked quietly, swatting at flies as the heat grew into the early afternoon.

The soldier made good time. He sipped carefully at his water. He knew it had to last at least three days. He didn't have any intel on the walking from the others who'd done it, he'd not talked to any of them but he'd figured it out by the days they'd taken to go and come back. He knew the goods train was out there but there was no water there either. So he'd ration his water, be sensible. Walk when it was cool, sleep when it was hot.

The gun was annoying to carry but he knew he couldn't leave it behind. They knew he'd likely killed people, so he'd not receive a warm reception, he knew that. He just wasn't sure how it would play out. But he'd worry about that when he got there, for now he'd just keep walking like he was on an endurance march, the stuff from his basic training. He'd breezed through that, had always been fit from footy and running, not like some of the others.

The dingoes came almost as one the next time. They were soundless, the approach only betrayed at the final moment by the shuffle of paws on the loose dirt of the maintenance road. They went low again, the way they hunted other prey, aiming for the achilles, grabbing and holding, forcing the prey to ground. The miner was slightly behind the woman, that's what saved her. He went down screaming his stick dropping uselessly out of his hands, clattering into the dirt ahead of him. The woman ran, she didn't turn to look, just ran, the screams driving her on. One of the younger males, who'd missed out on getting a grip on the miner ran after her. She could hear it behind her. The young dog was still uncertain of himself operating alone, the scream from the woman made him hesitate. When she screamed again he stopped and turned back to where the others were gathered around the kill.

The miner might have died more quickly had he not fallen on his stomach. The older bitch had gone for the throat, as she had done hundreds of times before on other game, strangling the life out of the prey. She grabbed at the neck worrying at the flesh, exposing the vertebrae beneath. She'd not killed a human before, the others had all been dead, rotting. She was confused, the screams making her doubt herself. The others were similarly troubled, especially by the backpack he wore. They'd largely broken the corpses open through the soft stomach cavity but couldn't reach it with the way he was lying, so they kept biting, tearing at his back, buttocks and legs, clothing torn, the flesh coming away in chunks. All the while the miner screamed, swinging his arms ineffectually back at the pack

214

working at him from above. Eventually the bitch got her nose in beside his throat, into the softer flesh and cartilage. She reefed and his head came around more to the side. The screams abruptly stopped as she clamped the wind pipe. He snatched a final breath as she released for a better grip and then bit down and held fast.

Tattoo ran until she dropped, her breath coming in ragged bursts, sawing at her lungs and throat, burning. She could still hear the screams. And then they abruptly stopped. It drove her on. She could smell the piss that had run down her legs, could already feel the chafing where the inside of her thighs had rubbed on the wet cloth of her jeans. She staggered on and then stopped.

She had to get back to the train. It was the only safe place. She cut into the salt-bush off the maintenance road, heading away at right angles. She tried to run again but realised she couldn't. She walked fast, panicked, stumbling. She fell several times in the darkness, tripped over the low salt bush, looking back into the darkness every few seconds. Had she looked up she would have seen the Southern Cross leading the way south.

21

The miner didn't hesitate, he swivelled and ran back the way he'd come, around the corner and along the shower block, past the charnel house, and across the hardscrabble, past the lonely caravans and into the scrub beyond.

He slowed when he was in cover and then cut back towards where he'd left his bike.

Fuck, what do I do, I've still gotta get past the roadhouse. Have they got guns? How else could they have done what they've done? Those poor old bastards. I'm sure at least one of them is still in that room. Should I try going around, through the scrub or wait it out and move at night. It'll be a long bloody day, and what if they come looking. Maybe I should just head back up the road a bit and then come back in the dark. But they'd be waiting for me. That room, the coppery smell of blood. It's like it's worse than the little girl on the plane. But how, I didn't see anything. It was those bloody knives. Bastards. And there's one of them still there. At least one. I'm sure I heard it. Sounded like a woman.

He was still squatting when he heard the jet approaching. It must have been following the highway. It came low, he saw it clearly, could see the pilot. He didn't recognise the airforce roundels on the fuselage. He jumped up and waved frantically. Not really sure why. It passed by in an instant, the noise taking minutes to fade away into nothing. He looked into the east, the direction it had gone, not able to see it, watching the sound. He snapped from his reverie and picked up his bike and made his way back towards the highway, thinking about what he'd seen.

But then he heard voices. They were coming from the black-top. He dropped the bike and lay down behind some salt-bush. He could see snatches of the highway through the branches. It wasn't far but the saltbush was thick. Flies buzzed his face. And then he saw them. Two men, older men, walking the edge of the road. One was carrying a rifle.

He watched the men move up the road. Could hear the murmur of their conversation but not what they said. They didn't go far, just couldn't see them. He left the bike and half-crawled-half-crouched back the way he'd come. He moved quickly, knew he wouldn't have much time. He cut through the side of the camping area, a shorter route and ran across the dry surface to the accommodation block. He couldn't see anyone. He ran to the door of the accommodation block, the one next to the slaughter room. He didn't hesitate, driving his shoulder into it. He heard the crackling of stressed wood, felt the door move marginally. He stepped back and hit it again, it gave this time, swinging open, smashing violently into the door stop attached to the wall behind it. He stepped into the gloom. It took a second or two, heard her before he saw her, lying there on the bed, bound hand and foot, gagged.

He didn't think much about what he was doing. He attacked the ropes that bound her hands. While he worked on the rope on her feet she pulled away the gag.

—Thank you. Thank you, sobbed the voice.

—Shhhh. He didn't even stop to look at her, kept tugging at the ropes. We need to move. They'll be back soon. He freed her feet and helped her up. What was he going to do with her. It was only now that he thought about it. He led her to the door and pointed to the scrub.

—Quick, move that way. I'm going to try and find some water. He saw that her feet were bare. Do you have shoes in your caravan? Get them and some clothing, a hat. Be quick keep moving to the scrub and hide.

She moved off, unsteady on her legs. He went back into the room. There was a half-full bottle of water beside the bed, he grabbed that and headed out towards the shower block. The 'blokes' side of the block was open. Relief flooded through him, he ran inside and filled the bottles in his backpack from a tap, the water running slowly, listening intently for any sounds.

He moved outside, darting his head quickly to check if he could see anyone. He paused. And then made a decision. He went left at a run, across the gap between the buildings to the rear door where he'd seen the man the first time. The door was open. It was as he hoped, a kitchen, a commercial kitchen that serviced the roadhouse restaurant. He saw no one, could hear no one. A huge silver pot sat bubbling on a low heat on the gas stove. Otherwise the kitchen was spotless. Huge expanses of stainless steel, empty and clean shone in the light that the sun sent through the eastern windows. He found the pantry through a door off to the side. He grabbed at the few tins that stood on the shelves, shoving them into his pack. He heard voices coming from the front of the building. Male and female voices. He sprinted across the kitchen and then out and along the wall past the men's shower room and past the back of the accommodation block. He ran to the corner and looked out across the camping area. Nothing moved. So he ran. He saw his walking stick leaning on the van and snatching it up as he ran past. He felt something tug at his backpack before he heard the shot, felt the warmth running down his back.

Tattoo kept moving as fast as she could, beating her way through the scrub, the saltbush rubbing along her legs. She prayed she'd done enough to lose them. She knew they'd come looking for her once they finished with the miner. She turned hard left, her reasoning that this would have her heading back the way she had come, back towards the train, to the east, back to safety.

She walked for an hour and then turned left again, knowing this should bring her back to the railway line, hopefully not too far from the train. She'd heard no more of the dingoes. Her panic had subsided.

She walked for hours before stopping to rest. She felt the panic rise again. She knew she was lost. Had no idea which way to go. She told herself to calm down, that she'd wait for the sun to come up and then she'd be fine. She just had to head north and then she'd hit the rail line eventually.

The Kalamazoo clattered into the siding a few minutes after midnight. They'd left the goods train in the late afternoon, not wanting to delay any longer. The Captain knew that the final part of the journey shouldn't take long and that they'd likely arrive in the middle of the night but that was okay. He just wanted to get there, as did the others.

The Captain knew the siding, had stopped there a couple of times in the past, usually to let another train past, pulling off onto a spur line. He'd never had time to go more than a short distance from his train. He'd occasionally share a word or two with the family who lived here, often chatting with the children, who were always excited to have someone new to speak with. He'd let them climb up into his cab and sound the massive air horn. They'd watch the other train thunder past on the main line and then he'd say his farewells, waving as he released the brakes and pushed the throttle control lever into the first notch, a thousand tons moving forward slowly back onto the main line. He'd get the all-clear over the radio from the father and then he'd increase his speed and leave them to their lonely existence.

So it was a new experience for him to walk among the buildings. The group was giggly as they moved towards the shop. They'd made it. They all felt it. Even the Matron was happy. They talked quietly as they walked, the darkness and lateness of the hour making them feel like trespassers. A couple of kangaroos hopped away in the scrub, spooked by the group's approach.

The man rapped on the door of the shop, twisting the knob and pushing it open. It was the twin they saw first, coming out from behind the counter rubbing the sleep from his eyes. Seeing him, Matron quickly lost any sense of joy that they'd achieved something, had survived.

The man followed him out from the door behind the counter, along with another short, older man. The man made the introductions. Matron could see the twin swivelling his gaze among the group. He looked back at Matron. There was no concern on his face. She could see that it didn't occur to him that anything was amiss. That there was a rational explanation.

When she told him it was like she had sucked the life from him in an instant. Later she thought of that science experiment where you heat a sealed can and then cool it. How it seemingly buckles from the inside. The exterior pulling in towards the centre. That's what she saw.

She and the man lead the twin away, outside. The Captain followed. The four of them sat on the verandah and told the story of what had befallen them before they left. The Matron talked about his heroism, his brother's and the manager's. That they'd given their lives for the others. The tears rolled down the Matron's check as she talked. She sniffed them away several times but was determined to finish her story.

It was quiet in the end. When the Matron was done no-one spoke. The sliver of moon sat high above them, at it's zenith for the night, throwing a dull light over the scene. The four sat there for some time until the twin rose and walked out into the night.

The group were shown to the quarters, the others waking with their arrival. Izzy ran forward with a cry when she saw the Matron, knocking the portly woman backwards a step or two in her enthusiasm to take her in a hug. The story was repeated. The room was quiet, the details digested. The man suggested they convene the next day to talk about what should happen next and that they should get some sleep.

The miner careened into the scrub, expecting at any moment to feel the pain of the bullet wound in his back. But he was able to keep running. He could feel the dampness on the back of his legs but couldn't stop. He knew he had to keep going. The thought of what awaited him if he didn't, drove him on. The image of those knives.

—Where are you, he yelled as he moved deeper into the bush. He almost knocked her down. She was directly in the path he'd taken. He grabbed her hand and reefed. Quick, we need to keep moving.

He wondered which way to go. East, back to the bike but then potentially trapped again, or west without the bike. Would it be of any use to two of them? But if he was seriously wounded. He'd been

221

dragging the woman's arm, pulling her behind him, heading deeper into the bush. He stopped, pulling her down.

He reached a hand behind him trailing his fingers along the back of his legs. I've been shot. He still couldn't feel the pain but knew that it was likely adrenalin keeping him moving. He brought his hand up to show her. It was more orange than red. He could smell it now. More sweet than the coppery smell of blood. Tomato soup, he said out loud. The can in his backpack. He laughed, so did the woman. He pointed her to the west, a tree in the distance they could see. He told her to go there, that he needed to get his bike, that he'd meet her there.

It was the first chance he'd had to look at her. She wasn't as old as he'd first thought. She didn't want to leave him but he knew he'd do better getting the bike alone. He forced her to go, her west, him east.

He worked his way back through the scrub. Stopping and listening frequently. They'd know by now what he'd done. They'd re-double their efforts to find the pair of them. So he moved quickly but with care. He overshot the bike, had gone too far east. He had to come out of the scrub near the black top to regain his bearings. He moved back into the bush and then cut back towards the roadhouse. He was relieved to see the bike was still there. But now he'd have to move it through the scrub, making a lot more noise than before.

He thought about it, thought about the risk and then scurried across the highway pushing the bike, hoping that no-one was watching in that instant. He squatted in the scrub on the other side, waiting and listening. Could feel his rapidly beating heart. He heard nothing other than the plaintive cry of a crow somewhere off to his left.

He moved deeper into the scrub and then turned right, saltbush branches catching in the wheels and the handlebars of his machine.

He lay the bike down at one point needing to head back towards the road to confirm his bearings. He was directly opposite the roadhouse. He lay and watched it for a time, peering from his stomach through the low scrub, his walking stick at his side. He could see a man sitting in a chair in the shade of the roof covering the fuel pumps. A woman came out of the roadhouse at one point and handed him a bottle and went back inside again.

The miner moved back carefully on all fours before rising. He found the bike and then kept moving to the west. He'd had to come back to the road several times to check his bearing before he eventually go to the point opposite the tree. He moved the bike closer to the road then crept forward to where he could see the black top and look across to the other side. He could make out the water tower of the roadhouse to his right. The road was empty, so he took the chance to run across, his walking stick in one hand. He could see what he thought was the tree that he had identified. He moved forward, his backpack catching on the bushes from time to time, pushing away at the saltbush with the walking stick.

She sat in a squat at the base of the tree, eyes darting. She'd obviously heard his approach. Was ready to cut and run. That was a good sign. She smiled when she saw him, moving forward and taking him in a hug.

—Thank you. I thought you'd gone.

—That's okay. He squeezed back. His voice sounded oddly alien to him. He realised he'd not spoken to anyone for many days, since he was at the caravans with the old people. Come on, let's get out of here. They moved back to the road and then crossed. He retrieved the bike. He looked back along the highway towards the roadhouse. It was hot now, the sun well up. The mirage danced, the roadhouse shimmering in the distance.

He offered the woman his water bottle from the bike. She gratefully accepted, slugging down long guzzles.

—You'll have to sit on the rear carrier.

—It's been a while.

He laughed. Me as well.

He took off his backpack, handing it to the woman. You'll need to wear it. It'll be in the way if I do.

He stepped over the bar and straightened up the bike. She clambered on. The front wheel wanted to rise off the ground. He pushed down on the bars and then rolled forward stepping up on to the pedals. It was shaky but there were off. The woman laughed behind him.

—We'll just get away a bit, he said. A bit of distance and then we'll stop in the shade somewhere and sit out the heat.

Tattoo woke with a start of fear. She thought the dingoes had found her, didn't know if it was a dream or whether she'd just woken in that state where you didn't know where you were. She couldn't remember a dream. The sun was still hidden but the sky was getting lighter. But not in the direction she had expected. No matter she thought. She took a long pull on one of the water bottles, and sat and watched the light flood through the saltbush.

The mood of the train had changed. More had died in the night. The living were confused. The word had been passed around that the leaders had gone, the Matron, the Captain, Tattoo, the soldier. Some had been killed. Rumour suggested that the manager was one of them. They'd heard the gunshots.

The deaths in the night were mostly among the old. Many had not had water for more than two days. They lay in the dining car on putrid mattresses stained with piss and shit, or lay in their cabins, the expensive ones at the front of the train, the ones with their own en suites and wood panelling.

There was no more conversation, they were too tired to speak. Tongues were too thick, throats too parched and lips too dry. Some lay with dead husbands or wives. The smell inside the carriages was thick and heavy, the odour cloying. The last body to be tipped outside the train, a man who had lost his wife days before, had been pushed out the door falling down the rail-bed embankment. The dingoes had come in to feed in the night. Right there in the rail bed. The people forced to listen for hours. The growling and snarling of the wild dogs as they fought over pieces, the rending of flesh and the crunching of bone.

The dingoes had ignored any effort to chase them away, turning and snarling, no longer fearing the passengers. It had ended badly for the last person to leave the train. A young woman, one of Tattoo's group, from the crew. She'd gone into the bush in the early morning to relieve herself and had not come back. There was no doubt what had happened, everyone left alive on the train could hear the screams. They went on for a long time.

The water was hoarded in the second dining car guarded by the remainder of Tattoo's group. They watched the old man approach. He shuffled on bare feet, barely having the strength to drag them along the corridor. The group sat around the dining car. It was midday, the heat was fierce, the smell rank. Death wafted in through the windows. Those that could still shit or piss did it in a bucket, maybe tipping the contents out through one of the missing windows. The dingoes waited for it.

The old man came on. It seemed a long time from when they first spotted him to when he arrived. His steel-grey hair was greasy

225

and lank, hanging away from his head in places. His eyes had almost disappeared inside the sockets. His spine was curved. He wore blue-striped pyjama pants and a white singlet. The flesh hung loosely from the back of his arms.

The group watched him. They sat torpid, transfixed. He placed a liver-spotted hand on the banquette table in front of two of the group. He looked down at them, his breathing hoarse, raspy. His lips wobbled from side to side as he tried to form words but no sound came out. The young man sitting at the banquette undid the lid from a water bottle and pushed it across the table to him. The old man's hands shook as he tried to grasp it, threatening to knock the bottle over. He pulled back from it and then gathering himself tried again. But any control over his hands seemed to have left him. The young man slid from the banquette, took up the bottle and raised it to the old man's lips. He tried to tip it gently but invariably any amount was going to choke the old man. He coughed, the water sprayed. The younger man was patient. He waited for the paroxysm to pass and then tried again. It happened two more times before the old man was able to hold any down.

A croaked thank-you came out of his mouth, before he turned back towards the front of the train. The young man watched him and then gathered up several of the remaining few water bottles and followed him. The others watched through haunted eyes. There was no disagreement or affirmation. They just watched as he followed the old man along the corridor.

And as they walked along the train the dingoes hugged the shade on the south side to see out the worst of the afternoon heat. They were healthy and well-fed. Only one lay dead. He lay in his hole in the sand of the culvert beneath the train line a short distance to the west.

22

She walked before the sun had breached the eastern horizon. She figured her east and then used that to guess where north must lie. She could feel the fatigue already. Her legs heavy. Her throat was sore from the frantic breathing while she'd been running. She'd not run since she was a kid. She could smell the stale piss on her pants but it was no worse than the body odour that had been building over the previous weeks. It was the inside of her thighs that hurt the most. She'd looked at the red-raw skin while she squatted to pee, where her piss-soaked jeans had rubbed away the skin as she ran. She'd winced, cried, as she used some of her water to rinse the wounds.

But she was confident. Now that she had the sun she could get back to the railway line. She told herself this and tried to walk with purpose. She moved for hours, until the sun was approaching its zenith. She knew she should've been at the line way before now, knew that she'd gone wrong somehow. She was so tired. She tried to curl in under the saltbush, out of the brutal sun. Just a few minutes of cooling shade. She said it out loud, it came out as a sob. Please.

She'd drunk too much of the water. She knew that. But she figured she'd be back at the train by now. She lay for an hour or more.

Sleep evading her, the sun cruelling her all the while. She rose again, unsteady. Tried to take a small drink but guzzled too much. She looked at the sun in the western sky, swore at it. Took a bearing, pointing her arm, walking.

The soldier saw the darker shape of the goods train in the distance, a darker blackness within the blackness. He'd rested during the heat of the day in a culvert. He was pretty sure it'd been used by some of the others. The sand disturbed, holes dug for hips and mounds built for pillows. He'd headed off in the twilight, rested. He'd slept well, figured he should make the goods train some time in the night, maybe another ten hours of walking. He'd checked his water supply. Sipped at it, rinsed it around his mouth before swallowing. It wasn't a lot but he'd make it last. He was disciplined.

He approached the train with caution, ever the soldier. He had a round in the chamber, safety off. He moved past the engine and could see the open door of the goods wagon. He shone the beam of his torch around, saw the cardboard in the rail-bed, knew they'd gone on.

He squatted and thought about it. He'd rest, wait out the next day at the train and then make the final push tomorrow night. He was pretty sure it wasn't far. He'd surprise them in the middle of the night. He just didn't know what he'd do when he got there.

He'd killed the boy, the twin and that old bastard, the manager. Oh, and the other one, he'd shot off the wagon as they'd pulled away. He'd forgotten about that one. No, he wouldn't be well received. He'd have to do whatever it was by force. He wondered if he could work the hand-car by himself. How much effort did it require? Maybe take a prisoner, force them to help him. Could he make it work? Take two? Sit on the little wagon and make them work. Load it up with supplies and make a couple of them work. That was it.

The kangaroo stew was well received. They'd set up a table in the quarters, two old doors perched on fuel drums and found enough chairs for everyone to sit around. The table was too high and it drew laughs from the group as they nursed the bowls of kangaroo meat. They all sported a mug of sweet tea. There was even powdered milk for those wanting it white. The twin had risen early and lit another fire and cooked up several dampers, pieces of which the group were gleefully dipping into the dark brown gravy of the stew.

The twin flushed slightly under the approbation he received but remained quiet.

The Matron was glad to see that Izzy was engaging with the group. She knew that the Dutch woman had been her constant companion and was thankful to her for that. She looked around at the group, shaking her head in amazement. It was hard for her to get her head around what had happened to them and where they were. The atmosphere was convivial, the food good, the tea sweet and strong. But she knew that it wouldn't last. A temporary positive hiatus. They were a long way from anywhere. They would talk about it after the meal. What to do next. The answer was obvious. She couldn't imagine anything else. Some of them would go west on the hand-car, but who and how many?

She didn't know what would be better. Staying here in relative comfort and safety but at the mercy of the effort of others. And what if no-one came back for them. They wouldn't survive here forever, would she even want to do that. But then what of the journey west on the hand-car. How difficult would that be?

—Alright, here's how I see it. It was Ticky who spoke. The Captain was happy to let him lead on the discussion. He'd had several days at the siding to consider their options and he was confident in the man's ability.

—There's three options. We can go back to the train and bring others back. He raised a hand when he saw looks of concern. Look, it's an option, just not the favoured one from my perspective. I just think we should put it all on the table. So, we can go back and bring others. But I don't see how that can work. We know that they're armed and prepared to use force. So it wouldn't be worth the risk to the hand-car as I see it. Are we in agreement?

He looked around the group eliciting nods. Right, option two. We stay here and wait for rescue. Again, not the preferred option I feel. It's been this long and no-one has come. Our mining friends who headed south have not returned with help, so here we sit. We could survive a good while, but food, rather than water, is going to be the problem. So that brings us to option three. Some or all of us continue west on the hand-car.

He talked about the distances. The goods driver and the Captain both offered information in relation to this, agreeing, that based on hand-car speeds to date that it was a four day journey to the first town. The discussion then centred on who should go and who should stay.

—Do we just send the hand-car and not the wagon? It was Izzy who raised the matter.

Ticky paused in his thinking. It's a valid point. The hand-car on its own would be faster, but then it could only carry four at the most, and with limited space for supplies.

In the end it was agreed that six would go on the hand-car and wagon.

—Six to remain. Who wants to go and who wanted to stay? The group looked at each other with little commitment to the raising of hands or otherwise.

—Here's what I think, said the Captain. He looked at the twin. As valuable as you'd be on the hand-car I think you need to stay. Your skills will keep people alive here. The Captain immediately wished that he'd chosen his words more carefully.

The twin seemed not to notice, nodding his agreement with the suggestion.

—We'll go. It was the older of the four crew members. He wore the button-up work shirt with the crest of the train company.

—And I think either you or I should go, said Ticky, smiling at the Captain, but probably me. It's an age thing.

The Captain laughed.

—We need one more.

—I'll go. It was Izzy.

The Matron looked to the Dutch woman who shrugged her shoulders but said nothing.

—Okay, we're in agreement, said Ticky, looking around the group. Let's leave the departure for a day, leaving tomorrow evening, to give everyone a chance to rest and for us to put together the supplies.

The two train drivers were designated to check the hand-car over. With the help of the twin they tipped it over onto its side and went over every nut and bolt in the apparatus, greasing and tightening and checking every function. They agreed that it was a sturdy craft with very little required to ensure its ongoing operation.

A drum with a tap was found, cleaned and placed on the wagon. The group then shared the work of walking buckets of water from the storage tank to the hand-car.

In the evening the twin hunted again for a kangaroo, snaring another large female at the water trough, the result almost a mirror image of the first. But no joey this time. Ticky was with him again and could feel the young man's pain. He didn't bother trying to force conversation, learning from his experience with Izzy that his presence would be enough, that it wasn't necessary to fill the quiet with chatter. Ticky tried to help where he could. But knew that his presence was largely one of companionship.

There'd been nothing said between them until the kangaroo had been hung and they were walking back towards the quonset hut, when the twin uttered a quiet thanks.

The woman asked the miner to stop after half an hour.

—I'm sorry, it's really uncomfortable.

—That's okay, we can stop and have a rest.

They hadn't spoken much beyond introductions. The miner focused on ensuring they stayed upright and the woman alone with her thoughts. When she stepped off the machine she burst into tears. The miner wasn't sure what to do. He dropped the bike on the blacktop and reached out a hand to touch the woman's shoulder. She moved towards him, clasping him in a fierce hug. They stood that way for some minutes, the woman sniffling but not speaking. She pushed back away and looked into his face and smiled through red eyes and a running nose and thanked him.

They sat and she told him the story. How they'd stopped for the night. Just them and one other couple in the camping area. That the power had gone out but they'd not thought much of it until the next morning. Even the battery power had gone in the van. Nothing. She laughed, telling the miner of the few things in the freezer that they were worried about.

—Chicken thighs. That's what I was concerned about. I wanted to make a curry in a couple of days and here the damn things were, thawing on me. They'd quickly established that the car wouldn't start and then gone to their neighbour, an older couple. They had the same issues. They'd gone into the roadhouse. They had no power. Their generator had gone and the backup. It was much more serious for them. There was no telephone, nothing. They wouldn't even be able to pump fuel if anyone came through. That's what they were worried about. Chicken thighs for me and fuel for them.

The miner sat and listened. She seemed to alternate between grief and humour. He struggled to keep up. She told him it was okay for a few days but then the owners, there were four of them, two couples, had become less friendly as it dawned on them that something had gone drastically wrong.

—And no-one came. Yes, there'd been two jets fly over but that was it. Nothing. Into the second week they didn't want to share the water or food. Even though we offered to pay. And then they came in the night. She sobbed as she tried to explain it.

He missed a lot of it. But picked up how they'd been trussed and locked in the rooms, separate rooms. She'd had no thought of what was to come. Would never have entertained that someone could do that.

It was her partner who'd gone first. She could still hear her voice outside her room. Asking what was happening, why they'd been tied. And then the scream. She didn't think it was from pain, more from the realisation of what was to come. The woman collapsed into the earth, like she was trying to be a part of it, to escape. She sobbed for a long time. She sat up again.

—And then they took the others I think. At least one of them. It all became blurred after that. So hot in that room. Not much water and

233

no food. I thought that would kill me before they did. And then you came.

She rolled over and clutched his legs and sobbed.

They stayed in the shade of the trees until late afternoon, the miner forcing the woman to take sips of water. He knew she needed to hydrate after her ordeal but she was reluctant to take too much from his supply.

—Well, if you don't drink enough, you'll die. And that means any water I've given you until now will've been wasted. So you'd better drink what I tell you.

She smiled and took another sip.

They mounted the bike in the early twilight, the woman sitting on the folded blanket on the carrier. The miner wished he had a pump, with both of them on the bike the rear tire was looking squishy. Despite it, they made good time as the night moved over them. He pedalled steadily not pushing hard, the speed was down from what he'd been able to do by himself, but still much faster than walking.

He thought a couple of times about whether he'd done the right thing. Going back for her. That he might've signed his own death warrant by doing it. But he realised it was the only thing that had made sense to him throughout the whole deal, saving this woman.

It made him think about the murder he'd committed. Here he was, determined to rescue this woman, keeping her alive when he'd not hesitated for a moment to kill that bastard. He wondered whether he was trying somehow to balance out the equation. Saving one to make up for the one he'd killed. But he didn't think that was it.

He told her the story of the train. Such was her own trauma and grief that she'd not wondered how he'd come to this point. She didn't believe him in the beginning. Couldn't believe what had happened

234

aboard the train, couldn't believe that he'd traipsed across the desert. His friend dying from snakebite. Couldn't believe that the plane had fallen from the sky.

He didn't tell her about beating his friend to death. He smiled in the dark, thinking she might feel a trifle uncomfortable travelling with him after that. He told her that he'd wandered off while he was asleep and that he'd never seen him again. The woman seemed to accept it.

They stopped several times during the night. Even with the blanket the position was uncomfortable for the woman. She walked around when they paused, urging the blood flow back into her lower legs. The riding was good otherwise, the moon casting a dim but serviceable light into the highway swales stretching out before them.

They stopped at one point to watch five adult camels and two young ones cross the road in front of them. The woman commented that it was eerie, how they didn't seem to make any sound, that somehow she'd expected a clip-clop on the bitumen surface. They just seemed to float there in the half light of the waxing moon. Ethereal was the word the woman used. The miner rolled it around his mouth a couple of times like he was tasting wine. He liked the word.

The woman had been driving west so neither she nor the miner had much of an idea of when the first town might appear. There'd been a road sign near the roadhouse but when they'd emerged from the scrub onto the highway it lay behind them, back towards the roadhouse, and there'd not been another one since. The miner figured it would be at least another couple of days. There might be another roadhouse. But he almost hoped there wasn't.

The soldier was tired. The effort had caught up with him. And his water stock was low. But he knew there couldn't be far to go. And then there it was. He saw the shape of buildings from a long way out. The skinny moon caught the whiteness of a wall, a dull sheen, but visible from a distance. His demeanour changed immediately. Gone was the slouch and the tiredness. A surge of adrenalin set him up for the arrival.

He kept to the service road, all the buildings on his right hand. The first thing he came to was the hand-car, sitting alone on the tracks. He walked up to it. He'd only seen it in the distance, shooting at it. Hitting the bloke cranking on the side closest to him. He'd fallen between the rails that one. He was still alive when he'd had stood over him, breathing heavily, his chase of the hand-car finished. He'd left him there, to go back and get his supplies. He wasn't moving when the soldier had returned.

He thought about it now, wondered whether he should feel something. But didn't. Kill or be killed. Or end up dead at least, he thought.

He walked past the hand-car to the wagon, laying down the shotgun and opening the tap of the barrel sitting on the bed. Water came out. They're getting ready to go. Must be tomorrow, they wouldn't bother leaving the water there otherwise. He filled his bottles, took a long drink from one and then refilled it.

I could go now. He checked his watch. After two. I need some chow. No idea how far it would be. Two, three, four days. I'd need food. He stood, staring at the hand-car.

She tripped on the embankment of the rail bed without realising what it was. She collapsed into the blue metal, the dry stones crunching together beneath her like she'd fallen into a giant bowl of cereal, the thick layer cushioning the fall. She'd fallen many times in the last couple of hours. Had almost stayed down the last few times, the stingy shade of the saltbush almost enough. But then she'd rise again. She'd finished the water in the middle of the day and kept walking through the heat of the afternoon. She tried to stay to the right of the sun. It had to be north, she wasn't stupid. So where was the rail line?

It was dark now, early evening, the moon sliver visible, low in the eastern sky. She pulled herself through the stones, up the embankment. She knew where she was now. She cried when her hand touched the smoothness and coolness of the burnished rail. She laid her cheek on it. So wonderfully cool.

The dingoes prowled outside the train, day and night, around and around, the soft pads of their paws soundless against the chalky loam of the dry, hard earth. There seemed to be hundreds now. That's what the passengers thought. It wasn't so. Just that the constant movement made it seem that way. The dingoes would stop only briefly to peer up into the empty window holes, time enough to send a shiver of fear into anyone who may have been looking out at that moment to see the menace of the almond eyes and the perpetual grin.

To an outsider, someone who had just happened on the scene, the ever-present half grin of the native dogs and their proximity would have made them seem friendly, tame. That the dingoes were approachable. Like the travel spots in the north where stupid tourists might end up on the local news, paying the price for the too-close selfie.

And that'd probably been the case for most on the train while they had rolled along in air-conditioned comfort pushing a finger excitedly against the glass, yelling at a partner to come and see the

237

wild native dog. But now those views had changed. The passengers saw the half grin as menace, evil, knew themselves to be the prey.

It was the white dingo which made the first foray up the stairs. They'd finished the corpse that had been tipped out of the train, down the side of the rail-bed. The feeding frenzy had haunted every surviving passenger for hours. But the dogs knew there was much more to be had inside the train. The smell of death all-pervading.

The big dog moved around, sniffing looking, whining, pissing, snapping at others. But he kept coming back to the steps of the second dining car, glancing up. He'd watched people go in there, could see them occasionally inside the dark hole of a window. And could smell them. Could smell the corpses at least, but it didn't matter to the dog. Alive or dead they were the same now. They'd run down the woman in the scrub, torn her to pieces. Carrion or not, it was all food now.

In the end he turned, seemingly feinting his intention to move on, cutting back at the last and darting up the steps. The door was open. No-one had given thought that this was a possibility. They were busy dying or trying not to.

The remnants of Tattoo's group were in the dining car. Some lay on the putrid mattresses, the flies black on their faces, moving from the orifices of corpses, through the piles of human waste alongside the train and back to the barely living. Some sat in the banquettes, upper bodies splayed across a table top. Spread like a spilled glass of water ready to run off onto the floor. They were all filthy. There'd been no personal hygiene for days. But the smell of unwashed bodies was nothing compared with the cloying, fetid odour of the dead that wafted the aisles.

Things had changed. The aggression and anger had long gone.

Hadn't even dissipated, had just disappeared with the departure of Tattoo and the soldier.

One of the crew took the last sip of his tepid water. He knew that maybe there were a few sips on the whole train. Someone would have a bit left somewhere. He could smell the smell from the top of the water bottles. The smell of uncleaned teeth, rank breath, food bits. All stuck around the neck of the bottle. He had a thing about it. He'd not drunk from anyone else's bottle on the whole trip. And when he'd seen someone drink from his bottle, back when there was water, he swapped his bottle out, discarded the other. He wondered if anyone on the train knew this about him. It made him smile into his arms, his head tilted sideways on the table top, peering towards the blackened backs of the window blinds.

He saw the flash of white from the corner of his eye. Such was the incongruity with the drab, dirty surrounds, and even in his semi-deliriousness, it was enough to make his head turn. Then he stood, coming bolt upright. He and the big dog looked at each other, the gap between them small, enough room for a mattress and a body on top of it. The dog turned his head slightly to the side, a look of mild curiosity, the grin set. Nothing changed outwardly that the man could see, that might've given any indication of what the big dog was going to do. The man just stood there. It wasn't that he didn't believe what he was seeing, more that the big dog seemed to be holding him trance-like. He snapped from it when the dingo lunged. The miner's head shot up in surprise, and then he was down on his back, the dingo snapping at his face and neck. The man could feel the teeth worrying at his flesh but he had nothing to offer. Others yelled and screamed but no-one came close. People ran to other carriages. No-one helped.

The activity was enough to bring other dogs, soon there were four or five, tearing at the man. He never uttered a sound.

239

Tattoo found the strength to climb to her feet. She turned west and began a stumbling walk. Her strength may have been enough to take her back to the train. Had she looked at the bare earth of the service road when she crossed it, she would have seen sign of people passing on foot. Had she been thinking clearly she would have realised that she'd passed the train and was now heading away from it in their wake.

She lay down for the last time somewhere approaching midnight, her head on the burnished rail, like a pillow. The night was clear. Orion the hunter moved across the sky, his faithful dogs in his wake, the Southern Cross pointing the way south.

23

The woman cried in the night and he held her. They'd ridden for many hours. He knew that she was in agony. Her arse and legs. She could barely stand when he helped her off the bike's carrier. He said it was enough for the night. That they'd sleep. She'd laid down beside him on the blanket in the wide semi-circular table drain beside the black-top. The dry spinifex had crushed down under the blanket and made for a softer mattress than the bare ground.

He'd fallen into a deep sleep almost instantly. Her quiet sobbing woke him. The moon was low in the western sky. It was close to morning. He could tell that now. An hour or more. There was no tell-tale rosiness yet in the eastern sky.

He pulled her close. She rolled onto his outstretched arm and he closed it over her drawing her in, her back to him. He put his other arm over the top and lay there, saying nothing while she sobbed, the tears rolling off her cheeks onto the blanket.

He knew he had to wait until morning, to see who was here and where they were living. Stumbling about in the dark would only get him into trouble, even though he had a gun. What if they had another one? He hadn't thought of that.

So he crossed the rail bed, past the hand-car, and lay down in the saltbush, grabbing snatches of sleep but with the flies waking him, that and his nerves. They were up and about early. At least eight of them he thought, maybe more. Hard to tell from here. They were using two of the buildings that he could see. The store-front and the old hut. He saw the old Matron and the driver—the Captain he'd heard him being called—and others he recognised. And then there was the twin. He knew there'd be trouble there. Even if he could somehow get a reprieve from the others he knew there'd be no way the twin would not want to attack him. No, seeing the twin made him realise that he needed to go, and take some people with him. It'd be under guard initially. He wondered whether there were any that would be more likely to come around to his way of thinking.

There were a couple from the crew. He saw them. They'd be the best ones. They wouldn't be close to the others, not like the Matron, the driver, the other guy, the dutchies. And then there was the barmaid. She'd be no good. He knew about the rape. She'd be a mess, wouldn't be much use. No, a couple of the crew would be best. He could make that work, could probably make them see sense in it after a time.

He decided to wait and watch for the day. Let them make their preparations. He was patient. It wouldn't be comfortable, here in the scrub. But he'd done it before. Waited, hidden, for long hours. Not so long ago. But he'd not had a chance to do it for real, in the field. He liked the idea of being a bad-arse in one of the special ops regiments. He'd thought about trying out for it. Reckoned he had the goods for it. Maybe after this. He wondered whether that option was still there for him. He hadn't thought much about what had happened, what lay at the root of all this. But he knew it couldn't be good. Whatever, his skills would be in demand in any outcome. He just needed to get out of this place. That was his focus.

So he'd wait. Let them make their preparations to go. If he came out now, he reasoned, he'd need to be on his guard for the whole day. It'd give them a chance to do something. But if I wait I can just come out when they're ready to go, and take over and not give them a chance to organise anything. That's the smart thing to do.

He pulled back away from the hand-car, into the shade of a stand of acacia trees. He'd be able to see the people coming and going.

They're all happy. Happy to be here. Happy to be alive I guess. Survived what went on at the train. Made the journey here. Probably the biggest adventure in their lives, for most. Pushed aside for now, the death and the carnage. Maybe not everyone. I can see it in the twin's face. The loss of his brother. I guess for a twin it's like losing a part of yourself, a limb. That you'll never be whole again.

I'm not sure about the young woman, Izzy. I don't imagine one ever gets over that kind of thing either. But she has a steely core that one. I can tell. It's like she refuses to let it beat her. Day by day I can see the return of her spark. I imagine it will haunt her but I can see her using it. Using it to make herself stronger.

But the others, it's almost festive. Even the Matron. A night's sleep on a full stomach and waking up to hot, sweet tea and some of that bread that the twin made. What did he call it, damper. We're simple creatures at heart. For all our desire to build and consume, when it comes down to it all we want and need is friendship, somewhere to sleep and a full stomach. It's a shame it takes this kind of scenario for us to realise it.

I wonder how long it will last. The ones that go will know first. Know what's out there. I can tell them now, it's not worth going to. They might as well stay here, see it out in this unique environment. As good a place as any. We can decide when it's been enough, we don't have to wait until the end.

It was broken long before now. Maybe it had never been fixed, that since we first stepped from a cave and picked up a weapon we were on a trajectory to self-destruction, annihilation. The die had been cast. We just didn't know it.

Ticky oversaw the preparations. The water tank was full and the food was packed. They loaded most of what remained of the tinned fare. It didn't leave a lot for those staying behind. A few other tins and the big bags of rice and pasta. It really puts the pressure on us to hunt, he thought. We really need those kangaroos around. If they go we're in trouble. Let's hope the twin can keep us in the style to which we're accustomed. Seems ridiculous when you think about how close we were to death from a lack of water and now its food. It's a shame we don't have that gun. It'd be so much easier to hunt.

The soldier tried not to sleep. Was frightened that they might load up and head off without him knowing. But the heat and the long hours of walking to get here made it impossible. He woke with a start in the middle of the day having not realised that he'd dropped off. He raised his head in a panic. But the hand-car was still there on the siding tracks, no-one around. He figured they would leave in the early evening, travelling at night, if they were smart. But he wasn't prepared to take the risk that they might leave earlier, so he tried to stay awake through the long afternoon.

The Matron was feeling relaxed. Enjoying the relative comfort and safety of the siding. But then her thoughts would shift to those left behind. So many would be dead now. All the older folks she thought. None of them had any water left when she'd gone. Many wouldn't have survived that day. And those that did would certainly not have survived the next. There had been no point going back, she realised that. The only people alive would be the ones that would make trouble for them. The tattooed monster, the soldier, the other miners. They couldn't risk it.

She kept an eye on Izzy and the twin. Her two patients as she saw it. She'd seen to the man's hands each day. The broken skin had healed without infection. She thought they'd be fine during his journey west. Especially now that he'd found gloves to wear.

No it was the twin she worried about most. The young woman was stoic. That was the only word for it. She'd talked openly to the Matron about what had happened. She'd shed tears but mostly it was anger. The Matron was no psychologist but she thought that her mental state was as healthy as could be expected. She wasn't convinced that leaving on the hand-car was a great idea, heading away from the support of her and the Dutch woman. But maybe she needed the focus of the journey.

The twin was another matter. He'd never been overly communicative, she thought, but she could see it in his face, when he was around, that his world had collapsed. She thought that the journey would be a logical thing for him. Like the young woman, something to focus on. But they really needed him here. It was selfish, she thought. But they'd made no bones about telling him. His skills were needed if the rest of them were to survive for any length of time.

She smiled when she thought about the Captain. Her friend. They really had become inseparable. She could see it on the faces of the others. The Dutch woman had even made a subtle comment about

245

it when they were alone together. She didn't bother explaining. She didn't care. And it would sound lame. We're just friends. Or, oh no, I'm a lesbian.

She'd had relationships with men. But not for many years. It'd been a long slow road for her to accept who she was, what she was. She'd grown into womanhood in an era when it was far from accepted. She was thankful that she'd not had to tell her mother. It would have driven them apart. And while the pain of waiting for so many years had been terrible, once it happened it didn't seem to matter. And what residual bitterness might have remained was washed away when she met her. There'd only been one woman in her life. Yes, she'd had to wait a long time for it but she never believed for one moment that it had not been worth it. Even when she was with her, lay down next to her, that final time in their bed, holding her hand, listening to her soft breaths, it had all been worth it.

And now she had to survive. She thought about that as well. What was she going back to? Who knew what was there? What had happened? It had to be bad to put them in the position they were in. Then why am I so desperate and so happy to survive? Human nature I suppose. Those old survival instincts.

The dingoes were manic. Feeding in the closed environment of the carriages meant that they were close together, no running off to eat unless they were prepared to run back down the steps.

And more had come. The smells had floated across the desert to farther reaches, inviting more and more, some from the crashed plane. The old people at the front of the train were now all dead. The handful that hadn't died of thirst had given themselves up to the pack. The last to go was the old man in his white singlet and blue-striped pyjama pants. He'd survived longer because of the water that the young miner had given him.

When the dogs had come for him he'd backed up into the corner of his bunk, sobbing. The dogs had hesitated in the closed setting. He hadn't tried to fight them, he'd just sobbed. His knees drawn up, the tears wetting the filthy material of his pyjama pants. But then they'd come. It was the white dog. He came in behind those that were hesitating, charging in, clamping and tearing at the wrinkled throat. The old man died about as quickly as one could reasonably expect.

The others, the handful, were locked inside the second dining car. There were only a dozen or so. They lay quiet, the screams, the snarling of the dingoes, the crunching and tearing of bone, long a part of their environment. And when the last screams had died away they knew that they were the only survivors. A day maybe, and then that would be it.

The woman was adjusting to her position on the rear carrier. She was able to go for longer and longer periods without stopping. They'd ridden past a handful of cars and trucks. They'd found bodies. Some next to vehicles, some along the road where they'd dropped and were picked over by the birds, or worse, torn at by the dingoes. At one they'd found a huge goanna, all yellow and black stripes, tearing at the flesh of one corpse. It had scurried off but not until they were close. It had clearly been feeding for some time. It's crab-like gait slow as it lumbered into the nearby scrub.

The miner stopped when they approached the signpost. The town was close. Closer than he'd realised. No more roadhouses. They'd talked a bit about what they might find when they made it to somewhere. But it'd seemed a bit abstract to the miner. But now it was real. The sign made it real and suddenly he wondered about whether he wanted to get there.

But he knew they had to. The water was almost gone, just a single bottle, sitting in the holder on the bike, and only half full. They'd been sensible. When the water level had become a concern they'd started riding only in the cool hours of the night and early morning, but making good progress on the spongy tyres.

There were more signs as they drew closer. He wondered that there was still no sign of life. His passenger said as much. They could see buildings from a distance. A reservoir standing on a hill to the south of the town.

24

They'd forced the soldier's hand without realising it. He'd watched them, the pair moving down to the hand-car. It was Ticky and the twin. Stumbling under the weight of a box, dumping it next to the water barrel on the wagon. They stood for some time looking at the wagon, talking. The soldier could hear them but was too far away to make out what they were saying. It made him edgy.

And then the man climbed aboard the hand-car. The soldier watched as the twin bent down and shoved against the front of it to get it rolling and then jumped on board.

The soldier was panicked. He couldn't believe that there would only be two of them. It didn't make any sense. And where were the others? Why hadn't they come to farewell them. But he couldn't risk it. He rose from his hide.

Ticky asked the twin to help him to take the food box down to the wagon. They'd leave in an hour or so. He'd warned them against bringing anything much of a personal nature. They would take a couple of the foam mattresses and a few blankets to make themselves comfortable, but that would be all.

As it was Ticky was concerned about the weight of the whole rig. With six of them on board, along with the water and food, it was going to reduce their travelling speed. He'd wondered at the optimal numbers and thought that maybe too many people were going. But then, the more that stayed behind, the more that would need to be fed. There was no easy solution. And he knew changing the numbers now would upset people.

They dropped the food box onto the wagon.

—Let's take it for a spin and see how she handles.

The twin shoved and jumped up onto the platform as the little machine gathered momentum. They were going backwards on the spur line, heading east, the shortest distance to the main line, the wagon in front of them. The speed was slowly building when the man looked in disbelief as someone charged out of the scrub at them brandishing a gun.

—Righto, stop it there, the voice yelled at them, the twin turning at the sound of the voice.

Both men stared, not talking, releasing the handle, the little cart clanking to a stop within a short distance. No-one spoke for a moment. The soldier walked up into the rail-bed directly behind them. He gestured with the barrel and nodded his head to the side.

—Get off.

It was the twin who recovered first, his face twisting into a bitter rictus as he recognised the soldier.

—You fucking murderer.

—If you don't want the same then I'd recommend you get off.

The man could see the twin thinking about what he should do. He reached for his arm.

—Not now. Not now.

The twin released a long breath, his shoulders dropped. They stepped between the rails.

—Why only two of you going?

—We weren't. We were just testing the load.

That made sense to the soldier. He thought briefly that he could go now, but not with these two. No, these two would be staying behind.

—Right, let's head up to where the others are. He nodded the other way and gestured with the barrel of the gun.

—Did you come by yourself?

—Yep.

—Nice.

—Fuck off, you left us.

—Wonder why. The man knew his comments weren't helping but he couldn't stop himself.

They were down to their last few mouthfuls of water. They lay about, moribund, in the stifling heat. It took some time for one of them, a woman, to notice that the dingoes had gone. She'd grown used to the sounds of death around her. It'd been a day or more since the final screaming. That had been the worst. The last she could hear was faint. Somewhere towards the front of the train, the first car maybe. It was a man she could hear. The sound travelling as much along the side of the train, through the empty window holes, as along the corridor.

She'd once dared to look through the glass partition in the door, leading to the carriage entry area. It was like he knew, the big white one. He was sitting there staring up, that grin that they all had, that made them look friendly, happy. She was transfixed by the almond eyes, held his gaze, until he'd lunged at the glass. She'd screamed and fallen backwards, a warm squirt of piss running down her leg.

They'd sat through a day or more of feeding. She knew that the crunching of bones was something that would have stayed with her for the rest of her life. But she'd laughed at that thought. She knew her life was over. It was only a matter of a day or so at that point. It was a strange feeling. She'd cried a couple of times, mostly to herself. They'd all kept to themselves. She figured, like her, they were coming to terms with what was approaching, maybe having thoughts of family and partners. That's what she was doing.

But it was so quiet. Even when the dingoes rested she'd hear the occasional whine or growl. They were only outside the window. She used some of her precious energy to rise and move across to the empty hole where the glass had been. It was late afternoon, the train shadow was vast across the saltbush. She poked her head out, looking down the side of the carriage. She could see where they'd been laying around the edge of the rail-bed and the service road, the chewed segments of bone like autumn leaves on the ground. The loamy soil was dark where it had been disturbed by their movement. But they were gone. She stood for minutes, nothing. Not a dog anywhere.

She moved slowly to the door, a couple of others watching her, wondering at her effort. None of them had moved for hours. She thought they looked dead, eyes sunken, haunted. It was only when she pulled on the door handle that life flooded back.

—NO. It seemed to come from most of the others. Several shot to their feet. One man, a crew-member still in his rail-company shirt, ran towards her screaming as she tugged at the handle.

—They've gone.

—No, don't. They'll still be there. Waiting for us. The man was on the verge of tears, pleading. The woman had no patience for it. She hauled the door open and stepped into the breezeway, looking through the open door and out across the saltbush and into the desert beyond. She thought it looked beautiful, the ochre red of the sunset pushing through the low scrub. She'd not seen it look so lovely.

The man slammed the door behind her, looking at her through the glass, frantic. She gave a back-handed wave, dismissing him, and moved to the stairs. The effort of climbing down cost her. She stopped and sat on the bottom step, her feet resting in the blue metal of the rail bed.

She was mesmerised by the view. Like she was seeing it for the first time. She felt tired, bone weary. The smell of death had dissipated. The dingoes had been efficient she thought. She looked at the bones, but they looked innocent enough. Picked clean, gleaming almost, chewed into pieces they presented no more fear or loathing than the skeleton of a dead kangaroo or cow.

She wanted to walk. She wanted to get away from the train. Like it would somehow make her feel clean. Well maybe not clean but certainly it would take away the claustrophobia she felt. She stood on unsteady legs and slipped down the side of the rail-bed, happy to make it to the service road without falling. She turned to the west, chasing the dying rays of the sun, its warmth against her face. One foot in front of the other. She laughed at her faltering steps. It reminded her of crossing the sports oval in bare feet in the small town where she'd lived as a child. Watching out for the cat's eyes. She was surprised when she looked to her right and could no longer see the gleaming silver carriages. She stopped and looked back. The train was some way behind her. It made her smile. She came to a culvert running under the rail line. It looked like a quiet and comfortable place to rest. She stumbled down the incline, could see bones but they didn't trouble her. The sand in the bottom looked warm and inviting. She lay down and rolled onto her side pulling her legs to her chest and closed her eyes.

It was as if one of them, maybe the white dingo, called an end to it. A silent signal. They moved almost as one, rising from their afternoon slumber and then taking to the scent of the people who had gone west, following in that mile-eating trot.

25

The Captain had seen it happen. But it took some moments for him to figure out what he was looking at. He'd been about to walk down to the hand-car and see what the two men were up to, lend a hand for the final tasks before the others departed.

It was some distance but he could clearly see three men. It was the gun that filled the gaps in his understanding. He stepped back inside the building, quickly gathering and quieting the others. He knew they wouldn't have much time.

The man and the twin walked through the doorway into the accommodation building, looking across at the group sitting around the table. The soldier ushered them further into the room before he entered. The crew member, a man in his late thirties dropped from above the doorway. It wasn't perfect but it was enough to knock the soldier off his feet. The two train drivers moved quickly, before Ticky and the twin had any idea of what was happening, moving past them and into the melee behind. The gun fired, the pellets peppering small holes through the corrugated iron wall. The Captain swung the rolling pin he'd taken from among the kitchen implements, catching the soldier on the side of the head. The blow slowed him but he continued to struggle with the crew member. A second blow stilled him.

When he came around he found himself chained by the ankle to the water tank. The goods train driver sat at a distance on a chair, the shotgun across his lap.

The group waved and cheered as the Kalamazoo built up speed into the west. With the arrival of the soldier the departure was a little later than planned but Ticky saw no reason to delay departure. All the preparations had been made, it was time to go.

He'd taken the first shift and was facing east so he could see his friends growing smaller in the distance. He thought about the twin and the soldier. He'd chatted briefly with the Matron and the Captain about what to do with him. They couldn't very well take him with them. It was bound to cause trouble but having him remain at the siding would be a taunt for the twin, a constant reminder.

There was no solution. The group needed to go. So he left it to his friends, hugging them both before mounting the platform of the hand-car. The Matron and the Dutch woman cried along with Izzy. The Captain had to separate them in the end.

He stood back beside the Matron as they watched the odd little group disappearing into the desert twilight. The Matron took his hand on the walk back to the accommodation block.

The Captain was satisfied that the chain was safely and securely fixed to the soldier's leg. He saw no need for anyone to stand watch over him during the night. The soldier had remained quiet, saying nothing, ashamed that he'd been taken so easily. But he was prepared to wait for an opportunity. His biggest concern was the twin. He

256

realised his mistake when he admitted to killing the other one. He realised that if he'd been smarter he might have sown a seed of doubt that he had been the culprit. But as it was he was concerned about what the twin might do. He wouldn't blame him. He'd do the same.

The twin was mulling it over. The sight of his brother's killer sitting outside taunted him. He knew that killing him wouldn't help the way he felt, wouldn't bring his brother back. But to see him sitting out there, alive, when his brother was dead, it didn't seem right. He wondered what his father would do, or say.

When the soldier screamed the Captain woke, stumbling out of his bed onto the floor, confused, lost for a moment. The scream was so close it might have been at his bedside. He quickly realised that the twin had taken matters into his own hands.

Others were now awake. Questions flew. The Captain pulled on his pants, feeling around for his boots in the dark. All the while the screaming continued.

—Please everyone, stay in the room, he said. Let me deal with this. The Captain had taken the gun the night before, wanting to remove the temptation from the twin. His hand touched the cold steel of the barrel as he reached for it. All the while the man screamed, begged for help.

The Captain moved through the darkened room. Someone grabbed his arm.

—It's not me out there. It was the twin's voice.

The two moved together to the door. They could hear it before they opened the door, the snarling of the pack as they tore at the soldier, the chain clinking as they dragged him. The Captain shoved the door open. There was enough moon that the two men could see dogs running to and fro, working themselves into a frenzy. The white dog shone in the pale light. He was standing over the soldier. The soldier was quiet now. Some of the dogs turned at the sound of the door opening. The Captain fired into the air. The dogs scattered, running for the safety of the saltbush. The white dog paused. The Captain drew a bead. It was a long shot with a twelve gauge. The pellets spread but there were enough to pepper the big dog. He yelped, turning his head and snapping at his flank where a pellet bit like a scorpion sting.

He turned and ran after the others.

—Wait a sec, said the twin. He returned with a torch. He shone the beam towards the inert figure of the soldier and then around in an arc. They could see no dingoes, no eyes shining in the beam. The soldier was still alive. His throat was torn, it gurgled softly. Red blood bubbles formed in the torch light as he tried to speak. His face was a mess. One eye was gone and his nose and lips were torn. His shirt was open and his stomach bloodied. The soldier could form no words, he reached a hand out towards the two men and then it dropped into the bloodied dirt beside him.

They buried him immediately. The four men taking turns on the shovel, the torch beam swinging constantly on the look-out for the native dogs. Several times red eyes shone in the beam. A shot from the gun scattered them. The men returned to their beds to grab what little sleep they might before the sun rose.

The white dingo went from leader to prey in a short space of time. Several pellets had pierced his gut. It didn't take long for the contents of his stomach to poison him and less time for the pack to turn on him and choke the life out him.

With the white dog gone the pack began to disintegrate. Several dogs moved off immediately, heading back in different directions to the territories from which they'd come. One group went back towards the train into the east. Some stayed. The smell of humans enough to keep them there.

The travellers made slow but steady progress. They rotated through, someone new moving in every half hour, each person having a half hour on each side of the handle before several hours of rest. The wagon had been made comfortable. The foam mattresses meant that the four passengers could lay down and rest while the other two worked. They halted in the heat of the day. Ticky guided them into culverts to rest, chasing a huge sand goanna out of one and a gwardar out of another. He was satisfied with their progress. It might have been faster, he thought, but they were healthy and rested. They had a good system for water rationing and the food was enough for now.

He knew the town must only be another two days at the most. They had begun to discuss what they might find when they got there. The fact that no-one had been to look for them was something that they talked about. The man suggested, that because of this—the fact that no-one had come to help them—that they should temper their excitement about what they might find.

Izzy knew the town. She'd been there several times. It lay a day's drive from where she worked. It wasn't much of a place, she'd explained. A pub, a few shops, a supermarket, a service station, a few hundred people she reckoned. It was the final resting place before the desert. A place to top up your fuel and your supplies. The place where the train line and the highway separated if you were heading east.

The man wished they'd been able to bring the gun, but he realised that those staying behind needed it more. It would make the hunting much easier, there was no question that it would stay with them. But even so he worried for their safety. After what had happened on the train who knew what might confront them, where populations were larger. Maybe people would get together and be smarter. Organise themselves better. But he doubted it.

The Captain moved tentatively outside the next day, the shotgun poised, the others remaining inside the hut. He saw a couple of dingoes, but only in the distance, on the edge of the scrub. He moved towards them and they ran away.

He walked back towards the hut, past the chain laying on the ground, still padlocked to the leg of the water tank. Even with the dark colour of the links he could make out the black, dried blood around the end of the chain. And there was the patch of blood-stained soil. He kicked at the soil, turning it over. He took the key from his pocket and dragged the chain back into the shed. No-one needed to see that.

When he turned the twin was behind him. There was a moment of awkward silence.

—How do you feel?

—Not sure.

—Probably the best outcome, the Captain said.

—Probably.

26

This is what life should be about. Living simply. The bare essentials. It should be about people, not about things. Accumulation of wealth, needless technology. Look where that's taken us. We have what we need. We are all working together for the common good. Even the one who drove the goods train, he is helping, is finding his niche in the group. There is no hierarchy. We talk things through, make decisions as a group. Everyone has an opportunity to speak. It hasn't been organised this way. It has just happened. Where did we go wrong? Why could we not have evolved this way. I wonder if out there in the galaxy there is a parallel culture, the same species evolving along a similar time line in a similar environment. But that somehow they've taken this path, the path that we are on now. I do not wish to be found.

The miner pedalled slowly into the town.

—Where is everybody? asked his passenger.

He didn't respond, but indicated with his right hand, a small joke, turning across the street and into the driveway of the roadhouse. She laughed. He laughed. Neither had done so for as long as they could remember.

He put a foot down, stopping the bike in the forecourt, careful to take the weight. They'd already toppled on one occasion and almost on a couple of others. He felt a brief moment of panic thinking that riding in like this was foolish, given what he'd been through on the road. He wondered why he felt more secure here. Would people be more reasonable in a town? But they were here now, and no-one had shot them, not much point turning back.

June climbed off the rear carrier—that was her name, it had taken him a couple of days to realise that he didn't know what it was. She said she'd told him at the beginning, in the bush west of that other roadhouse, when she thought that he wasn't coming back. He didn't remember her telling him her name but then that didn't surprise him.

He leaned the bike against one of the petrol pumps and they walked towards the shop, the place to pay for fuel.

—Hey. Hey you two.

If he'd not thought about his previous experience the miner thought about it now. Another garage, another voice. But this time it wasn't from the garage, it came from behind them, across the street. A shout.

They both turned to the sound but neither could see where it was coming from.

—What do you want? The voice again. Authoritative.

The miner thought this an odd question. He looked at June as if for confirmation. Gave her the facial version of what-the-fuck, tightening of the neck muscles, the bottom lip pulled tight against the bottom row of teeth, eyebrows up.

—Some water, maybe some food.

—There's nothing for you here.

The voice was coming from the window of a cottage across the street. The window was open but it was darkness behind, a bit like his memory of the train. But he could see something, long, thin and black protruding over the old-fashioned sash.

—We've come a long way, said June. We're tired and have very little water left. What's happened, why is everything like this?

The pair could hear quiet discussion, more than one there.

—Can you tell us what's happened?

—What do you mean?

—Like, what's going on. We've been in the desert. I was on a train. June was driving. We met. He tried to summarise. He had so much he could say. It was like he'd just realised all the things that had happened. He wouldn't know where to begin.

—Nothing works.

He looked at June again. He tried to imagine what the speaker looked like. Short, a bit fat, a bit older than he was. That was as far as he got.

—Can we come and talk. He stepped towards the voice.

—Stop. Stay there.

He stopped. They were standing in the sun on the footpath. The sun, as ever, was fierce, and no cooling breeze from the speed of the bike.

—We just want to know what's going on. Here, and in the rest of the country, in the world. Fuck. Please. Just tell us.

Hushed conversation again. And then a door closing. But nothing to see.

—Just stay there for now.

—Can we move back into the shade.

A pause.

—Sure, go back to the garage, to your bike.

263

They walked into the shop. Ignoring the order. Nothing there. Shelves stripped of anything edible or drinkable. Fridge empty. Freezer a sea of ice-cream wrappers floating in their putrid ex-contents.

—I love Magnums.

June screwed-up her nose.

—Hey. It was the voice from the house.

—Stay where I can see you.

—Just looking for water.

—It's turned off, none there. Back where I can see you.

They sat on the plinth of concrete alongside the bowsers, both leaning forward between knees, waving flies away.

—What do we do if they won't let us stay, or give us water and food? We won't get much further, will we?

—Let's hope it doesn't come to that.

—Why won't they tell us what's happened?

The miner laughed. You keep asking me questions that I don't know the answer to.

June laughed as well. And then she took his arm and moved closer.

—I can't believe we're here. That we made it this far. I'd be dead now. She shivered as she said the last part. Thank you.

He squeezed her hand.

—You want to fuck me?

—What. His head shot up in surprise.

—You want to fuck me? I suddenly feel horny.

—I thought you and your friend, were like, lesbians.

—We were, are. But I like men too. And I want to fuck you now, while I feel like it. Who knows what's going to happen.

—This is nuts.

—Do you want to?

—Yes.

—Quick, come back in here.

—Where are you going? I told you to stay there. The voice from the window. They ignored it.

June grabbed the miner and kissed him. Their teeth bumped. She reached for the front of his jeans. He was already hard, she could feel it. She undid his belt and zip and reached in. He gasped.

—Quick. She pulled down her jeans and panties, stepping one foot out of them, grasping the edge of the freezer.

He moved behind her. She reached back and guided him. He almost finished with her touch, jumping like he'd been shocked. He plunged into her. Three thrusts and he groaned, pushing hard into her, holding it, legs straight, back arched. Her pleasure came as a squeal.

—Fuck, I can barely stand. Sorry it was so quick.

—That's okay. That's all I wanted.

She turned. She had tears streaming down her face.

—Shit, I'm sorry, I...

—No, it's okay. Stop. It's all fine. She touched his face with her fingers. Just find me something to clean myself with, it's running down my leg.

He pulled serviettes from the metal holder on the counter. He had an image of kids with melting ice-creams, parents plying the serviettes in the heat. She wiped between her legs and threw the wad in the corner, stepping back into her clothing.

—If I didn't need a wash before, I do now.

—I'll be better next time.

She punched his shoulder gently and smiled.

—Sport, who says there'll be a next time.

He didn't know quite what to make of that.

Then they could hear the muffled talk across the road again and walked outside.

—You two don't like listening. It was a different voice. Much older. Another man.

—Can you tell us what happened?

—Where are you from?

—What does it matter? He wondered whether the sex had emboldened him.

—Because we want to know, and because there'll be nothing for you if you don't tell us.

—Look—it was June—you've already said there's no water for us, so what's the point of telling you anything. Why are you wasting our time?

There was a pause, more hushed conversation.

—How do we know that you don't have the virus?

The miner and June looked at each other.

—What virus?

More quiet talk.

—Just tell us where you've come from.

—I was on a train, coming west. June was driving in a car. We were both stranded in the middle of the desert, met up on the highway, came here.

A pause while the pair inside the window talked.

—You're saying you rode here together on a bike?

—Yes.

—Are you well? Do you have a fever?

—Apart from being tired, hungry and thirsty, yes, we're pretty good, all things considered.

—But do you have a fever?

—No, the miner said, no fever.

—We don't know what you're talking about, said June. We don't know anything about a virus. We're not sick. Just worn-out and hungry.

More talking.

—Just wait there.

—Will you give us more water if we finish ours, we're very thirsty.

—Yes, we have water. Finish your water.

And they did. It was only half a bottle. Tepid, the top stinking of uncleaned teeth. It was the most either had consumed in a single sitting since they'd started riding.

—Feels a bit naughty. Drinking this much at once.

The miner laughed.

—Funny idea you have about naughty.

June laughed. And they drank the warm liquid sitting together in the shade of the roadhouse forecourt.

It was more than an hour later the woman approached them. They'd both fallen asleep. The flies on their faces not enough to keep them awake.

—Hello?

The miner woke with a start, wiping at the corner of his mouth. The woman was standing in the sun, at the entrance to the driveway. She was wearing a surgical mask and gown, her head covered in a skull cap, the type he assumed that went with the rest of the outfit.

—Hi, he said in return, June awake now as well.

—I want to take your temperature.

—Why?

—The virus. If you've got a temperature, we can't let you in. It's too much of a risk.

—Look, we have no idea what you people are talking about. We've come from the desert, we don't know anything about any fucking virus.

He wished straight away he hadn't sworn.

—Sorry, he said, meaning the swearing. We're just a bit frustrated. We survived so much and this feels, well… He let it hang.

The woman spoke as if she hadn't heard him.

—I need to take your temperature. I'm a nurse she added, taking a few steps forward.

As she drew closer the miner realised she was wearing gloves and safety goggles as well. She was now in the shade with them.

—We're taking a risk, even considering you. We've turned others… She stopped saying whatever she was going to say.

The miner decided not to pursue it, suddenly concerned that they could be turned away.

—Please turn to the side, and step away if you need to cough or sneeze. I'll just check your temperature in your ear.

She raised the device she was carrying. The miner recognised it as the same one his mother used, something from a chemist shop. It beeped and she pressed it lightly into June's ear, pulled it back on the next beep and repeated the process on the miner before stepping back.

—Please sit again.

They obeyed. She took the mask and googles from her face.

—Your temperatures are normal.

—That's good. But what now? asked the miner.

The woman arched her eyebrows. I don't know. I'll go and talk to them.

—Can you tell us what's happened, how did things get like this, why did my train stop?

268

The woman looked back towards the window and then back to the pair.

—A virus in the cities. That's all we know. Don't know where it came from. It spread quickly. The government did something. Pushed a button somewhere. Everything stopped. Everything. Planes, trains, cars, trucks, television, radio. The whole lot. We have an engineer in our group. She said it was some sort of pulse. Shut down all electronics. Instant. They wanted people to stop moving straight away. We don't know much. One of our people has a radio. He got it working again. It's our only link. He said he'd never heard the airways so quiet. He has a friend in Sydney. That's where we got our information from. But even that stopped a couple of days ago. We don't know what happened to him. He was talking to our friend and he was cut off. He just disappeared. But he said he'd been worried. He said Sydney was a mess. It seems so unbelievable. He talked about gangs, and fights over food and water. People killing and people just dying. Dead bodies. Lots and lots of dead bodies.

The miner watched as she began to cry. Despite tears she kept talking.

—I've got family in other places. I haven't heard from any of them.

—And here in the town, what's happening here?

Before she could answer a voice rang out, the same older voice from before.

—I have to go, she said scrambling to her feet.

—What about us now?

—That's not for me to say.

—This is ridiculous, said June. Can we get water and food at least?

—I'll ask.

—What's your name? the miner asked.

She didn't answer.

269

A few minutes later the voice called out.

—Stay there, we'll bring you water and food.

They walked through the restaurant. It was hotter inside the building, no point being in here. And there was nothing to eat or drink.

The man in the window was a hunter. His usual targets, pigs, donkeys, sometimes camels. Pests. He thought himself ethical. No native fauna, that was his rule. He'd drummed it into his kids. He was a logical choice for the role he'd been given. He took it seriously. He was under orders, that's how he viewed it. Didn't have a military background but felt comfortable under orders. It freed him.

He was kneeling—the gun stock resting on a pillow on the window sill—looking through the scope of his Remington. Watched the darkness of the restaurant doorway. It was the woman who appeared first in the cross hairs.

It was the other young woman on the hand-car, Dee, who saw the smoke first. She had the best eyes of the group. Ticky had said as much several times on their journey when she'd pointed out things they were passing. Things that no-one else had seen, and Ticky sometimes never saw. It was only that morning they'd stopped to admire a python. Ticky had been amazed how she'd seen it off in the rocks twenty eight metres away—he'd paced it. She also knew snakes, told them it was a Stymson's python, how it wasn't venomous, that they made good pets. He was horrified when she picked it up. She'd said they were sluggish in the mornings. That he—she said it was a male—was warming himself.

Ticky stood well back, but then relented, his curiosity getting the better of him, and moved forward to touch the scaly skin along with the others. Cool and smooth. They'd all laughed when Dee offered to let him hold it and he'd quickly moved away. His memory of that other snake, the Gwadir the twins had called it, was still fresh in his head, at least the part about how deadly it was.

She was so gentle with it, that's what impressed Ticky, letting it move around her arms and neck, no attempt at restraining the head of the thing. It was as if the snake knew she was no threat. He envied her the calmness she exuded, handling the thing. Izzy was the only one of the group to take up the offer of holding it. Ticky wanted to say no. Didn't want someone getting hurt. But had stopped himself, trusting Dee's judgement that it would be okay, realising that it was a good moment for them, breaking the monotony and tension around what it was they were doing.

It was only a few hours later Dee saw the smoke.

It was a single plume, narrow. It'd taken Ticky another quarter of an hour of travel to really see it. It reached high and straight, a thread of cotton connecting the heavens and the earth. That's what Ticky thought. Tenuous.

It was another hour before they came up on the town. The landscape had changed in the last half-day as they neared. There were more and taller trees—stands of stringy gums with smooth, fluted trunks. More bird life. It meant that they couldn't see as far ahead except along the line of the track. And that had changed as well. There were now bends in the tracks, no more straight lines for hours on end.

And then they saw the highway, coming in on the south side at an oblique angle, moving towards them like the sunrise through the saltbush. But once it was there, running along beside them, it was as if it had been there the whole time, a trusted companion. A fence of rusting barbed wire atop rusty sheep netting—stalks of dry grass weaving through—the only thing separating them. But no traffic. A couple of advertising signs extolling cheap fuel and another spruiking the fine fare of a cafe, told the travellers that they were close. That and the plume of smoke.

And then they saw the low buildings in the distance.

They'd eased their speed downwards to where it was barely above walking pace. Nobody spoke. But it was trepidation that curtailed the conversation, not excitement. Ticky nodded to Izzy. They released the handle and it moved up and down a couple of cycles before stopping.

The quiet after they stopped was always a shock to the travellers. They'd all referenced it at various times on the journey. The syncopated rhythm of the hand-car gears, clanking and grinding, the squeal of the small wheels not quite comfortable against the rails. And then nothing when it all stopped. The quiet of the desert. Maybe the scuttling of a startled goanna, or the dirge of a lone crow. But often nothing, maybe just a soft breeze rustling the dry grass.

They had grown accustomed to staying quiet for a time when they stopped. It had become something of an unspoken ritual. Often it was the movement of one of them that would break the silence. The rustle of jeans against the mattress on the wagon, a sniffle, or even a breath drawn. It was like the moment was gone, so talk would be permitted. Mostly it was Ticky who broke first. An observation about their position, or maybe the effort of a period of travel, or an opinion on the landscape. It made them smile at each other. But not this time. They stayed quiet for a long period. All of them looking towards the distant buildings, hands shielding eyes against a setting sun, smoke streaming into the air from somewhere in the town.

The whole town lay on the south side of the tracks, the rail line the barrier between bush and civilisation. It seemed to say do not cross. Ticky hadn't thought about this moment. His focus had been on getting them here. But now they were here he was unsure of what to do.

—Let's just ease back a ways.

No-one protested. They could all feel it.

—Nice and slow and easy, he said to Izzy, after she had stepped off and given the hand-car a shove to get it moving backwards. They rolled slowly back to where the highway separated, in the shade of a stand of tall gums.

—That'll do us I reckon.

—What should we do? It was Izzy who asked the obvious question.

Ticky was surprised at how no-one had questioned his action, to move away from the town. He knew that they sensed his unease, probably had their own.

—I reckon we rest up here. Have a drink and something to eat and when it gets dark I'll sneak up and have a look around, just to get a sense of what is going on. Concerns?

They sat through the hours before dark in the cool shade of the eucalypts. No-one slept. They talked quietly, occasionally, glancing often along the tracks towards the town, the smoke obvious, not abating, seeing no-one. The afternoon dragged for all of them. The sun seemed to tease them, refusing to drop that last distance behind the hills. But then it was gone. The twilight dropping over them. Ticky rose.

—Can I come? It was Izzy.

Ticky thought about it for a moment. Sure, but just two of us okay. No-one else argued.

—What should we do if you don't come back? asked Dee.

—I don't know. If we're not back by morning, sit out the day here and move past the town tomorrow night and keep going west. That's all I can suggest.

Ticky regretted the comment as soon as he said it. It didn't help. He could feel the pall that it had cast over the group. That there was a good chance that something untoward awaited them in the town.

—Look. We're just being careful. Let's not over-engineer this. But given what we've been through I just think we need to be sure.

Ticky carried a bottle of water in a small backpack, along with his torch. When they rounded the bend in the rails—the point they'd come to earlier in the day—they could make out the faint outline of the town in the closing gloom. But no lights. They stopped and looked for a long time but saw nothing, heard nothing to suggest people were nearby. It was the raucous cry of a kookaburra that told them that there was other life here on the edge of the desert.

As they moved closer they walked quietly, stepping on the concrete sleepers, avoiding the noisy blue metal between, almost tip-toeing. When they came to the roadhouse on the edge of town they moved off the rail-bed, climbing through the rusting wires of the fence and along the back wall of the building to the vast concrete apron.

It was full-dark now. The sliver of moon that they might expect was still some hours away. Neither spoke. They stood and looked and listened. Nothing.

The heavy glass door leading into the garage store was propped open. Ticky reached into his pack and took out a torch. The batteries were almost gone but it was enough light to show that the place had been picked clean. The shelves of the few aisles were empty of food. The only things remaining that he could see were a few spare parts;

fan-belts, bungee cords, nuts and bolts and the like, hanging on their racks and spikes.

—Smells like rotten milk. Izzy said it in a whisper.

They soon found the answer. Ticky pointed his torch into one of the big freezers, the bottom a melange of multicoloured wrappers floating in a soup of spoiled ice cream.

—Rank said Izzy.

The upright fridges were empty. Izzy sighed. Ticky looked at her.

—I was thinking about a can of coke.

Ticky gave a snort of laughter. Would have been fairly warm I reckon.

—I'd kill for some sugar, warm or otherwise.

They moved along to the restaurant door. Tables and chairs upended, cutlery strewn, an obvious pathway cleared towards the kitchen. And carnage in the kitchen. Cupboards and fridges open, the floor littered with whole and broken plates. A soup ladle caught the weak beam of Ticky's torch, hanging alone in its place above a stainless steel bench, the other implements scattered to the floor.

Ticky reached under a bench and came away with a tin.

—Baked beans he said, putting it into his pack.

—What do you think?

—Let's go. He reached and touched her on the arm before they moved off. Really careful now, okay?

—Okay.

They moved outside and onto the footpath, towards houses lining both sides of the street. A white four wheel drive was parked in the middle of the roadway. Abandoned there.

They both froze at the sound of the shot. Just one but it seemed to hang in the air. Not like an echo, more a warning. It wasn't close, a few streets away. Close enough. Ticky grabbed Izzy's arm—probably more firmly than he'd intended—and led her into the yard of the nearest house into the shelter of a side wall. He proffered his water bottle. Izzy took a sip and passed it back. Ticky took a gulp. His mouth was dry.

—Fuck.

—Indeed.

—What do we do?

Ticky paused, mouth drawn, lips tight. He had nothing to offer.

—Not sure.

27

The room is quiet. Relatively. My Captain is snoring. He makes me laugh. Says he doesn't snore. Tells me to ask his wife. I say I will one day. We laugh a lot. Not just he and I. My Dutch friends. Josefien especially. I call her Yozi. Closer than friends, we're sisters—we agreed on that. Laughing and crying, both. For whatever time we have. We've talked about that as well. She wants me to come and live with them in the Netherlands if we ever get out of this. A university city. I'm to stay as long as I want, forever's fine. They have the room. And she told me with a wink she knows lots of gorgeous lesbians.

We're comfortable for now. Death seems abstract again, now that we're settled here. The human psyche is bizarre. What we've been through, what we've all seen, where we are, how we're living. But it's a kind of happiness for now.

Our young farmer keeps us fed. His name is Josh, no longer one of the twins. His brother was Jack. I cry sometimes about that. Out of everything that's happened it's the thing that's hit me hardest. Words can't describe Josh. He's a wonderful wonderful boy. I want to cry when I look at him. I try to understand the hole that it's left in his life. I wonder when I feel like this that it's not just the sadness I feel for Josh, that it's somehow representative of the whole. The death of all those people in that horrid place. The dingoes. Maybe it's my way of finding a single point of focus. I hug him sometimes. I think I need it more than him. But he never turns it away. And we never speak about it. He just smiles at me.

And he keeps us fed. Kangaroo stew. The gun has made life easier. Thankfully the kangaroos haven't moved away. It's hard to fathom that they stay around when we chip away at their numbers. One every few days. That's about as long as we can make the stew keep in this heat. Wrapping pots of it in wet hessian has helped. Our refrigeration. We're running low on additives. Yozi and I have been experimenting with wild herbs. We found something like a lemon myrtle and another like rosemary. It makes a difference and we haven't poisoned ourselves yet. And there's something appropriate about it, eating the flavours of the bush.

We've still got some potatoes and flour. But they won't last much longer. It'll be hard to stomach the stew without them.

And we need something green or we'll end up with scurvy. I've experimented with a few different plants, hoping to find something like lemon grass. No luck yet. But our walks have taken us further and further into the bush. We get up early, before the heat, just on sunrise. We treat it like an expedition. And its wonderful. The shadows of the saltbush across the plain, and the rich colour of early morning. It's the time to get anything done, before the heat. It's almost cool, and those bloody flies aren't too bad at that time.

We've been lectured by the Captain a few times about the potential to get into trouble, 'out there', he likes to say with a grand sweep of his hand. We've seen a couple of snakes. I'm surprised that Yozi is so relaxed around them, coming from a country where they're rare. But relaxed she is. In fact she loves it. Gets way too excited for my liking. And too close. She's a real earth mother. There's something so warm and caring about her. And so beautiful. Elegant. Tall and graceful. She's older than me by a few years but makes me feel like a galumphing elephant. We laugh as I stumble about, her shushing me when she's seen something, me scaring it off.

We've taken to sitting around a big fire in the nights. I love it. The best show in town. A billion stars above. Not much conversation. A few housekeeping comments from the boss, my Captain.

I've thought a couple of times if I wasn't gay whether he'd be a man for me. Initially I might have said he was. But that was more about feeling protected, safe. Because that's how he makes me feel. But I know now he'd drive me nuts. Must drive his wife nuts. Don't get me wrong. I love him. I doubt I would've survived as I have without him. But he waffles and he dithers. We wouldn't last long. But I hope we can stay friends if we survive this. I wonder how his wife would feel.

The other driver is the laziest person I know. Bob. He's last from bed and first into it. First to line up for stew and last to be seen when we clean up after eating. And doesn't seem that fond of bathing. It's hard to dislike him but he's definitely a passenger. But thankfully the only one. One can be tolerated.

We've talked about the family who lived here. Wondered what happened to them. The Captain thinks they might have gone away for a break. They'd be able to catch the train, he said. No vehicle tracks or signs they had a vehicle.

Yozi's husband, Dirk, is a nice man. He and my Captain have become fast friends. Yozi and I laugh about them talking. Probably having separate conversations together. Happy to have someone to talk at. No need for a relevant response. It's a bit unkind. But true.

But what will become of us, this strange little group? We're here for good if no-one comes. The town is much too far. Josh the only one who would

279

stand a chance of walking anywhere. There's still plenty of water. But if the kangaroos desert us and the potatoes are gone, we'll need to confront it at some point. We're already losing weight.

I'm not going to go like so many on the train. Drawing it out. The thought of those poor old couples lying in filth. I don't want that. Maybe when it comes I'll think differently. Cling to any shred of survival in the hope that someone might be coming. But I doubt it. But then could I put that cold black barrel in my mouth and pull the trigger. I don't know about that either.

—We need to see, don't we, see what's happening here? It was only one shot, it could be anything.

Ticky could hear it in her voice. That she wanted to believe what she was saying. He felt the same.

—Yes, we need to see. He was glad she was with him. It wasn't fear, he couldn't quite understand what it was. Maybe protecting her would make him more cautious, keep them both alive. Maybe that was it.

They moved away from the wall and into the front yard of the small house but stopped in the cover of a tree. Ticky wanted to watch and listen before they moved. He could smell smoke. Nothing to see, nothing to hear. And then kookaburras. The raucous laughter in the twilight. It was so out of kilter with how he felt. Or maybe it wasn't. The manic laughter of crazed people. Maybe that was it.

They moved onto the footpath.

Izzy whispered and pointed. That street leads to the centre of town. To the supermarket and the school.

They crossed the street in a running crouch. Fugitives escaping justice. At least there was no moon, thought Ticky. But he still felt vulnerable. Front fences blocking a quick evasive manoeuvre. Houses sitting quietly on their plots, no lights, doors closed to them.

—It's like something from a Stephen King story, said Izzy.

—But there's someone here somewhere.

They kept moving. Wraiths. More houses. More darkness. More silence.

But then something else. They'd stopped, like the sound had halted their progress. A wall.

—Singing? Ticky said it but couldn't imagine how it could be so. The last kind of human utterance he could imagine in this time. In this place.

But then something else. He knew the sound. A bolt being worked in a rifle and then a voice telling them to stay where they were.

28

And then the kangaroos were gone. Vanished. Josh had been out for hours. Hours longer than normal. We'd started to worry. A brief moment of relief when he walked in, and then concern again when we saw his face.

He told us he'd seen nothing, heard nothing. They'd just gone. We knew it had to happen at some point. Hoped it'd take much longer. They'd already become skittish, harder to approach. But they were still around. Until now.

Without them we were nothing. From relative comfort to the unspoken truth, that we would die. We were already thin. I'd laughed with Yozi, that I hadn't been this thin since my training days. We laughed but we knew.

The potatoes lasted only a day or so longer. I thought of Matt Damon growing them on Mars. We'd talked about trying to grow them. But couldn't wait the ten weeks that they'd take nor spare the amount we needed to grow them from.

My Captain looked drawn. His beard seemed too large for his gaunt face. His clothes swam on him. We rested more now.

The men had pulled the generator to pieces but couldn't get it to work. That'd been the last project. Motivation had gone. And we needed to conserve our energies. We chewed the few greens we thought were edible.

Made soup from some. We'd had one day of reprieve when Josh had shot a huge goanna he found prowling in one of the sheds. The flesh was delicate. White. Somewhere between fish and chicken. More than edible. Especially when one is starving. But it was only a short reprieve. Within days we were back to starving again.

He said he'd wounded a camel but that it'd run off. It was hard with a shotgun, he'd said, not the gun for camel. Would need to get much closer. But then even Josh didn't have the energy. Lying down with the rest of us in the long hot part of the day. Much more pleasant than the train. We even managed to keep most of the flies outside. But we all knew where our lethargy was taking us. Except maybe for Bob. He'd not been on the passenger train, to see so many, moribund.

I thought about the end again. What I'd thought about before. Whether I could do it. When was the point? When was it lost? This is what I had thought about, talked to Yozi about. When do you give up?

Dying of thirst seems so much more logical in this heat, in this place, than dying of hunger. I knew the stages. Are we were all at stage three? Fat reserves depleted, energy requirements eating away at our muscles. The signs are there. Apathy, listlessness—I think Bob started in this stage.

Dirk is probably the worst of us. He's lost his spark. And makes no effort to hide it. I think it probably bothers him the most. He was so excited by the life we were leading. Like we'd found some example of Nirvana. He talked about it a lot. How well things were working. How we all worked for the greater good. Naive. I try to keep an eye on him. But then I feel like I'm back on that accursed train. I realise the images and memories are just there. I don't like them. I hadn't realised how much I hated it now that I was away. And Dirk is taking me back. Washing his forehead with a cloth. His raspy breathing. It was the same. He'll likely die of a heart attack like most of the others I tended. Thirst or hunger ending at the same point. Two different paths with likely the same outcome.

Yozi stays with him. He can't rise now. My Captain sits with him. But I see it in him as well. Fighting to rise from his bed. The flesh of his neck hanging. I wonder if it's time to have a conversation about it.

We should have sent Josh on his way days ago. It was selfish and cruel that we didn't. The only thing that saves me from hating myself for this is knowing that he wouldn't have gone. I can say that with certainty. He wouldn't have gone. And now it's too late for him. It's obvious that he's still the best of us. But that's not saying much. And it's not the golden ring, the prize. Being last. Watching everyone go. Hasn't he suffered enough? Who wants that?

No, maybe it's time to talk about this.

29

I wanted to pee myself when he came up behind us. It was out of nowhere. And that great big gun. Ticky looked as frightened as I did, I could see it on his face. It didn't help me.

—Back to the roadhouse he said.

Ticky took my hand.

—What's happening? I asked.

—No talking, walk.

So we walked. Up the middle of the road. I looked up, could see the stars. Spotted the Southern Cross. This is crazy. It suddenly struck me. I was being marched at gunpoint in my own country. What the fuck? It made me angry. I stopped and turned.

—What the fuck are you doing? I mean what the fuck.

—Izzy.

—No, this is ridiculous. This is my country. What are you doing? We've done nothing, nothing except to survive that fucking horrible train, hundreds dead and now our friends out there, maybe dying. And this prick is threatening to shoot me. Go on then, fuckin' do it. I could feel hot, angry tears running down my cheeks. Just fuckin' do it, I said again. I've had enough of this shit. I walked towards him. I could see him more clearly now. Bearded, older. Rough-looking. He looked unsure of himself.

—Don't, just keep walking.

I ignored him.

—Izzy no. I felt Ticky's hand on my shoulder. But I kept walking. A couple of metres to the end of his gun barrel.

He took a step backwards.

—Just keep walking. Don't do this.

—Fuck off.

He stepped back further.

—What if you've got the virus?

That stopped me. We all stopped. It was quiet. It was bizarre. I could hear the singing again.

—Singing?

—From the school.

—Why?

He shrugged. People seem to like it. Keeps 'em sane. Me not so much.

—What virus? asked Ticky.

—Look, we need to test you. We can't let you in if we don't test you.

—We're not sick, I said.

—We don't know that. There's been others. We need to check first. It wouldn't be fair. He lowered the rifle. His shoulders sagged. Just, please wait. Sit inside the roadhouse, I'll get our nurse. Promise you'll just wait here.

We looked at each other.

Ticky spoke, sure, we'll wait here.

He walked back up the street, his rifle carried low in one hand.

It was the miner who made our entry into the community simple.

He came back with the nurse and a few others. She'd started to speak, about what she needed to do. And he stepped forward. I didn't recognise him at first.

—I know you two, from the train, he said it stepping forward and shaking hands with us both.

We sat inside the roadhouse and he told us the story. About the virus, what had happened, why the train had stopped. His journey. And about the four who'd come from the west. They were sick. It was obvious. The town put them in a building, an old shed, stocked it, furnished it, let them die in relative comfort, a couple of days, alone. And then they'd burned the shed and everything in it, including the bodies. He said he'd manned the bushfire truck, standing by so the fire didn't spread. That's the smoke we'd seen.

He said the committee had talked about the train and all those people. But they had no way of reaching them.

—What could I do?

He sounded defensive. But really, what could he have done?

We told him our story. It didn't seem to shock him. I wondered whether it should have. Probably not surprising I supposed, given what he'd been through. I didn't mention the rape. I wondered whether he knew the filthy pig. That disgusting, fat, smelly pig. It was the smell of him I couldn't get out of my head. That was the worst of it. His rank body odour. Like some sort of crazed animal. I hated thinking about him. It made me feel like he'd won, every time I had a thought. Made me so angry. But he was dead. Dead like all of them out there. It didn't help, knowing that. I wondered what would help. Ever.

The miner walked with Izzy and me to get the others from the handcar. He seemed to take great delight cranking the little machine with me to the road crossing on the edge of the town, where we left it. I wondered briefly whether we should take it off the tracks.

We were assigned rooms at the town motel, it was all very formal he told us. There were a couple of other families there, they'd been travelling and been in the town when this thing had started. We had rooms to ourselves. Sleeping on clean sheets was heaven, we all said it. A good mattress and clean sheets. It'd been a while. But better than this. A shower. Not in our rooms, but at the school. I hadn't realised how badly I smelled until I walked into that cubicle and undressed.

And then a doctor gave us a once over. We were thin and exhausted, no surprises there. And then we crawled into those crisp, clean white sheets. Heaven. But I didn't sleep as well as I'd hoped. We had friends who needed rescuing.

The next day the miner took us to breakfast. Everything happened at the school. That's where the meals were prepared and eaten. It was a well-oiled machine. Seating times, hygiene, medical treatment and chores for everyone. And planning meetings. A town council. The mayor at the head of affairs. I was impressed with it all.

Afterwards he introduced us to his cycling companion and we walked the town together. The water was still flowing for now, he said, the reservoir staying full, the black pipeline, bringing the precious liquid from the somewhere in the west. But they'd already sourced a back-up. The water might stop any day. They just didn't know.

So they'd got the old bore working again, fixed the Southern Cross windmill. It hadn't been used in years but they'd fixed it. Still had the skills in the town. So they had a guaranteed water supply. They'd planted vegetables. Sweet potato, pumpkin, squash and beans. I'd seen the garden. It was impressive. Their sports ground, the fertile soil ploughed, fenced, netted against pests. The water system already there.

They'd have potato in a couple of weeks. Enough food until then. And they had meat. They had Scope, the shooter. Camel, the main source.

They'd had word from the outside. Days after the radio-man lost contact with his friend in Sydney they were contacted. The voice said he was military, that the country was under martial law for now. Told to stay where they were. Do what they were doing. That there'd be advice at some point, but for now to stay put. The voice, the radio guy said, had been formal but at the end it'd told him that they were the lucky ones.

I couldn't help thinking that they'd put a lot of store in a single voice on the other end of a radio transmission. Trusted the authority. But then what else could they do?

But all I could think about was rescuing our friends. We couldn't afford to wait. Izzy agreed.

I put the case for rescue to the committee. I'd workshopped the idea with Izzy. We'd need four people to work the little machine in shifts. Two less than before. But we needed to bring people back, so we couldn't afford the space for more. Even then, two would have to stay behind. There wouldn't be enough room. And who would volunteer to do that? To be fetched later.

I'd laid it out for them and they asked me to leave it with them, that they'd get back to me. It was frustrating. I wanted to push them to help then and there. There was no discussion to be had as far as I saw it. It was who and how, not if. But I held my counsel. I knew anger wouldn't get me anywhere.

The committee summoned me after breakfast the next day. An extra-ordinary meeting they called it.

The Mayor spoke. He was formal, old-fashioned, small, round and balding. Reminded me of George Costanza, even down to the glasses, which he removed and placed carefully on the table when he addressed me.

—We've considered your request to attempt this rescue and we support the idea in principle. The town will providore your expedition, as you have laid it out. But you will need to find volunteers. And provide a guarantee that you will take responsibility to retrieve those you will need to leave behind.

I agreed to everything. I just wanted to get moving. Days would make a difference. I was ready to move when Scope asked to speak. I was hoping he wasn't going to drag this out. We needed to get organised, sort the crew. But then he surprised us all.

—It's the old shunting engine. Been sitting in the rail shed for ten or twelve years. They used to use it to move the rolling stock, you know, carriages and wagons, around. It's old. Real old. But I reckon that'll be, you know, the good thing about it. Nothin' electrical on it. I reckon I might be able to get it running. She'll do about twenty miles an hour, forward or backwards. Not fast. But simple, reliable.

—How long would you need? I jumped in before the council members could speak.

—A couple of days at least. Hard to say without havin' a look at 'er.

—If it takes a couple of days to see if it's going to work, and it doesn't, that's a couple of days we'll lose. It's a great idea, don't get me wrong. I'd love nothing more than to not have to crank that little cart all the way back, but a couple of days could mean the difference between life and death for our friends at the siding.

Scope nodded. I liked him. A real bushy. He had a slow way about him. Considered. But smarter than he let on. He'd wanted to hear our story from beginning to end. He loved the Kalamazoo.

—How about this, he said in his drawl. You head off—he pronounced it 'orf', and if I get 'er runnin' I'll come fetch you.

I could've kissed him. Common sense.

—Deal, I said before the Mayor could think of anything to say. I almost ran from the room.

So we went. Four of us. Me, Izzy, the miner and a young strapping mechanic from the town, Darren.

—Bit bored, he'd said, as to his reasoning.

I'd said he might need to stay behind for a bit. Him and the miner—Lex, I discovered was his name. I figured they'd be good candidates to stay there until we could get back to fetch them. Lex didn't seem to mind. Darren similarly.

—I'll bring me rifle. We'll be solid. Bowl over a camel or two. Good eatin' those buggers.

The feel of the handle on my hands was something I didn't enjoy. It was a little too familiar but not in a good way. We'd loaded the wagon with food and enough water for a one-way journey. It was a bit of a risk. But no-one said anything and I didn't mention it.

Our stores were set out for us. It was all very formal. We had to sign for them. Everything edible and non-perishable in the town had been shifted to the school. Our allocation was outside the store room along with a four-wheeled trolley with pneumatic tyres. It took us four trips to shift everything to the little wagon, dragging the trolley down a couple of streets to the crossing. I laughed when we could see the handcar sitting there in the distance on the tracks and in the middle of the road.

—What? asked Izzy.

—Just seems so small and useless. This tiny contraption that saved our lives. And hopefully a few more.

The Mayor and several committee members, along with more-than-a-few of the townsfolk came to wish us well. Dee gave me a wave from the back of the scrum.

The first day was hell. It was like I'd never done it before. It'd only been a few days since we'd arrived in the town but it was like my body had said enough was enough. Even the gearing on the cart seemed to protest. I smiled at Izzy a couple of times. I could see she wasn't enjoying the experience either. We were both tired. We should've been recovering. But we had to do this. Our friends were out there. Izzy needed to see the Matron again. She'd said as much.

I wondered about the miner, Lex. It was hard to read him. He'd told us his story. It was worse than ours in many ways. He'd described the death of his friend when the snake had struck, and the scene of the plane wreck. These things would haunt him, I had no doubt about that. And then finding the woman. I couldn't begin to imagine how she was coping. At least they seemed to be close, they were sharing a room. But there was the other miner. The troublesome one. I sensed something in his reference to that. Too fleeting. Things unsaid. But I wouldn't pry. We'd all have our secrets after this.

Scope caught us on the second night. It was unreal. We heard the rickety old machine a long time before it arrived. The noise was so alien in the desert air. There was a moment of panic when we realised that maybe we needed to get off the tracks, that he wouldn't see us until the last and mightn't be able to stop in time. Darren ran back along the tracks, waving a torch. And then we laughed and ran around like teenagers when he hauled up behind us, a grin from ear to ear. Proud.

It was like a small old-fashioned steam train. Open cab, rattly, loud.

—She's not real quick.

—Like Donald Campbell's Bluebird, I said, compared to what we were doing.

He had a wagon on the back with drums of diesel and water. Plenty of water. It was fantastic.

I sent Lex and Darren back to town on the handcar, wanting to save the space. I could see the disappointment on Darren's face. He'd been set for an adventure. But there was much more at stake here than his feelings.

And then we were whizzing through the night, Izzy and I laughing at the novelty of a cool breeze through our hair and no effort required.

—We'll be there by mid-morning, I shouted. I shouldn't have said it. I'd barely finished the sentence when I felt the engine shudder and slow. I watched Scope's hands moving over the controls. I didn't like the look on his face. Concern.

The engine cut out before we'd stopped. We ground to a noisy halt. And then complete quiet.

—Fuel, probably the filter, he grunted.

Izzy held the torch. I handed him tools from his battered tool box. It wasn't long before diesel was running down his arms, Scope blowing through some part of the fuel system.

—Bit of grit in there. Probably from the drum we used.

He put things back together.

He stood at the controls while I used the handle to crank. I hadn't thought about it until now. But we'd be stuck here for a long time before anyone came for us if this thing didn't start. But worse, what would it mean for our friends?

—Keep winding until I flick this lever over, he said pointing to the top of the engine, but make sure you pull the crank handle out. If you don't, and the engine starts, the handle might fly out and kill one of us.

Not sure I needed the pressure.

—Now?

—Righto, into it.

I wound the handle, the resistance heavy at first but it got easier and before long I had it spinning almost as fast as I could keep up with. Scope flicked the valve-lift lever and I reefed out the handle. The engine coughed, a puff of smoke belched out of the exhaust and then something caught and the old machine rattled into life. Izzy cheered, I was relieved, Scope looked like it was never in doubt.

—Never in doubt.

It happened a few more times before the sun came up but it was only a short stop each time once we had the hang of things. And then we saw the buildings.

Those straight lines and square corners incongruous against the plain and the saltbush. All three of us whooped. Scope slowed the old machine as we approached.

But no-one came to meet us. I looked at Izzy and could see my concerns reflected in her face. We left Scope with his train and walked towards the hut, nerves jangling. It wouldn't be right, was all I could think. After everything we'd been through, that they'd been through.

It was the twin, Josh, who met us at the door. He smiled and hugged us both. Izzy burst into tears. He stepped aside to make space for me to pass. The Dutch woman was sitting on the bed beside our matron. She turned to look, a smile. Izzy ran forward, dropping to her knees beside the two women. I saw the matron's hand move towards my young friend.

I could see the Captain on his bed. I ran to him, willing him to be

294

alive. It looked as if he'd become part of his bed clothes. His frame was wasted. But there was life in his eyes. A merry twinkle in among the weathered cracks. I moved to him, lifting his hand. I had to bend my head to him to hear what he said.

—'bout time.

We buried Dirk and the goods driver in the little cemetery. Others had died here, the last fifty years before, a young child, from snake bite. Scope and I dug the holes. I told him about the train, what we'd had to do there. About the graves and what had happened after that. He didn't say much.

We fed the others, Matron gave her instructions. This was what I wanted to see. Her back in control. She told us to wait a couple of days before we left. That they'd all need strength to move. It was no great suffering to stay at the siding. We spent the days making small regular meals for them and letting them sleep.

The flesh seemed to increase on Josh's bones by the hour. And it wasn't long before Matron was up and about, fussing over everyone. The Captain had the worst of it. It embarrassed him to have so much fussing. But I figured this was a good sign, that he was strong enough to be bothered by it. But it'd be some time before he was his old self again.

The day of our departure Matron let him out of bed and we held a ceremony in the cemetery. Our words seemed inadequate and served only to fill the space of time that we stood there looking down at the freshly turned soil. I suspect the others, like me, probably thought about those out there to the east where the train still sat amid the saltbush.

We left the siding in the late afternoon, timing our run to arrive early morning, travelling through the cool of the night. Everyone was comfortable now. Mattresses, food. Even a couple of chairs. It was a ridiculous sight.

I took a final stroll through the buildings. I saw the chain, the one that had held the soldier for the dingoes. We hadn't buried him in the cemetery. I thought about that as well. I closed the door to the accommodation room and walked back to the siding where the little train was idling. Everyone was loaded up and ready to go.

We'd be reversing all the way back, with no way to turn the machine around. Scope had assured me it was of no consequence, the little machine was just as fast going backwards. And then we were on our way.

I looked towards the sun, where it seemed to be about to roost for the night behind the distant scrub. Funny now that it was a beacon of hope and life, rather than something to despair about. It was all a matter of perspective.

I turned one last time to watch the siding buildings disappear into the distance, the sun catching the glass in a window briefly like a wink.

30

The train waited patiently on the burnished rails. The sun bounced off the polished silver of the carriages. From a distance it looked as if it had only just stopped, that the passengers might disembark from the refrigerated air to have a moment to experience the harsh environment through which they travelled. It would be mostly the younger passengers—the effort of climbing the steep stairs a bit much for many of the older passengers. They might take a short stroll through the salt-bush and look out across the endless plain through the distorted heat. Maybe they'd see a camel or a kangaroo or dingo. Something to give them a story to tell the others inside the train, justifying the effort of climbing out into that furnace.

And then a whistle, back on board. Back into the chilled air, a cool drink served by polite staff in crisp, white uniforms. Laughs shared about the idea of being left behind or of living in such a place. And then the whistle again. The driver selecting the first notch on the accelerator, the train moving gently away, the driver careful to avoid spilling drinks.

The only witness to this scene, a solitary dingo standing outside a culvert, watching the silver carriages pass overhead, disappearing into the west.

Thanks for taking the time to read my book.
Please consider leaving a review at your point of purchase.

A big thanks to my beta readers, Fiona, Andy and Claire for their assistance and support. And a special mention to my brother-of-the-keyboard, Clive. Pain shared is pain halved.

CPSIA information can be obtained
at www.ICGtesting.com
Printed in the USA
BVHW031115121221
623852BV00015B/186